THE FOUR RIVERS
OF PARADISE

THE FOUR RIVERS
OF PARADISE

BY

HELEN C. WHITE, 1896-

THE MACMILLAN COMPANY

NEW YORK · 1955

210

To
Elizabeth M. Richardson

I
ROME

I

USUALLY MEN DO NOT KNOW THEIR GOOD
fortune until they have lost it. But that early winter morning
in the year of Our Lord 404, Hilary, grandson and heir of the
great Aquitanian landowner Postumianus, knew his. For he had
so nearly never had it at all.

The pre-dawn air was dank and cold here on this low hill
where Medoc had suggested that they pause to see if the mists
would not lift for what, he said, was for this western side the
finest view of Rome. But the heart of the young Hilary was
warm with excitement, for he was on the threshold of realization
of the dearest dream of his twenty years. All his life, it seemed
to him now, he had been gazing from a far shore across a great
sea of space and time and impossibility to this, the fountainhead
of everything he loved and dreamed of, the Rome of Virgil and
Augustus and Horace, and, yes, as his sister Blandina with her
woman's proper piety always reminded him, the martyrs. But
with his grandfather's hatred of the very name of Rome, he had
seen himself forever grounded on the shoals of Bordeaux with
only the younger brother's portion of books to tease his longing.
And now here he was, on the very rim of Rome and of all the
world's wonder.

And then as the air lifted again in the first stirring of the
pre-dawn breeze, a quite unaccustomed feeling of awe sobered
his excitement. For it had just occurred to him that his good
fortune had been at a price, and it was not he who had paid it.

3

His grandfather's sudden crumpling under the shock of his elder brother's death, from the presiding deity of all their Bordeaux world to a bewildered old man, had been appalling enough. But even more shattering had been the realization that when Postumianus had rallied his wits and blurted out, "Go to Rome and get it out of your system," he was afraid.

All through the weeks of their journey from Bordeaux Hilary had been trying to puzzle it out. He knew that Vincentius the priest had said that it served the old heathen right. He had refused to let them cut down the sacred oak, because Martin of Tours had been driving at its destruction when he changed his mind and took Postumianus' heir, Desiderius, instead. And now in a sudden freak of wind the old tree, from which their Druid ancestors had cut the mistletoe, had fallen, catching Patricius and crushing the life out of him. But Postumianus had always laughed at the Christian priest's threats, and Hilary could not see him even now easily yielding to what his philosophical eclecticism must still regard as superstition.

Patricius had wanted to go to Rome, too. But he was like his friend Fortunatus, who loved to say that one is nothing but a provincial until he has been to Rome. Postumianus knew that his elder grandson would never be carried away by any impersonal passion of the imagination. But of Hilary, the birth of those incredible days of desolation after the flight of Desiderius, Postumianus had never been so sure. He was quieter than his brilliant and often defiant older brother, and his love of books should have won the sympathy of his grandfather's own book-loving heart, and yet even in that, Hilary's enthusiasm for the Rome of the poets and the orators and the historians had frightened Postumianus. And now that Hilary was the last hope of his family, Postumianus could not shake off the fear that like his runaway father he might yield to some passion beyond any reasonable man's comprehension, and complete the ruin of his grandfather's life.

All this Hilary had slowly come to see in the long meditations of the road when his companions for very weariness fell silent and left him free to ride for miles with his thoughts. But what

4

awed him was the still incredible realization that at last Postumianus, who had always been so uncompromising with the recalcitrances of life, had come to recognize that there were some things beyond his control and tried a compromise. So he had summoned his old friend, the trader Medoc, and bidden him procure everything needed that Hilary might go to Rome in the style that fitted the heir of a Roman senator. And though he had often enough in the lifetime of Patricius grumbled at the light-headedness of the grandson of his old friend the poet Ausonius, he had invited Fortunatus to accompany Hilary to Rome and see the city as young men should.

Hilary, suddenly conscience-smitten, had protested that he should stay and help him with the estates, but Postumianus had snorted and reminded him that his brother-in-law Cerealis had always managed the estates very well with little help from the proper heirs. Hilary's sister Blandina had looked very proud of this vindication of her low-born husband. But for the first time it occurred to Hilary to wonder if the grave and laborious Cerealis, for all his good luck in winning even a crippled wife in a family so far above him, might not sometimes wonder as to why others should spend so lightly what he worked so hard to gather. And yet when Hilary asked his brother-in-law for a bag of gold for the little Greek girl whom he was leaving behind in the street of the silk-weavers in Bordeaux, Cerealis without comment gave him more than he asked. And now irrelevantly remembering this, Hilary wondered if perhaps Cerealis would have liked to be here, too, waiting for the sun to rise on Rome.

And then he forgot everything but what was before him. For all at once the night mists lifted and blew into nothingness, so that they looked across miles of brightening air to the shadows of the low hills beyond, with a gleam of light where the sun had caught a river. And then the shadows flushed, and fell away, too. And they saw that the hills were a city, such a vast city as these young men from Bordeaux had never imagined even in their dreams. And from the throat of slave and master alike, both Christian and pagan, broke the same cry, "Rome!"

At first to their enchanted gaze it seemed to be all white and gold, gleaming like a heap of jewels in the sunlight against the gray-green hills, and here and there, where they rolled apart, against the clear-blue sky itself. Shining in the winter air, it seemed not so much to reflect the sun as to light the clear space with its own brilliance. And then one became aware of the river over to the right, gleaming through the gray-green and the marble and gold, and of the aqueducts dripping silver in the winter sunshine.

But as they gazed, they began to pick out faint shadings of other colors, of bronze and terra cotta on the sloping roofs, of red in colonnades and porticoes, of lighter green in the gardens. And seen more steadily now, some of the white walls turned to yellow and saffron and, here and there, even brick. But still the white of the marble seemed to swallow up all color, and everywhere there was the glint of gold.

And presently the white and gold shimmer began to yield patterns of every conceivable size and shape, domes and towers and arches and pediments and colonnades and still more arches, every architectural motif of which one had ever heard flowering in undreamed-of splendor in one white and gold and green garden.

It was too far away to identify any of the city landmarks, but it was possible to guess at the types. That must be a basilica, that a temple, a palace, a theater—and then each man began to grope for something of which he had heard or read. That must be the Vatican hill there beyond the river with Constantine's great church gleaming among the trees, and directly in front of them the shining heights of the imperial Palatine. And all that gold and marble between, the forums of the emperors. But what are those great blocks of masonry, giant barracks rising in the brightening air like red and white islands above the floating treasure of the city?

Medoc, who had been listening with amusement to the various speculations, laughed now. "They are islands, indeed," he said; "that is what the Romans call them. And they are a sort of barracks, too, for many men live in them."

"They must be wealthy men who live in such splendid edifices," said one of the young slaves wistfully.

Again Medoc laughed. "Oh, it is in Rome as everywhere else. The rich live on the spacious first floor with the high windows, and the poor trudge up the narrow steps to crowd into the holes under the eaves."

"But even the poor must be rich to live in Rome," protested the slave.

"Rich or poor, what does it matter if one lives in Rome?" Fortunatus challenged.

"The young," said Medoc, not unkindly, "never make sufficient reckoning of the poverty of envy. But you are right. It has taken the wealth of the whole world to build that, and there if anywhere should men call themselves rich."

But Hilary said nothing, for he was thinking again of Patricius. When he was younger, he had often enough envied his elder brother. It was not so much his position in the household, for Hilary had early learned that the on-looker often sees more of the game than the player. It was his gayety, even his recklessness, and now Hilary wondered if from the high wall of heaven the blessed could see the things they had coveted on earth and failed of seeing. He was not sure it was a proper thought for a Christian, but he hoped so.

Presently, he was not so sure. For the broad highway was beginning to run through those stretches of warehouses and tombs and shrines and odd ramshackle houses that the receding farms and estates always leave on the fringes of suburbs, whether in Gaul or in Italy. And the narrowing roadway was filling with traffic. Part of it was familiar enough in kind to the Aquitanian visitors: country people in leather tunics, some leading pack-mules overflowing with garden produce, others driving farm wagons with heavy wooden wheels thudding hollowly on the stone of the roadway, and not a few afoot, carrying on their heads baskets of live poultry or fruit. There were gentlemen on finely caparisoned horses, with slaves on not so fine horses dogging their heels, and there were a few lordly figures elegantly driving light chariots with small iron-bound wheels clicking smartly on the pavement. And then out of a private side path came a litter, borne shoulder-high by half a dozen almost naked black giants, trotting easily with a rhythmic grace that made Hilary pull his horse to the side of the road to watch.

"They are Liburnian bearers trained to carry a litter without jolting," explained Maxentius, one of the older slaves, whom Postumianus had long ago brought home from Rome.

It was hotter now, and the dust was beginning to whiten the faces and the cloaks of the men from Gaul. And that mingled sense of the familiar and the strange, the splendid and the homely, stayed with Hilary as they left their horses at the gate of Rome and made their way into the streets of the city. For here were taller houses than Hilary had ever seen and narrower and dirtier alleys than any in Bordeaux. The stench that rose from the running gutters and the filth that spattered their boots seemed to the astonished provincial worse than any peasant barnyard in Aquitaine. And the noise of the crowds jostling through the splendor and the squalor of Rome paralyzed thought. It was a dream hovering on the edge of a nightmare.

Hilary was relieved when Medoc led them out of the uproar up a hill where the houses seemed at last to draw apart from each other and trees to peer above the bricked tops of the stuccoed walls.

But though there was no gainsaying the magnificence of the house on the Caelian Hill, the first floor of which Medoc's agent had engaged for them, the very motley impression of Rome stayed. One could still hear the uproar of the city even in the spacious and high-pillared peristyle. The private rooms were small and dark, while the air was stale as if some backwash of the stench of the city had overflowed even the ramparts of the Caelian. For the first time in weeks Hilary thought of the long galleries of the house at home and the sweet air blowing in from the miles and miles of fields and woods.

But Medoc was asking them for their plans, for he must hurry to his warehouses at Ostia. There was plenty to do if he was to get north in time to meet the agents who would have come through the passes before the winter closing.

8

There had been a good deal of jesting on the way as to what the young men should do with the letters which Maxentius was carrying. For they reflected very well the divisions of the family at home in Bordeaux. Postumianus had contributed several, of which the most important, he had repeatedly reminded Hilary, was that to Symmachus, the great leader of the Senate. Even Fortunatus, who had rather enviously quoted his grandfather Ausonius's description of Symmachus as a pompous pedant who kept burning incense in shrines that everybody else had forgotten, admitted that that letter was worth all the introductions his own not inconsiderable father had given him. But there were, also, the letters from Hilary's aunt, especially to the great ladies of the Anician and Furian houses and to the Senator Pammachius. Fortunatus had groaned at the last. "The man's a monk, a veritable sheep in wolf's clothing." Hilary had laughingly admitted that his family seemed to know all the best people on the wrong sides, and had proceeded to forget it all in the absorption of the journey.

But now Medoc soberly reminded them that their first visits had better be carefully chosen, for a young provincial calling on one of the leading men of Rome was choosing his patron and, for the first months at least, his circle of acquaintance. Apparently Medoc had taken to heart what Hilary had said about politics, for he made no reference to anything but social life. But Lupicinus, the steward whom Medoc's agent had hired to head their Roman household, looked so anxious as Medoc talked, that Hilary felt sure that more than social relations was at stake. He had not entirely liked the first look of Lupicinus, at once so much more servile and so much more knowing than the slaves and freedmen he was used to at home. But now he could not think of that. For already Hilary had begun to realize that his grandfather's heir was not so free to nurse his own fastidious likes and dislikes as the studious on-looker of the days before his brother's death.

Fortunatus' alarm at the prospect of attachment to the Senator Pammachius amused Hilary. He had often enough dodged his sister's and aunt's demands for what might be called feminine frills in devotion, but on one point he had been well taught by his masters, pagan and Christian alike, and that was that a decent piety was the foundation of a Roman's character. He would never go to the extremes of the Senator Pammachius any more than he would follow his own father's example. But he could not accept Fortunatus' picture of the monk-senator. For Pammachius was a Roman, too.

But now that the decision must be made, Hilary suddenly saw with a clarity that surprised him that all this was irrelevant. He had come to Rome as his grandfather's heir. Whatever the obscure details of his grandfather's break with Rome, which had so long puzzled him, Hilary could not betray him. Postumianus had confidence in Symmachus, and he had directed his grandson to go to Symmachus at once. That Hilary would do.

He suspected from Medoc's quiet nod of satisfaction that he understood his decision, but when Fortunatus slapped him on his back approvingly, and Lupicinus twisted his hands in happy anticipation, Hilary was alarmed. For he suddenly saw that he was in the hands of people who had no idea of what kind of person he was. And perhaps for the first time in his life, the young man who had always so clearly known what he wanted, especially when he saw no chance of having it, was not so sure himself.

II

THE NEXT MORNING HILARY WOKE IN THE darkness, wondering sleepily what had roused him. It was not the flat pre-dawn chattering of the birds at home. It was a curious shuffle of hurrying feet, broken now and then by a cough, a muffled imprecation—Hilary remembered the crowd at the gate yesterday. But this seemed more deliberate, more systematic than any country movement.

Then he heard the silky voice of Lupicinus, almost in his ear, reminding him that it was the time for clients to salute their patron. Hilary had been warned that the hour for such formal visiting would be early, but it had never occurred to him that it would come so close to the inaudible cock-crow. Still half asleep, he threw back the coverlet and stood on the cold rug at the foot of his bed. Somebody held out a basin of water, and he was pleased to find that it was warm, and then startled to realize it was scented, too. But before he could protest, skilful fingers were draping the heavy folds of his mantle over his shoulders. The deft service of these Roman servants irritated him. For ever since a fever of a couple of years ago, he had been jealous of his self-reliance.

The irritation was not dispelled when he came to the door of the house and found all his train, including the servants from Gaul and the new Roman household, waiting.

Fortunatus emerged grumbling, too, behind him. "Now I know what my grandfather was talking about when he used to complain of the burden of the great. Imagine getting up at this hour to entertain half the riffraff of Rome!"

The light was breaking now, a cold, damp winter dawn, with marble porticoes riding coldly out of the fading mist and all the gilded statues dripping dully on the chill air. A few nondescript individuals in skimpy, grayish robes were hurrying by in soggy sandals, as if to catch up with a procession they had missed. But the narrow streets were filling up again with companies like Hilary's own, groups of household slaves strutting importantly ahead of and around and behind the litters and chairs of their masters, mostly middle-aged, with balding heads and richly embroidered mantles draped elegantly about their ample persons. As the companies jostled each other at a narrow crossing, the slaves cried the names and titles of their masters and claimed a doubtful precedence while their masters saluted each other ceremoniously.

When at last the procession halted before an open gate in a high brick and cement wall, there was already a crowd milling around the gate, and Hilary wondered how they were going to get in. But the new Roman attendants lost no time in clearing a way, shouting the names and family rank of their masters, and using their elbows freely when the obstructions were slow in giving way. Only as they passed into the house did the din of voices subside. And for a moment Hilary had a chance to look around the crowded anteroom with its slim columns of peach marble and its gilded stucco ceiling, and then the pressure of the crowd relaxed as they were borne more slowly into a magnificent atrium with great red-veined marble columns holding up the shining copper eaves, and gilded statues rising majestically out of flowering shrubs.

There was a numerous company here, too, but the voices were lower, more respectful, more self-important. And Hilary's own escort became suddenly quietly obsequious as they bowed over their charges to the waiting ushers.

With scarcely a word spoken the path opened to where the master of the house reclined on a richly draped couch. At first sight he looked formidable enough, a spare, wiry figure with a look of alert yet self-composed serenity that challenged any interruption. As the major-domo standing by his couch repeated the Gallic visitor's name and his grandfather's, Hilary presented Postumianus' letter. Breaking the seal, the old man glanced over it. Then his whole mien changed; he smiled austerely, and rose to embrace the two young men. Then he made them sit down at either end of his couch. The hum of conversation through the room, which had been suspended during the greetings, resumed about them, and Hilary had a chance to look more closely at his host.

He was not so old as he had first thought, and not quite so imperturbable for all that high-beaked sharpness of look. Now he was speaking with a slightly breathy urbanity to Fortunatus —"the greatest poet we have had in the language since Virgil," and Hilary was amused to see Fortunatus, who had always professed a low opinion of most of his grandfather's verses, expressing his gratification at Symmachus' appreciation. Then Symmachus turned to Hilary and politely inquired about his grandfather's health and his aunt's; indeed, he remembered all the family, including even Hilary's father, who had run away with Martin. Of him Hilary said only that they had heard that he had left Primuliacum and gone to the eastern frontier in Dacia. He was brief, too, on the death of Patricius, saying only that he had been crushed by an old tree, falling in a high wind. But Cerealis would have blushed at the warmth with which his usually casual brother-in-law spoke of his sister's husband, and even Blandina would have been satisfied with her brother's account of the promise of her two small children.

Symmachus professed himself delighted to hear of these consolations which his old friend had found in his extreme age. He had not had an easy life, Symmachus sighed. Postumianus was a man of deep loyalties, and had taken the death of the Emperor Gratian hard, as one could tell from the way he had declined to visit Rome since.

Hilary looked closely at his host then. Of late he had wondered a good deal what it was that had so terribly disillusioned his grandfather with the Rome where once he had obviously played so important a part. Hilary had been hoping that he might receive some light on that old mystery from Symmachus. The great senator had spoken, indeed, as if he had known Postumianus well, and yet how could anyone who knew his grandfather even slightly believe that he could ever have been so sentimental as to let grief for the dead emperor wrench him from all he must once have so much enjoyed? But Symmachus gave every appearance of believing what he was saying, blandly repeating that loyalty like Postumianus' was a very rare thing in these degenerate days.

Completely bewildered, Hilary groped for some polite word of appreciation, but he need not have worried. For at that moment there was a sudden pulse of excitement in the great room, and a slave rushed in with the news that a courier had come from the imperial palace. Symmachus excused himself with a sigh at the inevitable interruption of the pleasures of friendship by duty.

Everybody in the room fell silent and watched as the imperial messenger, a beautiful blond young man, carrying a decorated staff and a parchment scroll, made his obeisance to the master of the house. Symmachus unrolled the parchment and soberly pondered its contents. Then with the whole company respectfully hushed, he asked for his secretary, and a young man stepped forward with stylus and tablets. Symmachus seemed to consider. Then slowly and carefully he dictated his answer. At first, Hilary had tried not to listen, but he soon discovered that he was apparently the only one in the room who had any scruples about eavesdropping. Indeed, as Symmachus proceeded with his answer, his voice rose until it seemed as if he were delivering an oration.

It was a very formal letter with an elaborate apparatus of complimentary address and of expressions of appreciation of the honor of consultation, but so far as Hilary could make out, the issue was rather obscure, involving a point of order in a procession. However, the very considerable company that still remained in the magnificent atrium listened with the deepest attention, and when Symmachus had finished the reply, they broke into applause.

But Symmachus seemed to be lost in thought. When the hubbub of congratulation had at last died down, he called for another secretary, and when the man appeared with writing materials, he bade him make arrangements for the calling together of the senate the next morning, that both the Emperor's letter and Symmachus' reply might be communicated to them. There was a further point concerning the arrangements for the Emperor's games that really deserved the advice of the senate for its proper solution.

Again the chorus of praise arose all over the room, and Hilary concluded that the Emperor's recognition of the wisdom of the senate in consulting it on so important a matter as the games which he was giving in honor of his consulship had given the greatest encouragement to all solid citizens who looked forward to the restoration of Rome to her proper place in the imperial universe.

"It is all very well to talk of having the Emperor and his court within reach of the frontier and the legions which the

Emperor is to command," said a very distinguished-looking old man beside Hilary to a neighbor quite as distinguished-looking. "But in the greatest periods of our history the Emperor stayed in Rome and sent out generals to the frontier, and victory never failed to crown our eagles."

But even as the speaker talked, he looked uneasily toward his host, and his voice fell. Still other messengers had arrived, but Symmachus was contenting himself with answering their questions orally.

A young man next to Hilary turned to him suddenly and in an elegant drawl asked, "Don't you get awfully tired of all this talk about the barbarians? I think the generals don't really want to clean the thing up. They'd be out of all those fine chances for booty if they ever did."

Hilary was too startled to reply, but the young man only shrugged his shoulders and lounged away. Everybody in the room seemed to be moving now, taking leave of their host with salutations which he was for the most part too preoccupied to acknowledge. Hilary and Fortunatus began to move a little uncertainly toward his couch, and he lifted his head to smile wearily at them. "I am sorry that I have so much urgent business today that I cannot talk to you any more now. These games of the Emperor's are such an enormous undertaking, and there are so few people in Rome who have any experience of such matters."

Another very distinguished-looking gentleman passing at that moment paused smiling. "Symmachus is as always too modest. There is no man in Rome with his experience in giving games that really maintain the old tradition." But Symmachus waved his hand deprecatingly. And turning to the young men he invited them to return the next morning at dawn and to accompany him to the senate house.

To Hilary's relief, only about half their train was still waiting at the door, and everybody seemed to be moving more casually as if the day's business were done. Only now the streets were full of people, seemingly bent on the ordinary affairs of life. As they

15

were carried along also at their ease, Fortunatus whispered to Hilary, "Did you get what all the fuss about the letter meant?"

"Not much, except that all the important-looking people standing around were excited. Perhaps we'll learn more about it tomorrow."

But though the next day Hilary arrived at Symmachus' house before dawn, and the senator did him the honor of putting him on his right hand in his own litter for the procession to the forum, Hilary had to confess himself defeated. It was an exciting enough occasion, with processions of purple-clad dignitaries and their escorts coming from every direction to the senate house, so severely plain in the varied splendors of the forum. All around in the porticoes and on the roofs as well as in the forum itself a noisy throng of men and women of all races and obvious gradations of wealth and poverty paused to watch the senators go up the steps and through the great bronze doors into the senate house. Now and then cheers broke out as the crowd spied some favorite, like Symmachus. And sometimes there were murmurs and jeers and laughter.

Symmachus appeared completely unaware of the crowd but went on pointing out to his young guest various senatorial leaders as they came into sight. Some were names with which Hilary had been familiar since his schooldays. Others he had heard in his grandfather's reminiscences of Rome and in banquet conversations at Bordeaux. But many were strange Greek-sounding names. Finally, Hilary plucked up courage to ask whether there were so many Greeks in the senate.

Symmachus smiled wryly. "It is a fashion of these degenerate times. Men with great Roman names which every schoolboy knows have taken outlandish appellations from Homer and the Greek poets, and prate of their descent from Agamemnon and Achilles, if not from Polyphemus." At that moment a man, tall and thin and very patrician-looking in a monk's rough brown robe, walked rapidly up the steps alone. Symmachus frowned as he saw him but made no comment, and Hilary thought uneasily of his aunt's friend Pammachius. And like a shadow on the splendid scene came the thought of the father he had never known.

16

But before he could ask any more questions, they had reached the top of the steps themselves, and Symmachus had paused for a moment, putting forth his hand and then hastily drawing it back. He laughed uncomfortably, "I can never remember that there is no longer any incense there." And then at the puzzlement on Hilary's face he lowered his voice, "The fanatics have removed the statue and the altar. May the gods grant that they have not removed Victory, too, from Rome." And pointing out to Hilary the little courtyard in which the escorts might wait, he passed majestically into the already crowded senate chamber.

But although Hilary listened attentively to the gossip of other waiting members of senatorial escorts, and still more attentively to the self-important conversation of the senators themselves as they emerged some two hours later, he had to confess that he understood no more of the business than he had the day before. It was clear from the way in which his colleagues crowded around Symmachus at the foot of the steps to congratulate him, that he had acquitted himself with his usual distinction in reading both the Emperor's letter and his own. And it was equally clear that all these important-looking men, like their humbler escorts, felt that something of great importance was moving forward. Only the senator in monk's dress looked bored and aloof as he hurried off, still alone. And for the first time in his life Hilary wondered what his runaway father looked like, going about his incredible business in far-off Dacia.

Hilary waited for some time, hoping that in the graciously expansive mood in which Symmachus was obviously enjoying his little triumph, he might get some light on what it all meant. But Symmachus went off chatting with a couple of the older senators, without so much as looking in Hilary's direction. Fortunatus, who had been waiting at his side with considerable impatience, took his arm. "Now, my budding statesman, will you kindly tell me what has happened, or is happening, or may be going to happen?"

Hilary shook his head. "I have no idea; only it must be very important."

Fortunatus laughed. "When I was a boy, I once overheard my father read some verses of my esteemed grandfather on the senate. The most quotable part compared that august body to some outworn hens cackling over the eggs they could no longer lay. I have looked through all his papers for those verses, but I have never found them. Sometimes when fools prate about Virgil, I wonder what they would say about those verses and doubtless others which my grandfather, unlike Virgil, was wise enough to burn himself."

But Hilary rebuked him, reminding him that the sacred ground on which they stood was no place for ribald remarks about such an historic institution in which one day, doubtless, they would be proud to take their seats. Fortunatus, however, prayed heaven to postpone the day, and the two young men, free at last, plunged into the wonders of the forum. For a few hours Hilary forgot his astonishment at present-day Rome in the contemplation of the more familiar glories of her past. And for the first time he saw to his surprise that the books he had loved were not only the refuge of the idealist from the prosaic everyday but the magic key to a reality richer than even a schoolboy's dreams.

III

"ACCORDING TO JUVENAL, HE WILL NOT KNOW us today," grumbled Fortunatus a few days later, as, prodded by Lupicinus, they set out again for the house of Symmachus. But he was quite mistaken. The senator received them graciously and encouraged them to continue their calls. Before a fortnight was out, he recognized their assiduity by sending them on one of his innumerable errands. It was to see the dealers in wild animals who were keeping some importations from Africa for the Emperor's games in stockades down by the river. Everybody standing around in the atrium seemed much impressed by the confidence which Symmachus had put in the young

18

strangers from Gaul, and smilingly made way for them as they set forth. The detailed instructions, consisting chiefly of adjurations to take special care of the diet of the crocodiles, were entrusted to a steward. But Symmachus gave the two young noblemen a full account of his own disastrous experience with crocodiles which he had imported from Africa at great expense for the praetorial games of his son two years before.

There was no question that Symmachus' anxiety was justified, for they found the Emperor's crocodiles lying limply on the sandy rim of a shallow tank into which a couple of slaves were gingerly trying to drive them with long sticks, under the prodding of an overseer who kept cursing their cowardice. The arrival of the vistors was seized upon with alacrity by half a dozen slaves at once, who rushed off to inform their master of the arrival of the senatorial party.

The master, a weather-worn individual of undecipherable nationality, roundly cursed the overseer in turn, mixing up imprecations to strange deities and incredible sums of exotic money as he contemplated the loss of a crucial investment to the stupidity of the climate and the slaves of Rome. He turned a very jaundiced eye on the steward of Symmachus, and shrugged his shoulders contemptuously at his advice. But his whole mien changed when he saw Hilary and Fortunatus. Hastily summoning the overseer, he bade him listen to the steward's instructions and take them for his orders. As for the slaves, he would feed them to the crocodiles if they let another of them die. And then he turned ingratiatingly to the young men, asking if perhaps their lordships would not be planning games of their own presently.

But Hilary hastened to disclaim any such ambitions, and Fortunatus observed that the family had never recovered from the expenses of his grandfather's consulship. The animal dealer, however, was unconvinced and insisted on displaying a couple of mangy and depressed-looking lions in a cage with rusted iron bars, and a sick-looking python in a covered wicker basket. Hilary protested that he was quite content to take his strange beasts from the rolls of Pliny. But the animal dealer was no stranger to the persiflage of the young Roman aristocrat. He shrugged his shoulders and turned to one of the accompanying slaves for the necessary information as to family names and addresses.

Symmachus' steward, however, professed himself gratified with the success of their mission, and by the time they had returned to his master's house he was ready to give the young noblemen, particularly Hilary, all the credit. And Symmachus expressed his thanks at such length that several distinguished-looking gentlemen standing by came up to Hilary and recalled his grandfather with flattering pleasure.

Hilary was puzzled. He knew that he was tall and not ill-formed, and that long association with his grandfather had given him a restraint and a habit of respect that usually won the confidence of his elders. He had no thought of anything but seeing a little of the great world before he settled down in his new place as a provincial magnate. Fortunatus seemed even more completely carefree about it all. He had long ago professed himself interested in nothing but having as much fun as possible before his family married him off to the fortune of lower birth that would redeem his younger son's portion. Now he laughed at the attention they were receiving and swore that he was going to make the best of it for whatever it was worth, though he agreed with Hilary that it was not likely in the long run to amount to much.

But some days later both young men began to wonder if they had been too sceptical. For this time Symmachus declared that he had a really delicate matter to entrust to them. He had heard that the Emperor was expecting daily the arrival of some captives from the northern frontier. Honorius, who had repeatedly solicited his advice on every other detail of the games, had so far done him the honor of deferring to his experience. But at one point the Emperor had not seemed quite to understand what Symmachus was talking about. Or rather, said Symmachus, seeming to feel that perhaps he had been indiscreet, the imperial experience had been different. His generals thought of the barbarians in terms of the frontier. They assumed, not unnaturally, that men who fought hard in the field would fight hard in the arena, but it was not always so simple.

That piqued Hilary's curiosity. He himself seldom found things as simple as they were supposed to be, but he was surprised to find the great Roman of so doubtful a mind. His interest must have piqued the senator's love of sharing his experience, for he went on to explain with a sigh that he knew what he was talking about, indeed. His voice rose a little, and the company fell respectfully silent for the story.

"It was when I was giving the games for my son's praetorship. The Emperor honored me by sending me a band of Saxons who had been taken in battle. They were, I must say, a fine-looking lot." Ever so lightly his voice stressed the word "looking." "You know," he added, "tall, golden-haired with reddish brown mustachios curling fiercely. And somebody had fitted them from some stores that had been picked up on the frontier— fresh skins, and leather shields, and those long spears of theirs, all of the very best make, and fresh and new. The centurion who brought them marched them through the streets, and everybody ran out to look at them and said it would be the finest thing in the show." His eye flashed with pride at the recollection, and a light sigh ran through the bystanders. Then he fixed his glance on Hilary. "And what do you think those wretches did the very night before the games?"

"Ran away?" asked Hilary helpfully, remembering too late his aunt's advice about answering questions in the midst of his grandfather's reminiscences, "Make it good, but not too good." Now a hard shadow came into the eyes of his host, who for a moment clearly thought his promising young friend was trifling with him. Then he remembered, and with a smile of condescension shook his head, "Ah, you have not seen the excellent arrangements at the gladiators' barracks. They were cowardly enough for that, if it had been possible. But it was much worse. They hanged themselves from the hooks for their gear in the barracks, every single one of them. The whole amphitheater roared with disappointment when they heard of it the next day."

Polite sounds appropriate to the magnitude of the disaster ran through the company. Symmachus drew himself up authoritatively. "So tell the master of the gladiators to look over any captives he has, and cull out the Saxons. Huns or Dacians, once they are in the fight, will go mad with the urge to kill, no matter who is opposite them, but I would never trust Saxons again."

So again Hilary and Fortunatus with an escort of their own and Symmachus' slaves set forth in an atmosphere of mighty business afoot. Fortunatus laughed. "Give us a couple of weeks more and we shall be running those games."

But Hilary was thinking about the handsome Saxons. Surely they had not been converted if they had taken their lives so easily. But when he asked Fortunatus about it, the latter scoffed. "It wasn't a matter of religion at all. They were poor creatures. Their lives were forfeit when they were taken, and they begrudged anybody else the pleasure of their dying."

Hilary was so startled at his friend's matter-of-factness that he nearly ran down a little man in monk's dress who was charging through the crowd as if he were blind. Symmachus' steward shouted at the little monk, and the latter blinked as if he had just wakened to find himself in the middle of a crowd without knowing how he had got there. Hilary murmured a word of apology, and Fortunatus began to laugh, while the steward grumbled about the idiots whom the games had brought to the city. The little man looked around the company who had closed in about their master, as if he were trapped. He was a scrawny, dirty little fellow, but he had a curious kind of dignity about him, as if he, too, were on an important errand. And catching Hilary's eye he asked him in slow and halting Latin if he would tell him the way to the house of Pammachius.

"You look like the kind of man of whom one asks directions," jeered Fortunatus.

"No, I am dark like a proper citizen." Hilary laughed at the flush that rose almost to Fortunatus' brown hair. Then he turned to the steward. With a contemptuous gesture the freedman waved the monk back the way they had just come.

"Could you not spare one man to show him the way?" asked Hilary.

But the steward's mouth tightened. "Even if it is on the Caelian, it is no place to send a man from a respectable house. Half the slums of the Suburra will be there." But even as they talked, the little man had slipped from sight. And Fortunatus hastened to remind Hilary that the fate of the games waited on their errand.

But it was as if a shadow had fallen over the bright scene around them. The disappointing Saxons, the absurdly preoccupied little man, the contempt of the steward—the day that had begun so well had flattened out. And the sense of flatness persisted as the company swung away from the majestic amphitheater of Flavius to the barracks of the gladiators close by, low stone structures with high walls about them.

The master of the gladiators, a bull-necked tower of a man with the telltale red hair of his barbarian ancestors and the tacit autocracy of his army position about him, was clearly inclined to pooh-pooh the worries of Symmachus, but on second thought, after a good look at his guests, he thought better of it.

"We may have a Saxon or two, for we have a little of everything in this lot, but the chances are that any one of them will find himself facing a Hun, and I assure you that there is no love lost there."

An instinct of loyalty to the man whose errand he was doing made Hilary defend Symmachus' worry. "It's his own experience, I suspect. You probably have heard the story."

"Of course," said the master easily, "and I made my own investigations and sent a report to the frontier. It was their fault. I have a couple of Saxons in my own household, and they told me that anybody who knew anything about Saxons should have known that it was a picked group. They had some kind of oath to their chief, who was killed, or they would never have been taken. They should have been held as hostages, or sent to the mines, or the galleys."

And then having satisfactorily accounted for a mistake that was the fault of other men, the master invited his guests to look over the establishment with him. It was, indeed, impressive; the stone barracks were clean; there were spacious baths with every accommodation for massage and anointing of the body; there were exercise fields and halls with every facility for games and sports, and a whole army of coaches and trainers and servants for the perfection of the body and bodily skill. And as he exhibited his establishment to his admiring guests the captain expatiated on the problems of his job. "They used to dump criminals on us, but most of them were no good. Except for the bandits and a few of the murderers, they were a miserable lot, whining and cringing, until for very disgust somebody had to clear them off the earth. I'm glad they don't bother us with them any more. Now they go to the torturers where they belong. And I wish they'd do the same with half the captives. Let us pick out the ones that are some good, and train them, and we'll put on a much better show for the Emperor or anybody else."

Hilary found himself completely at a loss for anything to say to this serene and competent brute, but Fortunatus seemed to take the right tone without effort.

"In other words, you prefer professionals," he said gravely.

"Of course," replied the master, clearly gratified to find that one of his guests had sense. "I like a man with his heart in his work, and willing to use his head as well as his fists."

"You should like the Huns then," said Hilary dryly.

But the master shook his head indignantly, and then went on to explain as if to a very backward pupil that he did not care for the Huns at all. "They go mad after the first blood flows, and then all they do is try to hurt somebody. They make no effort to protect themselves. It's just slaughter, no art to it at all, nothing a man of taste would enjoy."

"But your professionals?" asked Fortunatus encouragingly.

"Ah," said the master proudly, "wait until next week. I have a score of men who will open your eyes. The kind of fighter who does not hang back but goes after his opponent, and yet he does not leave himself open. It is a joy to watch him thrust and dance back, feint and thrust again. If he gets his man, it is a triumph of skill not slaughter. And if he goes down, one knows that his slayer has really earned his triumph."

"But they all go down at last, don't they?" said Fortunatus musingly.

But the master scoffed, "All men die, don't they?"

"Surely most men want to live a little longer," protested Hilary, finding that the conversation was beginning to take a turn he could comprehend.

But the master was triumphant. "I have men who have been fighting for five years."

"That is lasting longer than some of the politicians at that, Hilary," said Fortunatus soberly.

"But what a life!" All the day's distaste came out in the single phrase, Hilary realized too late.

The master was indignant. "Training, the best of food, wine, women, sport, the glory of the amphitheater, and the certainty that, when your time comes, you will go out fighting like a man. What more could a man, a real man, ask?"

"He has you there, Hilary," said Fortunatus, but at that moment the steward of Symmachus reminded the young men that his master would be waiting anxiously for their report.

"What report?" asked Hilary absently.

Fortunatus nudged him sharply. "No Saxons with winged mustachios will be hanging themselves on the eve of the games, Hilary. He may sleep tonight."

The master looked disappointed at the unmistakably mocking tone of the young man who had been so sympathetic, and Hilary hastened to express their appreciation of his courtesy.

As they pressed through the increasing crowds in the streets, Hilary could hear people pointing them out, "They are from the household of Symmachus. They are arranging the games," and suddenly he began to feel a little foolish.

But this time the little procession took another route back to the house of Symmachus. As they came up the Caelian Hill, the steward pointed to a gate in the tufa wall around which a crowd was pressing. Hilary looked more closely. It was an odd crowd, thronging but quiet, shabby and patient. Unlike the crowds before the gate of Symmachus this one contained a number of women with children in their arms. And Hilary noted several cripples trying to get in on the edges of the throng.

"The house of the Senator Pammachius," said the steward. Hilary looked at Fortunatus, and the latter raised his eyebrows. But before he could say anything, a doorkeeper came to the gate, and addressed the crowd apologetically: "The Senator Pammachius regrets that he cannot see any more of you today. If anybody is hungry, he may go round to the little gate at the side, and he will be given food."

A number of the company, including several of the women, and a few of the cripples went around to the side gate. The rest moved away slowly but quietly. Only a little monk ran up to the steward and caught at his sleeve. "I must see Pammachius today. It is life and death." The doorkeeper looked at him wearily, "He cannot be troubled today. You may see him tomorrow." And apparently quite used to such importunities, he pushed the little man away gently and closed the gate. For a moment, the monk beat at the bronze-barred panels, and then he turned away with a look of utter despair on his dirty yet queerly dignified face. It was the same man whom Hilary had walked into that morning. "Tomorrow will be too late," the little man said to no one in particular.

"Come, my lord, the afternoon is passing," urged the steward, and Fortunatus took his friend's arm. For a moment Hilary hesitated, looking at the little man, but the latter gave no sign of recognition. With a sudden and unaccountable sense of helplessness Hilary yielded to the pressure of Fortunatus' arm and followed the steward to the house of Symmachus.

IV

SOMETHING OF THE SAME SENSE OF UNEASINESS remained with Hilary through the rest of the days of preparation for the Emperor's games. Even when the end of the week brought an engagement to which Hilary had really been looking forward—the banquet which Attalus was giving in honor of the games—Hilary still felt a curious lack of confidence. But there was something in the sight of Attalus, a large, assured man with a high arched nose and bold eyes giving character to an otherwise too fleshy face, and a jovial voice with curiously pliant undertones, that banished any scrupulous brooding over what could not be helped. And the pretty woman at his side had a certain Tanagran delicacy to her quiet elegance that made Hilary catch his breath—Rhodope? But when Prisca, the wife of Attalus, spoke, there was nothing in the artfully modulated harmonies of her voice to stir any uncomfortable memories of the little Greek girl whom he had left sobbing above her embroidery easel in the street of the clothmakers in Bordeaux.

"Ah, my Gallic friends," Prisca began with exquisite graciousness, "Attalus tells me that Symmachus has kept you so busy that you have had no chance to meet any of the ladies. That is the trouble with these politicians. They can think of nothing but their own obsessions."

"Beware," laughed Attalus, "she looks harmless, but she is the most inveterate matchmaker in Rome."

"But two such handsome young men are surely pledged already to Gallic fortunes."

The two young men hastened to reassure her. Fortunatus, as usual, took the lead, explaining that he was only a younger son, and therefore forced to seek wider fields, while Hilary was so recently an heir that the mothers and grandmothers of Bordeaux were only now making their plans for his return.

Hilary, who still could not bear to think of any mistress but the clever little comrade of his student days in Bordeaux, looked so sourly at Fortunatus' gay persiflage that Prisca quite misunderstood.

"We shall have mercy on him then," she trilled charmingly, "and begin with the ladies of the Cornelii. Laeta is a Christian and therefore has no choice but to stick to her Theophilus, and Gaia, who keeps the faith of her fathers, has just got rid of one husband, and swears she will have no other. Laeta is prettier, I think, and smarter, but Gaia has all the fortune of her branch

27

of the family. So Hilary may relax with Laeta, and Fortunatus may see what he can do to change Gaia's mind."

And she swept them through the knot of young men about two ladies, one short and plump with bright red hair, beautifully painted and jewelled in a magnificently embroidered robe, the other statuesque with dark hair plainly drawn back from a pale, haughty face quite innocent of any make-up, and a severely plain dress of heavy white brocade threaded with gold. As if drawn by a magnet, Fortunatus went to the fashionable beauty, while Hilary gazed in admiration at the face that might have come off an ancient coin.

But Prisca protested. "You have it all wrong at the very beginning. This is Laeta for Hilary, and Gaia for Fortunatus." And she insisted on making the young men change places, explaining to the young women the reasons for her choice of partners. Hilary looked at Laeta for a moment in embarrassed silence, but she only laughed, displaying teeth as delicate and gleaming as the pearls about her neck, and began to ask him if it was true that he came from the very ends of the earth, and did they have that wonderful Bordeaux wine to drink every day. It was a delightful voice bubbling with friendly curiosity. But Hilary was gazing in astonishment at her dress. For the amethyst-colored brocade was edged with an embroidered border of Christian symbols—grapes and leaves and fishes with the sacred letters in a monogram.

Seeing his eyes on the border, she picked up one of the draped edges and asked him prettily, "How do you like it?" and without waiting for an answer she went on gayly, "I believe in avowing my faith." And then as Hilary still said nothing, she turned with a pretty petulance to her cousin, "Gaia, this sober-sides here is your style. You take him and let me have Fortunatus."

The exchange was made laughingly, but Gaia gave Hilary a keen look. "You are a Christian, then."

"What makes you say that?"

She had a low, rich voice, in surprising contrast to the general austerity of her appearance. "You looked so shocked at Laeta's embroidery."

"Oh, no," Hilary hastened to reassure her. "But I had never seen anything quite like it—that is, on a dress."

Gaia laughed. "You have an odd way of telling the truth, my friend. And you are quite right. Laeta had the fabric worked for the pastor of one of their churches in the Suburra." She spoke in a low voice, but it carried to her cousin's ears.

"Really, Gaia, I don't see why you have to tell everybody that old story." Then Laeta turned to Hilary with a pretty air of outraged innocence, appealing to an understanding judge, "Gaia makes it all sound so vulgar with her 'pastor.' It was that handsome priest Celestius, who is all the rage now in the best families. He came to see me one morning when I was having my secretary get my accounts ready for Theophilus. I hate figures anyway," she shook the heavily piled curls with graceful despair, "and Theophilus does ask such stupid questions about where the money has gone, as if everybody didn't know that the freedmen are in league with the shopkeepers. But Celestius did not laugh the way most men do; he just asked if I had remembered the Church and the poor. And he talked about a very poor church in the Suburra. So I suggested an embroidered hanging, and he said that would be very nice."

"And then when it came?" prompted Gaia with a glint of mockery beneath her finely arched brows.

"Well, you can see that fine work would never show up at any distance," and again she held up a border, and all the group that had now gathered around the two ladies of the Cornelii laughed.

"Did Celestius let you get away with that?"

Hilary turned in surprise at the high-pitched sweetness of the voice that challenged so directly. The speaker was quite as statuesque as Gaia and as magnificently painted and dressed as Laeta, but she was older and, Hilary thought, less easy to identify, with a certain firmness about the mouth that might mean anything from obstinacy to scepticism.

Hilary suspected that Laeta was not pretending to be intimidated when she hastened to explain, "Of course, Proba Faltonia, I gave him another piece of cloth. Some very fine crimson brocade which I can't wear any more now that I have changed my hair."

There was a roar of appreciative laughter, and then the conversation broke up. "I'm no fanatic, but I like a priest to look like a priest and not like a eunuch," Proba Faltonia was saying in a firm, shrill voice.

"Oh, come, my dear aunt," a light but warm masculine voice broke in, "you know Attalus will never forgive us if we spoil his party with religion or politics." Hilary turned like all the company with relief to the handsome, laughing-faced young man who slipped a slim, ringed hand on Proba's arm.

One of the men at the edge of the little crowd laughed, and whispered, "Lucky for us all that nephew Faltonius has come to pour oil on the troubled waters."

But they needn't have worried, for it was hard to remember any of the world's troubles as the gilded doors of Attalus' banqueting hall swung open a moment later. Though it had still been winter on the rather tarnished-looking streets of Rome an hour ago, here a summer fairyland opened before their enchanted eyes. The whole room was ablaze with the light of countless lamps swinging from gilded holders and wall brackets while from the marble columns supporting the painted ceiling garlands of flowers swayed gently in the warm, scented air.

And when the guests had stretched out on the gayly enameled couches that ran along three sides of the room, a company of girls dressed as wood nymphs came dancing into the hollow square between the tables with their white arms dripping with garlands of fresh flowers, roses and lilies and violets, and still rarer flowers which Hilary had never seen. And at the end of their dance they draped the garlands around the necks of the applauding guests. And then came a couple of waiters with amphora and mixing bowl, and proceeded to fill the crystal cups with honey colored wine. And after them came a whole procession of waiters with the main dishes of the feast—peacocks with their proud tails arched over the succulent roast, suckling pigs with fruits, guinea hens and thrushes with truffles and mushrooms, and other delicious foods, always with some distinction of rarity or grace of service as well as costliness. But the greatest excitement came with a huge sturgeon which four slaves, dressed as Neapolitan fishermen, carried in on a wooden charger, decorated with shells.

At sight of this several of the men left their couches to gather around the great fish and exclaim at its size. Flushed with their congratulations, Attalus acknowledged that it had been brought by relays straight from his villa at Baiae. And presently he yielded to the entreaties of his guests and summoned one of his secretaries to measure it and make a record of the largest sturgeon that had ever been seen in Rome.

"Attalus will record it among the battles of his ancestors," said Gaia, somberly.

But Fortunatus, lying beyond her, laughingly pretended to rebuke her. "In these happy days a Roman has no battles to record. I don't mind saying I prefer the champion fish."

There was a laugh all up and down the table, and under cover of it Laeta apologized to Hilary. "I am sorry to have left you to Gaia even if you look so serious. There is no accounting for what she will say since her divorce. You'd think she was a Christian the way it has upset her."

"Oh," said Fortunatus, jealous of her obvious pique at Hilary's lack of response, "that is why that Theophilus of yours dares to let you come alone into a wicked world. He is too confident of your wifely faithfulness."

"Oh, no," said Laeta, "he would not let me come without Gaia. He doesn't like banquets—he says they give him indigestion and make him feel dull."

"A sad dog, Theophilus," said the young Faltonius lightly; "prefers to take his pleasures quietly at home. But we shan't blame him, Laeta, so long as he does not keep the chief of them away from us."

"Theophilus is spending the evening with his new philosopher from Alexandria," explained Laeta. There was a roar of ribald laughter from the young men.

31

A little color came into the pale face of Gaia, and she turned to Hilary, "I have a headache, and I am going home. Won't you come to my house soon?"

And as Hilary rose, she smiled. "Laeta will be glad of the chance to come with me. She never really believes that her Theophilus prefers his philosophers to all the dancing girls in Rome."

Several other ladies rose to join the ladies of the Cornelii in their farewell to their host, among them Proba Faltonia, who very noisily insisted that her nephew should not miss the dancing. The latter, after escorting his aunt to her litter, returned to his place on the couch next to Hilary's. "I'm never sure," he said cheerfully, "whether my aunt does this to show her confidence in my behavior or to remind me that she suspects the worst of my tastes."

"Some of the religious ladies in Bordeaux will not go to banquets at all," said Hilary.

Faltonius laughed. "Oh, they do things more by halves in Rome. But here come the dancers. Gaia must have a headache. Everybody knows that Attalus' taste in entertainment as in everything else may be counted on. But your friend who admires Laeta may find them a little dull."

Faltonius' prediction proved correct. The dancers, who returned in the guise of nymphs in Flora's train, proved charming but rather aimless. Then a group of tall, slim girls in light silk robes did a dreamy fountain-in-the-woods dance in which one golden-haired girl shot above the others in a leap that brought applause from the whole company, but there was something taut in the lines of the throat that broke the foaming-waters illusion for Hilary. Then as the nymphs floated away, a darker figure came gleaming, bronze and gold, through the vanishing draperies. And a cry of delight rose from all over the room.

Faltonius' bright face sparkled with enthusiasm. "Jove, Attalus has surpassed himself to give us Attis." And then he turned to Hilary, "A black witch from the Nubian desert, who can dance like nobody else in Rome." As the room quieted, the slim bronze figure in a long pleated tunic of gold brocade drew itself up to its full height. The bare, tightly-curled head assumed the dignity of some archaic bronze goddess, and for a breath-taking moment the exquisitely moulded arms stretched the gleaming gold taut over the shadows of the breast like metal. Then the superb head turned to face the banquet tables with flashing teeth, and it was as if the light flashed from mouth and eyes through the whole gleaming body, until before their astonished gaze the long shining limbs uncoiled and flung their bronze grace on the air. And as Hilary watched, the tight knot in the pit of his stomach unclenched, and a warmth of content flowed through all his limbs.

But it was not merely the incredible grace of the body as it took one pose after another that held Hilary spellbound; it was rather the miraculous fashion in which every so often the gleaming flesh seemed to dissolve into a flash of light. Then in the slowing rhythms of the flutes it was as if the light had taken body again in liquid bronze that seemed to melt into the tessellated pavement. But even as the applause broke over the heap of gold-shot earth, a flame leaped from it, and the earth itself rose in fire, and the air took fire from it, and all the dross in the fire burned away, and the golden light flashed again on the clear air. It seemed to Hilary that never had he known such a clear certainty that the beauty of the heart's dream is not an illusion but the surest reality. He heard the applause break forth again, but he had no impulse to join it, or to do anything else to break the sheer completeness of his content.

"May I sit here beside you?" asked a low voice, speaking perfect Latin but with a warmth that went to the heart.

For a second Hilary fought against the chill of waking, but the low voice carried with it the warmth of the dream. He looked over the cushioned edge of his couch, and the eyes of the dancer, now flashing with mischief, looked up at him from under the rigid helmet of the tightly curled hair.

"But come up here and sit on the couch," he protested.

Attis laughed.

"Not, thank the gods, in the house of Attalus." And then as Hilary looked embarrassed, she went on more gravely, "Every dance has its rules, my lord, and only the inefficient fail to turn them to good account."

"But you are real," he said, and cursed himself for his stupidity.

Attis laughed a low throaty laugh that took off all the sting of his inadequacy. "Do you wonder why I have chosen you to sit with?" And now for the first time Hilary became aware of the teasing voices about them.

"Where did you learn to dance like that?"

She laughed companionably. "That is why I noticed you, my friend; you were not thinking of yourself or of me, but only of the dance. That is the purest kind of worship, the only kind worth having."

"You are right; it did not seem of this earth."

"Oh, it is of this earth, and of a good deal of it, too."

"The great desert?" he asked.

For a moment her face looked thoughtful, and he saw that she was not so young as the movements of her body suggested. "That is the beginning," she said, "and Egypt and Syria, and Armenia, and Greece, and now Rome, where the whole world ends."

"Is that what you were dancing?"

"If you like," she said lightly.

"It was more than that, I am sure."

A mocking look came into the dark eyes, and that incredible light flashed again. "Then, if you wish, what all the songs and the dances tell, the creation of beauty and"—the eyes seemed to melt like the gleam on the surface of the oil in a lamp—"its destruction."

"The end of it looked final, certainly," he said, trying to catch her tone.

"You may call it the destruction of the city."

"Oh, come now," said Hilary, "you have never seen a city burned."

"But I have," she said quietly. "It was in Armenia. My husband did not think they had taken the measure of the Romans. So we got out just before they closed the gates, and hiding in a wood on a higher peak we saw the city burn."

"It was probably a flimsy thing," Hilary said half to himself.

But she shook her head. "It was solid stone. But the stone crumbled in the heat, even the high temple of the god. A woman came out on the temple roof that night with her arms stretched up to the sky, and the flames leaped up at her, and she burned there against the sky as if she were tinder, and then the flame fell."

Hilary shuddered, but she looked at him thoughtfully.

"Like my husband, who pitied her, too, she is a cool shade among the shades these many years, my lord," she said reprovingly, "but for one moment she was beautiful, and that you saw tonight." She lifted beautifully moulded brows and sprang to her feet. "It is growing late for metaphysics, my lord. Come to my house on the Aventine, and we shall talk philosophy in earnest." There was no mockery in the soft eyes that looked down on him for a moment. Then she was gone in a flash of gold. Hilary turned to find Fortunatus watching him a little sardonically. He looked for his host, but he was gone; so was Faltonius. He nodded.

It was cold in the anteroom, and as the slaves lighted their torches, Hilary sighed. The dance of Attis had brought something to the threshold of his memory, but he could not lift it across. Now he remembered with sudden clarity—it was the flaming Dido in the golden fire on Rhodope's embroidery easel. And the choking sound of the little Greek girl's sobbing thudded in his breast as he went out into the dank Roman air.

V

THE DAY OF THE GAMES, HOWEVER, BROUGHT RE-assurance. It was, to begin with, beautifully clear and sparkling weather that lifted even the winter heaviness of the narrow Roman streets. And it was impossible to resist the excitement that pulsed through the crowds thronging every alley and portico and forum in the city. For the first time Hilary wondered if perhaps he had not been too sceptical of the incessant bustle of the house of Symmachus.

Indeed, when Symmachus and his train with a great flourish arrived at the senate house for the formal procession to the Flavian amphitheater, Hilary wondered how he could ever have been so unsympathetic. For not only the company of Symmachus but all the senatorial escorts were in their most splendid array, and between the self-congratulations of the senators and the plaudits of the crowds that swarmed over every available portico or roof it was difficult not to feel that something very important, indeed, was going forward. And when the great procession reached the vast arched circumference of the amphitheater, it was impossible to resist a quite personal sense of triumph. For a moment they paused under the great vaults of the entrance, and then at a blast of trumpets the senatorial company emerged into a glare of sunlight, in the center of what seemed to be a great bowl lined with flowers blowing in the breeze. And then as the eye steadied, Hilary saw clearly the tier upon tier of shouting and cheering men and women, rising to the bright blue sky.

"And the order was right," said Symmachus to a friend of his own age, as he took his place in the front row of an empty stretch of marble seats. And then he signalled his young guests to sit beside him.

But they had hardly settled in their places, when another blast of trumpets dwarfed all the noises of the vast crowd and brought everyone to his feet, shouting, "Caesar." And the most magnificent procession Hilary had ever seen swept on to the sand of the arena. First came a company of the Praetorian guard, bronzed figures with short tunics, gilded breastplates, and flashing helmets. They marched with a steady tread that struck the wooden floor of the arena to muffled thunder, and brought the whole vast throng to its feet, roaring with pride. And the roar deepened as a single giant figure with uncovered head brought up the rear of the company, flanked on either side by young

36

soldiers, carrying golden shield and helmet and sword, while he strode forward with majestic freedom.

"The Emperor?" Hilary asked involuntarily. The finely moulded lips of Symmachus straightened in a surprisingly hard line, but before he could reply the crowd had broken out in wild shouts: "Stilicho, Stilicho!"

It was hard for Hilary to believe that this was the barbarian upstart whom he had heard his grandfather so often blame for all that had gone wrong with Rome in these degenerate days. As he looked down, Hilary saw that Stilicho was older than he had first seemed, with white hair and a harder set to the jaw and a tighter throat than had at first appeared, but he kept the march of his troops with an ease a youth might have envied and a majesty that suddenly dwarfed all the dignity of the senate, now alertly silent in the popular uproar.

"There are those who say that that is what he aims at," said Symmachus in a low, cautious voice. But looking down into the proud, serenely confident face, Hilary grudgingly reflected that nowhere in the city, save for the marble statue of Augustus standing above his forum, had he seen a figure that more completely embodied the majesty of Rome. And then as Stilicho came to the marble barriers above which the senate sat, he gravely saluted the fathers of the city. And Hilary saw how in spite of himself the firm mouth of Symmachus relaxed.

But more trumpets were blowing, and now came the household troops of the Emperor in shimmering chainmail vests over purple tunics with great purple cloaks floating from their shoulders and purple plumes from their gold-crested helmets. After the thunder of the legions of Stilicho's company, these moved so quietly in their gilded shoes that Hilary thought of the chorus in a play which some Greek players had once brought to Bordeaux. Apparently he was not alone in this idea, for he heard one of the officials standing below the marble balustrade on which he was leaning say to his fellow, "I'd like to see those pretty mimes on the frontier."

Symmachus cried sharply for silence, and the two officials, undeniably old soldiers, shifted their position. And one of the

37

senators sitting behind Hilary muttered, "How the empire was won and will be lost in two acts"; but a companion corrected him, "No, here come the ones who will lose the empire."

"The Emperor's household," said Symmachus, as a group of richly dressed figures in long many-colored robes followed the guard. There had been a good deal of applause for the imperial guard, and Hilary felt that they had deserved it on appearance at least. But there was a curious silence as this new company appeared. They were, in a more elegant fashion, quite as pleasing to the eye, and they moved with great grace; and then Hilary realized that that was the trouble—they moved with an almost feminine grace. And then Hilary understood the word that was being whispered with various intonations of curiosity and contempt up and down the tiers, "The eunuchs."

But now attention had shifted to the imperial box beside the senatorial seats. There a number of very different-looking men had appeared, still richly but soberly dressed, with a look of power too sure of itself to be concerned with its effect. And then the whole great audience was on its feet, crying, "Caesar, Caesar," in a rhythmic chant that seemed to shake all the tiers of the vast amphitheater. There was no mistaking the Emperor in his purple robes with a diadem of pearls on his forehead.

He looked younger than Hilary had expected, though he carried himself with a casual indifference that suggested an older man, looking neither to right nor left but walking straight ahead with his head thrust a little forward and down. As he came down the marble steps, Hilary caught sight of his face for a moment. It was absolutely devoid of expression. He might be deaf and blind so far as any sign of awareness of the cheering was concerned.

At that moment a slim young woman in purple robes and diadem appeared at the rear of the box and moved diffidently forward. As she did so, a very handsome older woman leaned over from behind her and adjusted the crown on her fair head.

"It is the Lady Serena, the Empress' mother," said Symmachus in his best schoolmaster's manner. And then the Emperor, still as oblivious to his surroundings as if he were a sleepwalker, took his place on a low-backed throne in the front of the imperial box. Timidly the Empress took her place on a similar throne at his side. She looked at him as she did so, but he gave no sign of awareness of her presence.

Now all eyes had turned back to the arena, which had suddenly filled with a very different throng coming up from the doors beneath the marble barrier. Several processions seemed to be converging at once upon the space before the Emperor's box, hunters with spears and nets and bows and arrows, wild-animal trainers cracking their whips, grooms and slaves in every sort of costume, flowing cotton robes, short trousers, skins, bright colored loincloths—the variety seemed endless, and the delighted crowd laughed and shouted its identification of the various peoples. Some carried short sticks, others little whips, still others tridents and goads, and long poles.

With every accent in the world this motley throng shouted its salute to Caesar. But the Emperor still took no notice. Only when an attendant thrust an ivory staff into his hands, did he seem to rouse himself, and with a lazy, indifferent gesture let the wand slip from his fingers. A great cheer rose from the arena and echoed through the tiers of the amphitheater. The show had begun.

Afterward in dictating a letter home to his grandfather Hilary tried to recall what followed, but found himself bewildered. It seemed as if the pages of Pliny had suddenly come to life in that arena. There was a constant thudding of iron gates, as ever fresh species of animals leaped into the arena. At first the theme of the show was plainly costliness and rarity. There was a display of magnificent horses from Spain, of bloodhounds from Crete, of hunting dogs from far-off Ireland, of sheep with very finely curled fleeces from Persia. Then came a procession of elephants, and ostriches, and finally the crocodiles were shot upside down from the gates to the sand of the arena and forced to show some signs of life to right themselves. There was a scurry as the riders pulled the horses away, and sent the ostriches flying to the delight of the whole crowd. But although instructions had clearly been given to get the rarer species to safety, one of the

Persian sheep was overlooked. With a snap of its jaws an alligator sliced the creature in two and swallowed half, while another of the great reptiles snapped up the other half. A roar of delight went up from the crowd, and Symmachus smiled with satisfaction.

But that seemed to be the signal for the end of the exhibition. Now the fighting beasts took over, at first a couple of young lions evenly matched, and then several goaded into battle, and, finally, whole droves of wild animals in a tangle of combat that filled the arena with flying fur and squeals and howls and roars that made the women screech and the men yell with delight, as the frightened beasts leaped at the marble barriers. And then came the hunters, pitting their skill and arms against the maddened beasts, charging across the smoking arena.

At first the cheers rose for the skill with which the men extricated themselves from the paws of their prey, but presently a tension came into the air, and when one luckless hunter slipped and fell, this time before a charging elephant, a roar of savage delight rose, it seemed, from every throat. A couple of the hunter's fellows rushed to his rescue and snatched him from under the uplifted foot of the elephant, and the roar of delight turned to growls of disappointment. A few minutes later the rescuer just missed the hapless wretch who had been knocked down by a charging lion, and as the beast tore the man to pieces, the yells of the spectators rose to the clear blue sky, and the winter air warmed with the sickish-sweet stench of blood.

"A bold and warlike people," said Symmachus approvingly.

Hilary looked at him in astonishment, and then feeling an unspoken challenge in his haughty glance, he slowly turned his eyes back to the arena. One of the hunters had thrown his spear into the lion, while another held his net poised. A few feet away some tigers had leapt on the torn carcass. There was a hush of expectancy as several of the hunters closed in on them, and a groan as the hunters despatched the tigers and the lions without further incident. A bevy of slaves rushed out with shovels and pails, to be followed by another with fresh sand and brushes. A hum of conversation rose all around the vast arena.

"Those hunters are not much good," said Symmachus. "To simply panic like that and just slaughter the beasts!"

Then there was a shout: "The gladiators!" Like the hunters they seemed to pour in from all directions, but there the resemblance ended. For these men fell sharply into two groups. One group was made up of Roman professionals, or perhaps one should say the men who had become professional, for some of the gladiators were red-skinned and fair-haired. These rushed with enthusiasm to the area before the Emperor's box. The others were hardly inferior to the gladiators in physique, though few of them looked as well-nourished, but there the resemblance ended. For where the professionals moved with confidence and even alacrity, these seemed bewildered, and the arena slaves had to prod them with goads and tridents much as they had the wild animals. It was, however, a large company in sum, and a roar of approval rose through the structure when they gathered before the Emperor's box.

As they shouted the traditional "We who are about to die" salutation, the Emperor seemed to wake up and, with more energy than he had yet shown, he again threw down his staff.

"After that fiasco with the beasts, I hope they get this off to a better start," muttered Symmachus.

Then the gladiators withdrew to the barriers, leaving two men alone in the center of the arena.

"They say they are going to pit fifty gladiators against one hundred of the barbarians," said one of the younger voices behind.

"That is overdoing it," said an older voice; "with such numbers it will be no better than a vulgar brawl."

Then a joyous shout rose all over the arena: "Alexas!"

The favorite saluted and then turned to the man in a shaggy hide, watching him uncomfortably ten paces away.

A shiver ran through the audience. "A Hun, a Hun!" Hilary looked with sudden curiosity at this first specimen of the dreaded Huns, of whom he had heard so much from Gothic slave and Roman soldier alike. He must have been a large man, but now he was crouching uneasily. He held the long sword of his people in one hand.

Symmachus watched with the eye of a connoisseur. "They are never at ease off their horses, our generals say."

The Roman gladiator lunged at the Hun with his short sword, but contented himself with lifting the man's long hair. A roar of laughter went up from the marble seats. The Hun rose a little on his lean haunches, and one could hear the sharp breath of expectancy whistle through the tiers of the amphitheater. The gladiator thrust again, this time nicking the oxhide on his opponent's chest. Again a roar, and then the Hun seemed to realize that he was being mocked, for he flung out his sword in a sudden fury that nearly swept the Roman off his feet. This time the cheers redoubled, for the fight had been joined in earnest.

"He will wear himself out the way he is thrashing about," said Symmachus judiciously. But a movement on the opposite side of the amphitheater caught Hilary's eye. Something dark was coming straight down the white tiers. People were pulling away, leaving a curiously straight path down the rows of seats, and apparently paying little attention because the Hun in the arena had begun to press the gladiator. Hilary tried to make out what was happening, what the dark thing was. Then as it reached the second tier of seats, Hilary saw that it was a man in a brown robe. Even as he gazed in astonishment, the man leaped to the first tier in one remarkably sure movement and for a moment paused, drawing himself up to his full height, on the edge of the marble barrier. It was too far for Hilary to see his face clearly, but he certainly looked like the little monk whom he had seen in the street and at the house of Pammachius. For there was that same air of calm assurance so absurd in such a squalid figure.

The Hun seemed to have gone mad, flailing wildly with his sword, but moving with such strength and speed that the Roman gladiator was clearly put to the test. Every eye in the amphitheater was glued to the fighters. Hilary wondered if anybody else had noticed the little man. What on earth could a monk be doing at the Emperor's games? But even as he wondered, the little man leaped into the arena and came running up to the combatants. As he came near, Hilary saw that it was indeed the same man. He was running quite steadily, with the same astonishingly clear and resolved look on his face, and stretching his hands out to the fighters as if he had some business with them.

They were too absorbed in their struggle to be aware of his approach, but the crowd had caught sight of him, and one could hear the sharp hiss of astonishment that ran through the vast circumference of the amphitheater. The little monk, however, seemed completely unaware of the shock he had caused. Reaching the fighters, he raised one arm, traced on the air a huge sign of the cross, and, so far as Hilary could determine, without saying a word, thrust himself between the two combatants. Through some miracle the broken thrust of their weapons missed him, and the two men, whether pushed back by some unsuspected strength of his, or frozen with astonishment, seemed to hang from his outstretched hands against the air.

"What is he doing?" rose from a thousand voices. And then with a mighty roar came the answer, "He is trying to stop the fight!" The gladiator and the Hun jumped away as the first tile came hurtling down from under the roof, to be followed by a volley of stones from the arena itself. And then from all over the amphitheater came a hail of missiles of every description, stones, bricks, tiles, water flasks, daggers, whips with leaden ends, anything and everything an infuriated mob could lay hands on. For what seemed to Hilary, frozen in horror, an incredible time the little man stood erect; then he fell to his knees, and toppled over in the sand.

The two fighters remained staring at him as if transfixed, but all around men were leaping from the marble barriers into the arena and running to the spot where bright red was coming from the brown heap upon the sand, like wine from a broken earthenware cup. Seeing the crowd piling up in a wildly screaming and flailing heap upon the fallen man, Hilary shouted, "Leave him alone!" but in the mad uproar only Fortunatus heard him, and he nearly choked Hilary, whispering, "Keep still, you fool; there is nothing you can do but get us all killed."

Hilary turned to the Emperor's box, but Honorius was standing before his throne, quite alert at last. Then two files of guards appeared and closed the Emperor from view. Hilary looked back to the arena. The heap of struggling bodies seemed to be disentangling itself while other men milled around them. Someone brandished a shockingly white arm dripping with blood, somebody else a bloody thigh looking strangely inhuman. There was a yell of triumph from the crowd, but now the guards were in the senators' box, directing them to follow the imperial party at once.

"It is an outrage! Those Christians!" muttered Symmachus, hurrying after his colleagues. As they reached the stairs, Hilary looked back. All over the great structure men were shepherding women and children to the invisible stairways. Even in the arena the crowd was melting away, circling about one area as if an invisible wall had been erected around it.

As they left the amphitheater, Hilary and Fortunatus fell to the rear of the senatorial party. Some of the guards still escorted them, but it was unnecessary. For in every direction all one could see were little groups of people clinging to each other and hurrying off as fast as they could.

"I did not know Rome could be so quiet," said Fortunatus, and then with a cry of surprise he caught Hilary as he reeled with nausea.

VI

IT WAS SOME TIME BEFORE FORTUNATUS COULD persuade Hilary that their staying away from the house of Symmachus too long would only aggravate any suspicion the great pagan leader might have of his young Christian friends.

And when they finally did go, Hilary was not so sure that he should have yielded.

Symmachus received them graciously enough, but he seemed rather remote and preoccupied. And he turned away almost at once to a little group of older men, from which cautious whispers spread through the room. Once or twice Hilary thought people lowered their voices when they became aware of his presence. But he knew that his nerves were a little on edge; so he tried to persuade himself that he might be imagining it all. Presently, the voice of Symmachus rose in the unusually quiet room. "It is more than a breach of the peace. They are determined to destroy the games." Then his voice fell, and a man standing near Hilary turned to him helpfully, "It is clearly the hand of Pammachius."

"But we saw the monk turned away from the gate of Pammachius." Hilary looked to Fortunatus for confirmation. But the latter muttered only, "Don't be a fool."

Fortunately, Symmachus appeared not to have heard, for just then he summoned Hilary to present to him a young man who had come up to his couch. He was his son Fabius, and he had just returned from the family estates in Campania. He was a rather austere-looking young man, with something of Symmachus' hauteur, but also a touch of pedantry in the carefulness with which he spoke. His father turned back to his older guests, and presently his voice rose again:

"There is no question that they have brought pressure to bear on the Emperor. This making a martyr out of a fanatic is an old trick of theirs." For a moment something sharp and exasperated flashed through the habitual modulation of Symmachus' voice.

"It's Stilicho I can't understand," said another voice, quieter, more troubled. Hilary looked to the other side of Symmachus' couch; and this time he recognized the speaker, the Senator Pompeianus. "He's always had a better sense of how things are here in Rome. Even if he's a Christian, Rome comes first—at least I always thought so."

"Stilicho!" For a moment the firm voice of Symmachus trembled with indignation. "When I reminded him that to touch the gladiatorial games was to undermine the warlike spirit of the Roman people, he asked how many men Rome had sent into the imperial army during the last ten years!"

"What else can you expect of a barbarian?" A little shock ran through the room as the old man's voice rose shrilly from the little group around Symmachus' couch, and all the other voices fell.

"Lampadius is right," Fabius whispered in Hilary's ear. And then his dry voice sharpened surprisingly. "The reason I had to miss the Emperor's games was that some recruiting agent of Stilicho's was trying to take our farmers, some of our best ones, too. How they think you are going to run estates like ours without proper help I don't see." And then catching Hilary's surprise, he hastened to apologize, "But there, I must sound to you like a grumbling bailiff."

Hilary started to murmur something discreetly sympathetic, but Fortunatus was at his side. "Come, everybody is moving on."

He was right. Symmachus' guests were slipping away, it appeared to Hilary, rather hurriedly. Only the little knot around their host's couch seemed completely absorbed in their low-voiced conversation.

"I don't know about you," said Fortunatus as they regained the street, "but I have had enough of the men of Rome for the present. How about trying the ladies this afternoon?"

Hilary reminded Fortunatus of the other letters they had brought, for instance, the letter to Pammachius. But Fortunatus would have none of it. "What are you dreaming of? Do you want to find yourself like that damned monk caught between two fighters?"

So they went calling among the great houses on the fashionable Aventine, beginning, at Fortunatus' suggestion, with the house of Laeta.

"She's very pious," Hilary took the chance to return a little of his friend's teasing.

But Fortunatus only grinned. "Not even piety can spoil a figure like that."

46

"Theophilus is an eclectic philosopher, they say, quite devoid of any sense of humor, or apparently anything else human. Such men—"

But Fortunatus laughed. "She's no fool, our little Laeta. She likes to play with fire, but she is not going to run any risk of being burned."

"Gaia seems to me much more interesting," said Hilary thoughtfully.

Fortunatus stared at him; then he laughed. "Bookworm that you are, you must like risks. Look at her record."

"She's pagan, and there are no end of divorced women in her circle. Anyway I'm sure her husband was a bounder."

Fortunatus' supercilious eyebrows rose a little higher.

"You do leap to conclusions for all your pedantry, Hilary. While you were extending your geographical knowledge the other night, I was acquiring a little information about our new friends. Laeta's Theophilus and Gaia's rejected Alexander are brothers, rich and Rome's purplest, and some sort of cousins of our two cousins. There the resemblance ends. Their uncle who was the guardian of the young ladies seems to have shared your preference; so he gave Gaia the livelier of his two nephews. Everybody agrees he's a charming fellow with usually very good taste in women. He appreciated Gaia, still does. But there was a dancing girl in a pretty little house on the Palatine. If Gaia ever heard of her, she kept her knowledge to herself. Alexander, who must be a bit of an ass, took his luck for granted, and proceeded to take up a little Persian girl at Baiae. Instead of finding a villa for her in a quiet spot on the coast, he put her in the household. Gaia is a housekeeper of the ancient model, who knows what is going on under her roof. And instead of spoiling the Persian's charms with a good beating or two, she simply gave Alexander the requisite notice and came back here to Rome."

"I don't blame her," said Hilary.

Fortunatus raised his eyebrows. "My dear Hilary, if you didn't listen to the gossip in the Bordeaux baths, surely you must have listened to the Lenten preachers. If you believe them,

47

no bishop in Gaul would grant a separation to a lady who had been defied by an impertinent maid, for fear of exterminating the best families of the land."

But Hilary would not yield. "Your cynicism is more revolting than Laeta's piety!"

Half an hour later Hilary was not so sure. Laeta was having a reception to display a new bust which she had just added to the already impressive collection around the walls of the spacious atrium of Theophilus.

"Come," said Laeta, taking Fortunatus' hand, "and look at my greatest ancestor."

"Collateral, of course," said a low voice, coughing respectfully. The speaker was an elegant young man with thick, curled hair. There was a muffled giggle in the company, and Laeta tossed her head prettily. "Oh, never mind the technicalities, Celestius. He is the greatest of my ancestors, and I want everybody to know it."

It was, to Hilary's surprise, a beautiful bust of the finest white Luna marble, representing the classic Roman aristocrat. The face had perhaps a little more assertiveness, a little more intensity than most of the genre, but as Hilary looked around at the other busts of the Cornelian family, he had to admit that it seemed to be a family trait. If anything, the latest addition seemed a little more urbane and elegant than the earlier. It was the more surprising, therefore, to find this member of the family not in the robes of a consul, but in a plain tunic such as a slave might wear, with the top of a staff against his breast.

"It is a beautiful statue," murmured Hilary. But a sharp high voice, the voice of Proba Faltonia, broke in, "But how do you know Pope Cornelius looked like that?"

"Oh," said Laeta, "I told Miron to study the family memorials and see if he could catch the family look, and I think he has done very well."

The sculptor, who was standing smiling beside his masterpiece, bowed.

"I think he has done better than that," interposed Fortunatus in his most gravely caressing voice. "He has even managed to

48

add to the pagan severity something of the Christian graciousness of Laeta." Hilary looked anxiously at his friend; but Laeta
was fairly purring with satisfaction, and several of the young
men looked enviously at Fortunatus. Only Proba Faltonia returned doggedly to the attack, her still pretty, high-bred features
sharpening as she turned to Laeta.

"But it doesn't look at all like that picture you used to have
of Pope Cornelius in your chapel, Laeta. Have one of your
slaves bring it out here, and let us see if I am not right."

"That dreadful old thing!" pouted Laeta. "You know it was
done by some wretched painter who couldn't even do his own
dark-age style well."

But Proba was not to be turned aside so easily. "I don't know
about that. It was obviously a poor thing as a work of art, but I
always thought it looked as if it might have come from the life."

"Proba!" Even Laeta was becoming a little exasperated. "I
sent it to the catacombs when I had our chapel done over. It
will fit in better down there."

Hilary had not yet seen the catacombs, but he could quite
believe that an old picture would fit in better almost anywhere
than in the bright and charming little chapel into which Laeta
now led them. An idyllic mosaic of the Good Shepherd, young
and handsome, in a short gold tunic, with snow-white sheep
gamboling on a flower-jewelled hill against the bluest of blue
skies filled the apse, while a radiant figure that might equally
well have been either Christ or Orpheus, followed by a troop
of beautiful youths and maidens in flowing robes of jewel hues,
adorned one wall.

"And the nicest thing about it is that Theophilus likes it so
much," said Laeta happily, as her friends admired the pretty
little chapel.

But when the company moved back to the peristyle for the
wine which the slaves were bringing in in crystal jars, Hilary
pleaded a promise to pay another visit. Fortunatus, however,
refused to accompany him. "Christianity is so much more
cheerful," he whispered as he stood aside to let his friend pass.

In contrast to the house of Laeta en fête, that of Gaia seemed

49

quiet, indeed. A look of pleasure lighted her austere face, however, as she greeted her guest, and then she proceeded to show him the large, bare atrium.

"It has not been much changed from the old days," she said quietly. "It has been enlarged, of course; everything is on a bigger scale now. And when you keep collecting things as a family like ours does—" she shrugged her shoulders.

As he looked around the great room, Hilary was struck by the extraordinary impression of spaciousness, even bareness, that it made on senses still overpowered by the lush beauty of Laeta's house. There were, surprisingly enough, quite as many statues and busts in Gaia's atrium, perhaps more, for the shadowy walls held some masks of a more primitive style than anything in the house of Laeta. But there the resemblance ended.

It was partly the nature of the basic architecture, all very substantial but austerely simple. But still more it was the total absence of clutter. A few flowering shrubs in white and gray jars softened the hardness of the stone, but an obviously ancient altar was quite bare. And the fountain fell from a beautifully fashioned bronze dolphin into a low marble basin. But it seemed to Hilary that the very bareness accentuated the charm of the sunlight through the open roof, the cool prattling of the water itself, the stillness of the shadows behind the pillars. It was all very restful and, he added, as he sat down on a stone bench warmed by the sunlight, very beautiful.

The mistress of the house completed the effect. Only a woman very sure of herself, or very indifferent, would have been content with that fine white wool robe falling so simply about her tall figure, with the dark hair drawn back so firmly from the broad brow.

"It is very beautiful," said Hilary. "And perfectly fitting," he added with a smile. An answering light played on the quiet face.

"Thank you, that is praise they would have valued." And suddenly Hilary wondered what it would be like to live day in and day out with all those ghostly presences looking on. She seemed to divine something of the direction of his thoughts, for a rare flick of amusement came into her steady gaze as she said, "If you have lived with them most of your life, you rather take them for granted."

Hilary laughed. "It is as well that we do not have this in Gaul. To say nothing of the competence of the sculptors, some of my ancestors would not cut so dignified a figure."

For a moment Hilary was a little surprised at what he had said. It had been very hard for him to find anything in common between himself and the few statues of Gallic warriors which he had seen from the hands of Roman or Greek sculptors, and he could find no common ground at all with the fantastically rude effigy of a Druid priest which had been dug up on his grandfather's estate.

It seemed to be a new idea to Gaia, for she looked thoughtfully at him for several moments before she responded. "That's an odd notion. There's plenty of violence here, one way and another—battles, riots, assassinations—one never knows how human life will end. One of them was even beaten and beheaded as a common criminal."

There was a touch of irony in that sentence, and he looked at her curiously.

"He is not here, of course. You will have to go up to Laeta's house to see him."

He smiled. "As a matter of fact I have—with Fortunatus," he added, surprised a little at himself that he should be so anxious to have no misunderstanding. But her mind, as always, went directly to the point.

"What did you think of the new bust?"

"Very fine, quite worthy, I assure you, to hold its own with the rest. Pope Cornelius restored to his family!"

A shadow crossed the clear face. "But what did it look like? Did it look like the old picture at all?"

"I should think not," and he went on to tell her about Laeta's sending the picture down to the catacombs. She seemed amused.

"That is where it belongs in more ways than one. He's buried there—if they have not been moving his bones about the beastly way they do. And down there," she looked at him thoughtfully, "there will be other people who look like that."

"That is probably what Laeta had in mind."

For a moment something unaccustomedly speculative came into her clear gaze. "You know," she said thoughtfully, "Christianity would never be what it is today, whatever you think of it." She added hastily, as if she had suddenly recalled her responsibility as a hostess, "if it had depended on people like Laeta and her friends. You understand," she seemed to find again an unaccustomed difficulty in clarifying her meaning, "let us say what happened, when you see that old picture. It's not much—successful artists did not turn Christian in those days, I am sure. But there is something in the look."

"I must go down to the catacombs; you make him sound interesting."

But she hastened to put him right. "Don't misunderstand me. I think they were quite right to kill him. He betrayed everything his family stood for, just as they did." To Hilary's surprise she pointed to a couple of very fine busts of the Gracchi. "The gods have not made one man as good as another, and to take from the strong to piece out the weak ends only in mediocrity."

Hilary noticed that under the pressure of her conviction her voice did not rise but swelled rather with an astonishing vibrancy. It was startling to hear so terse a summary of a very complicated business from a woman who looked like that. With her usual quickness of perception she caught his puzzlement, and her voice softened. "Of course, I know that, being a Christian, you can not see it as I do."

Hilary hastened to reassure her. "You know my grandfather is still a philosopher of the old school, even though he allowed his Christian wife to bring up the family."

She seemed not to have heard him, for she went on, "I do not mind Christians being Christians, for themselves. What I am afraid of is that Christianity will be the destruction of Rome."

Then she must have realized that Hilary was not following her. She checked herself and apologized, closer to embarrassment than she had yet been, for troubling him with worries he could hardly be expected to share. He protested his concern, but she declined to talk any more about it. So he took his leave, wondering if perhaps she had not had too many lonely nights of late to brood over the fate of empires.

He remembered then the dancer Attis, so swift of perception, so impersonally gracious. Her house was higher up the Aventine, where the villas had begun to pull away from each other among the gardens. To his surprise he found it a small, obviously old house, set primly behind a high yellow wall, with only a light balcony of blue-painted latticework across the deeper yellow front to set it apart from its neighbors.

He was surprised to find Attis in a long robe like any Roman lady of rank, but the wool was a raw-blue color that turned her brown skin to gold. And she was smiling a welcome of flashing teeth and eyes that made even that blue seem a quiet color. And then as quickly the radiance faded, and Hilary gazed with surprise into a face of great dignity with a certain ageless look of intelligence and composure.

She stood quite still while he looked around the atrium in deepening amazement. For instead of the usual tablets and busts and statues of the houses where Hilary was accustomed to visit, this room was decorated with an array of masks, and statuettes on pedestals, and strange objects of metal and semi-precious stones and ivory and gilded wood that Hilary had no way of identifying, for he had never seen anything like them in his life. Here in an outwardly conventional house in a quiet neighborhood Hilary had stepped out of the normal Roman world as completely as he had the night when he had first seen Attis dance at the banquet of Attalus.

He smiled at his own astonishment, and she relaxed comfortably. "In the oasis in the sands from which I come, my lord, all those things men talk about in Rome—family, ancestors, poor, rich, the city, the empire, even the individual soul—have no meaning. It is our people, our tribe, if you wish. All the men can ride and fight; all the women can dance."

"Have you ever gone back to your oasis?"

She smiled at him with a look of compassion that puzzled

53

him. "Life, my lord, is a road on which there is no turning back."
Then she slipped her hand through his arm and began showing
him her treasures.

The twilight was slanting in among them, deepening the
shadows of their mystery when they finished. "The world is a
vast place," Hilary sighed.

In the failing light the face of Attis looked remote and mysterious too. "It is a good deal bigger than Rome, at least," she
said soberly, "and even Rome has taken very little of its measure." As he left her door, Hilary wondered how much of his
confusion she had guessed.

VII

ON THEIR NEXT VISIT, A WEEK OR SO LATER,
things seemed more normal at the house of Symmachus, and
Hilary began to wonder if perhaps the leader of a lost cause
had not developed a special power of assimilating disaster. He
was as gracious as ever to Hilary and Fortunatus, but the former,
at least, suspected that his present preoccupations were of a
nature with which even the most casual of Christians could
hardly be expected to sympathize.

Hilary had thought a good deal of what Gaia had said about
the different kinds of Christians. Now as they took their way
from the house of Symmachus, he broached the idea to Fortunatus with a laughing reminder of Laeta's statue. As he had
expected, Fortunatus was not much interested in the different
kinds of Christians: it was the sort of thing he was inclined to
defer until the future when doubtless he would have to reckon
with it as men had to reckon with so many things when they
married and settled down. But Laeta's statue was a subject in
which he was definitely interested and that in the present.

"That sculptor," he said with what was for him surprising

54

vindictiveness, "is as unprincipled a rascal as I have ever come across even among artists!"

"He seemed to me to know his business," said Hilary cautiously.

"Know his business? He is probably the cleverest sculptor in Rome today. The man who did that statue could do anything. But what a thing for a man as good as that to choose to do—flattering his patroness by making the eminent ancestor, and a pope at that, look like a very pretty and very feminine woman!"

"That is probably the only way he can make his living."

But Fortunatus, who had a very cultivated palate and never neglected any opportunity to satisfy it, was for once severe. "He looked sleek enough to me. No, he is a Syrian freedman, and they're worse even than the Greeks."

But when Hilary wondered what the old picture of Pope Cornelius looked like, Fortunatus agreed at once that he was curious too. He warned Hilary, however, that though he was ready to go out to the catacombs to see it, he did not propose to get mixed up with any of the pilgrimages likely, from all reports, to infest them. "They say that veritable mobs of the lowest elements haunt the place, and every disease known to man is to be found there."

The throng on the Appian way outside the catacombs of Saint Calixtus certainly bore out Fortunatus' worst fears in its general effect of sordid misery. But even Fortunatus had to confess himself surprised at the first sight of the basilica of Saint Sebastian. Christian wealth had certainly been generous in the church it had erected over the entrance, but it had been also, it seemed to Hilary, quite tasteless. The walls were hung with tablets and offerings, not only of lamps and garlands but of various fragments of human anatomy in marble and alabaster and even silver and gold. And underneath were the monuments, in every degree of grace or lack of grace, of those latter-day faithful departed who had been privileged to lay their bodies beside those of the saints and martyrs in hopes of the resurrection of the blessed. The children and heirs of many of these had put their busts above their tombs, and as Hilary took in the rather prosperously commonplace aspect of the faces so represented by the on the whole not very inspired sculptors, he thought again of what Gaia had said of the different models of Christians.

A ragged woman with hollow cheeks and large wistful eyes, who had pushed in front of the two young men to look at one particularly imposing bust of a very thin-mouthed, dour-looking merchant, summed it up very well when she said enviously to a companion as miserable-looking as herself, "One must be very rich to be buried so close to the martyrs."

Fortunatus shook his head. "It would take a lot more than that to get that old skinflint into heaven. Did he really think huddling up to the martyrs like this would do it?"

But the two women looked so shocked at the blasphemy that Hilary hastily pushed his companion to the back of the church, where a motley crowd of men and women of all types were jostling around a low doorway. Taking one look at the generally ragged and mangy-looking aspect of the crowd, one of Hilary's slaves started importantly to clear a way for his master, but the latter bade him come back and wait his turn so sharply that several people turned to look at him in astonishment. Then they seemed to huddle a little closer as if for protection from even the kindness of their betters.

"Are you going to make martyrs of us all to this stench?" mocked Fortunatus, but he hastily sobered at the indignation in his companion's look. In spite of himself Hilary wondered from under what rotting stones in all the gleaming splendor of Rome such slug-like faces could have crawled, such broken and distorted bodies.

Behind them the voices of two women were rising with the freedom of old women in all classes of society whom the final disability of age had freed from the life-long restraint of pleasing.

"That old cheat always tries to get more than her share of any alms that's going, whether it's in her own parish or not."

"But my lady had no call to strike her just the same. A fine thing to do on the very steps of the church, and the blessed Apostle himself a poor man, as that preacher said yesterday."

There was a dry cackle. "Don't you be fooled. Preachers who talk to us like that in the Suburra don't get asked to preach to the Lady Laeta and all those haughty slaves of hers who push people around as if they had no feelings."

As the voices arose, there was an uncomfortable shuffle in the crowd around the two young men. Hilary was relieved to find the jam break in front of them, and to feel a sudden rush of musty air as they were pushed down a narrow wooden stair into a darkness broken only by the light of an oil lamp in a little niche in the brick wall at the foot. And then the air of that extraordinary underground world dampened down upon them, and Hilary began to wonder if he had not been too hasty in his rebuke of his friend.

Some of it was, doubtless, the flat chill of the sunless depths of the earth; some of it was the fetid dryness of rotting brick and stone; but more pervasive than anything else was the rancid sweetness of the decay of the human body itself, unwashed, starving, sick, dying, dead. The dimly lit galleries that opened out in every direction were swarming with shuffling feet and rough voices, muffled with awe and the plangent mutter of prayer. Sometimes it was a hymn, sometimes a litany chanted waveringly but persistently by raw voices; more often it was the hurried and piercing whisper of private supplication. More heavily even than the odor, the sharp insistence of human need stunned Hilary, and he braced himself against one of the shelves only to feel the thin cement facing give way under his fingers. As he recoiled, he knocked the candle a slave was carrying almost into the face of Fortunatus and saw his own nausea reflected in his friend's gray countenance.

Fortunately, at that moment the other slave returned with a sacristan, bustling importantly and inquiring if they wanted to make the whole pilgrimage. Hilary hastened to put him right. They did not have time to explore the wonders of the catacombs today; they had come simply to see the chapel of Pope Cornelius.

The guide nodded more soberly. "A great many people come for that. There have been some very remarkable cures."

The tiny chapel, really only a shallow recess in the wall with a bare stone slab over the gray tomb, was crowded. Indeed, they

57

almost fell over the crutches of a cripple kneeling in the corridor outside. Their guide started to push his way in, but Hilary stopped him and explained that they only wanted to see the picture.

The guide was puzzled. "It is a poor picture, and it has come here only recently. The Lady Laeta"—but as he lifted his lamp to light the picture hanging on the wall by the chapel, Hilary gave a cry of surprise, and stepped aside to let Fortunatus see too.

The latter must have recovered a little of his equilibrium in the more cheerful presence of the guide, for he laughed with something like his normal ease. "Not much resemblance to Laeta's pope there. This one looks as if he might get himself killed."

The guide protested with an indignation one would not have expected from his professional cheerfulness, but Hilary held up a hand warningly. "Does he remind you of anybody you have met?" he asked Fortunatus.

"I?" asked Fortunatus in surprise, and then he looked more closely. "Of all things," he exclaimed, "the mother of the Gracchi and your pagan charmer." For there was an undeniable family resemblance between the bust that stood in the atrium of Laeta and Cornelius, and still more astonishingly between the martyred pope and Gaia herself. Both young men stared.

"It isn't really the features," said Fortunatus at length. "It is the look on the face." And then more thoughtfully, he added, "They both look as if they would carry it to the bitter end."

It was an extraordinary thing, the same look on the face of the man who had so recklessly taken time by the forelock and that of the woman who had so resolutely refused to yield to its onrush. There had been something of the same look on the face of the little man who had stopped the games.

It was impossible to stand before the picture of Pope Cornelius lost in thought, for his clients kept jostling anybody who lingered by the niche. Mechanically, Hilary knelt for a moment and tried to collect his wits to ask Pope Cornelius to intercede for him, who wished so much to understand—Hilary gave it up.

It was so vague a yearning that he felt sure Pope Cornelius could take no interest in it, and with a strange chastening of heart Hilary contented himself with praying that Pope Cornelius would not forget before the throne of God the misery that had come to his tomb for succor.

After the catacombs even the crowded church seemed a spacious and sunny release, but Fortunatus hurried into the outer air and Hilary followed him.

"What an appalling place!" Fortunatus shook himself as if he were afraid some of the stench of the catacombs still clung to him.

Some vague distaste made Hilary object. "They say it was a place of refuge in the persecutions. They went to hide there until the Emperor's soldiers had gone by."

But Fortunatus looked at Hilary in horror. "What sort of people could they have been who would go there?"

"I suppose they looked a lot like those people today. There weren't many like Cornelius." It was a startling idea, and the two young men looked at each other soberly.

"Where on earth do you suppose they all come from?" asked Fortunatus.

"The country round?" Hilary tried the idea doubtfully.

"Did they look like country people?"

Remembering the gray, slimy look of some of those faces, Hilary shook his head.

But Fortunatus was beginning to take refuge in indignation. "I thought they at least had free baths in the Suburra."

Gaia was apparently of the same mind when Hilary went to see her a few days later.

"It is a dreadful place, isn't it?" And then as out of some obscure impulse of loyalty her guest said nothing, her manner softened. "Your Pope Damasus who built the church usually did better than that. It was he who organized the library which you will want to look at some day."

Recognizing the apology, Hilary met her halfway. "You don't like disturbing the dead, do you?"

59

She grimaced a little. "Or the living. You can't go to any of those tombs without meeting the most wretched people."

"It's still a place of refuge, in a way."

She caught the note of speculation rather than argument in his voice, and she smiled a little wryly. "I suppose," she said, "that is the thing that most puzzles me. I can understand how a man would die rather than burn incense if he really thought he would betray his"—she hesitated at a loss for the word—"honor, though it seems silly. But I cannot understand how a man of one of the best families of Rome would throw himself away among people like that."

Hilary thought of the pilgrims of the day before, and remembered his own wincing. Again an impulse he did not in any way understand made him say, "You realize I am one of them."

But she laughed. "What do you have in common with them? Give them an alms perhaps?"

He laughed, too, but there was no comfort in it. So he shifted ground. "You know, Pope Cornelius made me think of you."

"Of me?" For a moment he thought she was going to be angry. Then she laughed, "Surely you are jesting."

"Only partly."

He watched to see how far he might safely go. She was beginning to look a little curious.

"He looks much more like you than that statue of Laeta's."

"Oh, that," she laughed easily now. And then a more thoughtful look came into her face. "You think I would die before I would put a pinch of incense on an altar?"

"Not that perhaps. But I think there are things that you could imagine yourself dying before—"

He saw the quick intelligence flash in the deep-set eyes, and a little color quicken beneath the flower-like surface of her skin. She looked at him appraisingly. "And that you do not think foolish, even if it is something you do not believe?"

"No, I do not," he said quietly, a little surprised to find himself seeing it all so simply. He had all his life heard martyrdom spoken of with honor, and paid his own tribute of awe, but he had always been glad that he had been fortunate enough to be born in a later day. In the company of this pagan it suddenly did not seem so far away after all.

Indeed, it suddenly occurred to him that the little monk in the amphitheater might have seemed a martyr to fanatics like himself. Perhaps to his own father in far-off Dacia? It was the first time he had wondered how anything would seem to that strange being he could never quite believe had anything to do with him.

Something seemed to have surprised Gaia too, for a silence came between them, and he heard the water falling clearly, even sharply in the marble basin of the fountain. How absurd to be talking of martyrdom in this serene and beautiful place in the center of Rome's surety.

II
THE BARBARIANS

I

WHEN HILARY LEFT BORDEAUX, IT WAS AGREED that he should have two years to stay in Rome. After that he would return home, relieve his grandfather of the responsibility for the family property, get married, and in general take his place in the public life of the province. At the time it had seemed a generous provision for seeing something of the great world, and perhaps studying a little. And though no one said anything about it, it must, Hilary knew, have been in all their minds that this respite would give him a chance to get used to his new role in the world, so different from what his position would have been if his brother had lived.

The first year of free exploration of Roman life passed with astonishing swiftness. Postumianus wrote from Bordeaux with satisfaction about the letters he had been receiving from his old friends on the excellent impression which his heir had made in the highest circles, as if he had quite forgotten all his warnings about the illusions and deceits of Rome. Still Hilary found himself, as the second year got under way, growing a little restless. It was no flagging of enthusiasm for Rome or the new friends he was making. It was rather that in all the brilliant routine of his days something was missing.

In his first weeks in Rome Hilary had hired a Greek master with whom he managed to work for a couple of hours on all but his busiest days. Now he redoubled his efforts, but the Greek master, though a good scholar, was a freedman. He had too ingrained a habit of watching cautiously for the drift of his patron's opinion to give Hilary any pleasure in talking with him. When Hilary complained of this to Symmachus, the senator suggested that he and Fabius join forces in their studies; but that proved even less satisfactory. Fabius knew more Greek than Hilary, but all his mental processes were so much more deliberate that Hilary received no real stimulus from his fellow-student, and the Greek master became, if anything, more flattering and subservient with Fabius. So the Greek lessons faded out.

Then for some months Hilary made trial of the philosophers who haunted the libraries of Theophilus and other members of the Roman aristocracy, and even of the public lecturers who held forth in various places all over the city. But none of them ever really engaged his interest. The questions which they discussed were too abstract, too removed from the daily preoccupations of mind and heart, to give any real satisfaction. Indeed he began to regret the Greek master, for he at least dealt in the many colored riches of the poets with all their appeal to eye and ear and heart. Presently, Hilary began to suspect that he was tired of listening to other men's thinking.

So when in the late summer of Hilary's second year in Rome Fabius invited him to join a group of his friends who were giving themselves a little private practice in oratory, Hilary welcomed what looked like a chance for something in which he could take a more active part.

At first, the little group meeting in the middle of a pleasant courtyard of the house of Symmachus seemed lively enough. Most of the members were, like their host, heirs to great estates, but there were also several young men of less assured position, professionals making their beginnings in the law courts. Hilary settled down to enjoy the keen competition of wits, the swift give-and-take of debate. Then one day he discovered to his surprise a still rarer excitement.

They had been discussing the question of whether a barbarian could ever really become a Roman. When the topic was first proposed, Hilary was sceptical. It seemed the kind of abstract question that cuts life into too easy alternatives. But when one of the young aristocrats suggested complacently that most manifestations of Roman culture outside the city itself were constitutionally inferior, like those plaster imitations of Roman marbles that the traders brought back from north Africa, Hilary was stung into a rebuttal that in its edge and passion surprised himself quite as much as his companions. It was as if a spark had suddenly struck unsuspected fire in the very depths of his being.

He did not recognize his own voice when he caught it, quivering a little and then steadying. He was as surprised as anybody in the room when he heard himself maintaining that in his native Gaul he had seen Roman architecture as fine as any in the forums of the emperors, and had heard Latin spoken with as much purity and elegance as in any senatorial palace, and problems of justice and public order debated with as much clarity and precision as in any basilica in Rome. And then the stream of his own eloquence carried him away, and he found himself in command of a whole range of examples and illustrations that he had not known he possessed.

As he talked, he saw the expressions on the faces of the men before him change from surprise to astonishment, to admiration, to wariness, and then to a kind of veiled resistance. When he finished, there was a flutter of applause, and as the time had now come for the company to disperse for the midday meal, everyone crowded around Hilary to congratulate him. But when the new orator found himself alone with his host, he became aware of a certain embarrassment in the latter's congratulations, as if the performance, fine as it had been, had offended against good taste in some fashion he could not bring himself to mention. Fortunatus, who had that day come to visit, was more explicit as they went home together. "Better hold your horses. You were pretty well carried away."

Hilary said nothing, for he quite agreed. The reaction had come, and he found himself spent, drained, even a little sick. But in the next few days the mood of depression began to lift. For to his surprise he discovered that the report of his eloquence had traveled fast in the circles that spread out from the least stone dropped into the easily disturbed waters of the house of Symmachus. Attalus, at a modest supper in the lodgings of Hilary and Fortunatus, was most gracious. "A young man who can speak like that should stay in Rome and take a hand in public affairs." The Senator Pompeianus, whom Hilary in attendance on Symmachus encountered in the forum a day or two later, congratulated him in the presence of a most attentive company, and laughingly told Symmachus that if he did not know what a treasure he had in his entourage, other people did. Symmachus rather stiffly assured his colleague that he fully appreciated the parts of his young friend. And Faltonius who seemed to know more than any man but Symmachus of what was going on in Rome, and was far more freely communicative of his knowledge, reported that the poet Claudian, who was said to be taking care of Stilicho's interests while the latter was with the Emperor in Ravenna, had been heard to say that his master would be interested in knowing the promising young visitor from Gaul.

At that the old uneasiness returned, for even to think of association with Stilicho in the light of his grandfather's denunciations seemed a dangerous trifling with his basic loyalties. But all he said was, "What a fuss over a few words!" Faltonius, who usually smiled his way through the tensions of senatorial Rome, looked startled.

Hilary soon found that he could not escape the consequences of his unsuspected eloquence. Gaia seemed more withdrawn when he next went to see her, as if perhaps she had given her confidence a little indiscreetly. Attis was amused that he had apparently had to come to Rome to discover the wonders of Gaul, and assured him that it was not the first time she had known it to happen, which gave him little comfort. And he felt no comfort at all when Proba Faltonia made quite a fuss over him when he went to dine at her house, declaring that she did like to see young men have courage enough to be different, something which Hilary had never dreamed of wanting to be.

But before the year closed, all this personal embarrassment was suddenly ended. Fabius had just returned from another trip to his father's estates and had come to tell Hilary about the situation in the country, when one of Hilary's Roman slaves announced very importantly a messenger from the house of Stilicho.

Fabius' thin eyebrows rose, and he sprang to his feet, but Hilary motioned to him to stay. He had barely met Stilicho, and he had every reason to avoid the repute of an intimacy that did not exist. As it turned out, the soldier's message was simple enough. The general would be obliged if Hilary could come to his house at his convenience, a little later that week perhaps. This, Hilary saw clearly enough, was the moment when his grandfather's heir should find some courteous way out of an impossible relation, but he could think of none.

When the messenger had gone with his promise, Hilary turned to find Fabius looking at him intently. "I thought Stilicho was with the Emperor at Ravenna."

"I hadn't thought about it at all."

But Fabius looked grave. "Perhaps you had better. They say that ever since the death of the Empress Maria last spring Stilicho has been losing favor. And then there are those stories about Maria's death."

Hilary shrugged his shoulders. The court gossip of Ravenna had always seemed less real to him than even that of Rome.

"Have you ever been to his house?"

Hilary shook his head.

"It is a very tactful house," said Fabius.

At the time Hilary wondered if the phrase were perhaps a quotation from Symmachus. He was quite sure of it the next day when he was shown into the atrium of Stilicho's house. For "tactful" was the exact word for the cool gray room, gray marble pillars, light plastered wall, black and white marble floor. It must be an old house, Hilary thought, with the ancient altar still in place, and a plainly carved basin to catch the rain. Only the green of shrubs broke the prevailing gray, so firmly accented by the smoky dimness of the unpainted rafters under the tiled roof.

But something was missing from the traditional effect, and then Hilary realized that there were no tablets or statues, only three busts on slim pedestals: an older man, with a young man and woman facing him. The older face was a strong, even harsh one; in contrast the younger man's was gentler, even to indecisiveness. The woman's was quite pretty in a curiously unformed fashion, so that Hilary was not sure but it might be a very dignified young girl. All three statues were made of the same delicately veined marble, as if designed to fit as unobtrusively as possible into this, Hilary suspected, deliberately modest room.

A firm step broke into Hilary's thoughts. It was Stilicho himself in a plain robe of straight, old-fashioned cut, that emphasized both his height and the dignity of his carriage. Seen close to, the face of the great soldier was a little older, a little more careworn than Hilary had thought it. But in its lofty purposefulness, its fine-edged discipline, it still seemed to the younger man, much as he hated to admit it, the closest to his old ideal of a Roman senator that he had seen since he came to Rome. Only in the deep-set blue eyes which Stilicho fixed on his guest, something started forward and as quickly hid away.

After greeting Hilary, he nodded to the statue of the older man. "You recognize him, of course, the Emperor Theodosius." And turning briefly to the statues opposite, "Honorius and his late Empress." Was it pride or grief made him forbear to add that the late Empress was his daughter?

Then Stilicho came to the point. "They tell me you are active and eloquent as well as heir to a great Gallic landowner."

Surprised by this directness of approach, Hilary almost missed the mumbled deprecation courtesy demanded. But although Stilicho spoke with precision and refinement, he seemed unconcerned with the formalities, as he moved straight ahead, apparently unaware of the identity of that landowner.

"How much have you heard of the rumors flying around Rome?"

Startled by this turn of the conversation he had dreaded, Hilary floundered. "Not much," he said at last. "Only that the barbarians are supposed to be overrunning Raetia and Noricum."

"Raetia and Noricum!" The contempt was quite impersonal.

"They are well into the mountains now, and will be in the Po valley with the new year."

"But how can barbarians—" Hilary began, thinking aloud, and then remembering to whom he was talking.

"Barbarians who are not too proud to put their best into the fight. No wonder Radagasius sweeps all before him."

"Radagasius!" Hilary repeated the strange name. Stilicho had risen to his feet and begun to pace back and forth, his strong face growing still more taut under his white hair.

"Radagasius. Of course the rumors do not name the general. Too many people in Rome assume that all barbarians are nameless men, that they come in a human flood without any leadership. Savage that he is, Radagasius is a leader I could use without difficulty."

"One knows so little," said Hilary humbly.

"One makes so little effort to learn anything here in Rome. But it isn't Rome I'm talking about now. Have you any idea how those barbarians are going to be stopped from overrunning all Italy?"

At first Hilary thought it was a rhetorical question. But Stilicho was waiting for an answer. "The legions?" He knew it sounded childish, but he could think of nothing better than the old bulwark of the family conversations at Bordeaux.

"The legions! The legions!" The low, clear voice rose to a shout. A slave came around a pillar and then, seeing his master's eyes fixed on his guest, slipped away again.

"What legions?"

"But surely," said Hilary, "there must be legions in Italy as there are in Gaul." He found himself too unsure of his geography to mention the outposts along the Rhine which had constituted one of the legends of that suddenly very remote Aquitanian childhood.

The general looked at the young man with an expression which Hilary could not fathom—contempt, pity, despair? He could not decide. Stilicho stopped his pacing, and his voice fell. "The Italian legions are protecting Ravenna on the west, at least those that can be relied on. And for the east I have to depend on Alaric and his Goths. And only a few years ago Alaric himself was terrorizing all Italy!"

"Then—" said Hilary, and it seemed impudent for him to go on.

"Yes, call in men from the other frontiers. Men from Gaul!" Stilicho did not see Hilary start. "That is why I have sent for you."

Hilary forgot all about the defence of Gaul in sheer astonishment. "Me?"

"Yes." The blue eyes were glittering.

Hilary rose slowly. "But I know nothing of armies or war."

"Men are not born soldiers, you know. And for war, that is not your choice but your destiny." The voice had sharpened, but the light had gone out of the eyes.

"But what use would I be to you?"

"Many of the men come from Gaul. You know Rome and you know Gaul." The voice seemed to Hilary a little drier now.

"I think," said Hilary thoughtfully, "growing up in Bordeaux as I did, I know Rome better than Gaul." He was astonished to hear himself saying those words, but they were said.

Stilicho looked at him. Again Hilary had the sense of something stirring in the depths of those deep eyes, something less sure than the firm set of the clearly molded jaw. But before he could say anything more, a low, clear woman's voice rang out behind them, "You look so solemn, both of you. Are you sure you don't want to be interrupted?"

And then as Hilary turned, the voice softened to a cordial welcome. It was Serena with her arms full of flowers. She looked older and quieter than Hilary had remembered her. Yet the sense of complete possession of the scene which had impressed Hilary when he first saw her in the imperial box returned afresh, and then he looked at the young man trailing in her wake, with a couple of vases. Hilary tried to think where he had seen that fat but very solid-looking figure, that laughing face wreathed in curls, with the mobile eyes so alert and then so swiftly veiled.

"Hilary, you must have heard Claudian read some of his verses?"

72

"It is one of the hazards of life in Rome these days." It was a perfectly friendly voice for all its mockery. Hilary hastened to express his pleasure; he had heard Claudian read—he could not be sure—it must have been at the house of Faltonius. But Serena had caught his uneasiness, and as she laid the flowers down on the old altar, she smiled at him. "Hilary, has my husband been playing the general with you?"

"I have simply offered him a chance to serve Rome." Stilicho seemed curiously stiff. Serena came up and put a wifely hand on his arm. "Oh, my dear, one does not ask the heir of a Roman senator to join the legions."

Both men protested at once, and Claudian laughed good-humoredly. "The senate in the legions! That would be the end of Rome, indeed."

"Do not misunderstand me," pleaded Hilary, still more uncomfortable at the implications of Serena's cheerful defence. "I simply said I would be no use."

Claudian stared at Hilary, his slightly bulging eyes round with mock astonishment, and then he burst into laughter. "That is the most extraordinary excuse ever offered in the Roman army. Man, you don't think all those officers standing like herons in the marshes around Ravenna ever asked themselves such a question? No wonder Gaul is gathering up all the wealth of the empire when even Gallic senators talk that way."

"But you are a soldier, a professional," said Hilary, he knew lamely.

But Claudian shook his curly locks. "If I had been a senator's heir, I should have been a poet and nothing but a poet. Being the son of a penniless Egyptian priest, I went into the Roman army."

It was hard to see anything military in Claudian's appearance, and the poet must have guessed Hilary's thought, for he grinned. "You see me, my friend, in my Roman guise. A month or two of army rations and mountain-climbing, and I am a different figure of a man."

"No," said Stilicho firmly, "I have promised Serena that you will stay with her this time. I owe her something for rushing off again like this."

"You would owe me nothing if you would take me with you," said Serena gravely.

But Stilicho shook his head. "That is settled."

Then he turned to Hilary. "And my business with you is settled, too," he paused, "for now. But," as Hilary prepared to take his leave, he held up his hand, "there is one thing I should like to ask you before you go. Rome conquered the world with Roman soldiers in her legions. Today Romans will not even let their tenants or their freedmen go into the army. How long do you think Rome will hold her empire when she must rely on the barbarians she is fighting to defend her?"

For a moment Hilary stared at the great general; then he said slowly as if to himself, "But does it matter where they come from? I thought the citizenship of Rome made a man of any nation a Roman."

"Bravo," said Claudian, and then he, too, grew thoughtful. "That is a superb idea. Do you mind if I steal it?" And then he turned to his patron, "I shall use it in that poem I am going to write in your honor while you are running down Radagasius."

But Stilicho threw his arms above his head in a gesture of despair and stalked out of the room. Hilary took his leave more ceremoniously, but in no less inner confusion. Even the faint glimmerings of understanding which the great barbarian general had thrown into his astonished mind seemed a betrayal of his grandfather. Never had he felt more completely unsure of himself.

II

WITH THE COMING OF WINTER HILARY FOUND himself growing restless again. He began to suspect that perhaps he had had enough of fashionable Rome. The Senator Pammachius with his doorway crowded with the poor, and his hospital for sick and stranded travellers at Ostia, and all his other mysterious preoccupations would certainly pay little heed to such a tempest in a fish pond, if indeed anybody would be so foolish as to trouble him with it. But when Hilary finally got up his courage and went to present his aunt's letter he was not so sure.

Apparently the doorkeeper had received some instructions, for though Hilary did not make any effort to push himself through the crowd waiting at the gate, the man called out to him as soon as he caught sight of his, Hilary suspected, conspicuously well-dressed figure.

It was some time, however, before the senator appeared, and Hilary had plenty of time to look around the atrium in which he was waiting. It was, it seemed to Hilary, the most magnificent atrium that he had yet seen in Rome, with finely carved pillars of cool green marble and walls of a delicate amber-colored stucco decorated with fruits and flowers in a graceful design of ochreous roses and yellow greens. The room was lined, too, with busts and tablets of obviously fine materials and workmanship, and Hilary remembered that Symmachus had once said that Pammachius had the best of the treasures of the Furian family in his palace, though he doubted if he ever took any notice of them. But in spite of the statuary the magnificent room seemed astonishingly bare. And then Hilary realized that here was none of the usual decorations of the fine Roman house, no flowers or shrubs, no gilded furniture, only a couple of cheap wooden stools and a pair of ancient marble benches.

The same incongruity invested the statuesque figure that now came quietly into the room on sandalled feet. Hilary remembered the first time he had seen the monk-senator in the procession to the senate house. In all that solemn progress of Rome's proudest no one had come anywhere near Pammachius in that Olympian dignity which Hilary had expected of the Roman senate. Seen close to, Pammachius in no way disappointed his guest. Indeed there was apparent now a certain purity of look in the pale, high-boned face, in the clear eyes under the level brows, in the firm hand uplifted in greeting.

Hilary rather apologetically explained that he had called before but had not had the good fortune to find him at home. But Pammachius cut him short. He had been quite sure that Hilary would come when he had leisure. And when Hilary presented his aunt's letter, Pammachius glanced over it quickly, and then looked up at Hilary.

"I have had a letter from Severus too. How did he seem to you?"

Hastily, Hilary tried to dredge up from the lower levels of the memory of the last crowded months the picture of the surprisingly cheerful monk on the height by the river in Gaul. It was shadowy. That had been their one turning-aside from the straight road to Rome. They had gone to the cliff monastery of Primuliacum to find Hilary's father, who was last reported there, and to tell him of Patricius' death. When they learned that Desiderius had gone off on some incredible missionary venture to the Dacian frontier, Hilary had lost all interest in everything else there. So now he courteously murmured something vague about Severus' good health and spirits, and then he became acutely doubtful if those were the correct terms in which to speak of a monk. A gleam came into the eyes of Pammachius, and for a second Hilary wondered if he had understood his embarrassment. But apparently he had not, for he seemed to be looking quite beyond Hilary. "He is a great man," he said. And then something more humanly wistful came into his face as he turned to Hilary. "Did he say anything about coming to Rome?"

"No, he seemed very much absorbed in what he is doing there on the river."

Pammachius looked thoughtfully at Hilary, and for a moment the latter had an astonishing impulse to tell him about his father. But it vanished as Pammachius said with a quiet air of finality, "So you are interested in oratory."

Again Hilary was surprised at himself, at the impulse of self-defence that made him say, "Not particularly, unless the question is one that I am interested in."

The level brows lifted a little, and Hilary wondered if that were a note of mockery in the quiet voice, "What sort of questions interest you?" Hilary, still remembering the way he had lost himself in the debate, answered cautiously, "Questions that seem to raise real issues of," he was going to say, "moral importance," but that seemed to him more than he should pretend to; so he hastily amended it to "importance to men." It was feeble, and he knew it. Under Pammachius' steady eyes he felt that he was being weighed and found wanting. Something more than a desire for self-justification made him yearn to tell this man that he was not at all certain what questions did interest him, and that he meant to find out. But there was too great a gulf between them. For he had not expected Pammachius to be quite like this, patient and uninsistent, and he saw that whatever Pammachius had expected him to be, from what he had heard of him, it was nothing like what he was, and the monk had guessed as much.

But all Pammachius said to his guest was, "I remember your grandfather very well."

Hilary looked so startled that the monk hastened to reassure what he thought must be the young man's embarrassment. "Yes, I know that he is a stubborn pagan, but when he married your grandmother, he kept his promises and let her bring up their children as Christians, at least while he was here in Rome."

Again loyalty to his grandfather overcame Hilary's uneasiness in the presence of the monk-senator. "He has never interfered with the religion of the household." And then he was embarrassed afresh as he realized too late the negative implications his host might read into that defense.

But Pammachius apparently did not notice, for he went on, speaking slowly like a man who is trying to be fair in an old controversy, "I never believed that he would have anything to do with that superstitious nonsense about the auguries."

And now Hilary's failure to understand was so obvious that Pammachius looked at him sharply. "But surely you have heard?" And for the first time he hesitated.

Hilary shook his head and looked so bewildered that Pammachius began apologetically: "I thought he must have told you.

Everybody here in Rome knew that he was accused of being implicated in that pagan conspiracy against the life of the Emperor." And then all the lines of the sensitive face tightened. "It was a foul business, using those silly auspices to foretell the death of the Emperor and to suggest Heaven knows what treachery. But it was no excuse for such a charge against a man who was always, however wrong-headed, an honorable man."

But Hilary said nothing. He was sick at the abyss of pain that opened behind the carefully cool and detached words of Pammachius. Anybody who had ever known Postumianus even a little would know that he would not be able to bear the suspicion of his integrity that such an accusation implied, to say nothing of the outrage to his intellectual pride that anyone would believe that he, who had such a contempt for what he called the magical rites of Christianity, would ever have condescended to the vulgar superstitions of the auspices. No wonder he had shaken the dust of Rome from his feet, no wonder—but Hilary could not bear the thought of the years of suffering that lay behind all those gibes of his at Rome and at Stilicho, the symbol of the Christian politicians who had made such unscrupulous use of the folly of their enemies. And with horror he saw how every careless plea of his for a visit to Rome must have been a fresh opening of the wound of that experience which had sapped all his grandfather's confidence in the world he had made so much his own.

With his characteristic sensitiveness Pammachius divined his guest's distress, but there was no way in which he could guess its cause, and Hilary, even if he had wished to explain, could not have found the words for the staggering revelation he had just received.

For some moments nothing was said; then Pammachius roused himself to a host's duty. "You should not be distressed over your grandfather's paganism. Think of your own father. I have often thought that his conversion was a sort of compensation for his father, a reward for his sincerity, if nothing more."

"But my father was brought up a Christian," protested Hilary, realizing only after he had spoken what Pammachius' opinion of the easy-going Christianity of the great Bordeaux landholders might be.

It was Pammachius' turn to be uncertain. But Hilary saw that there was nothing he could do to help; so he said with finality, "You know I never knew my father. He ran away before I was born."

"Ran away!" repeated Pammachius with indignation. "He went to join Martin of Tours!"

But before Hilary could find words for an apology, Pammachius had also realized that he had gone farther than he had intended. For in the more normal tone of a host trying to be helpful to a newcomer to town, he asked, "Have you been to the house of the Lady Marcella?"

For a moment Hilary stared at him. Then he remembered the other letters, of his aunt, the Lady Claudia. His first thought was that masculine monasticism was quite as much as he could manage, but then he remembered how much he owed to his uncomfortable host, and how rude he must have seemed. So all he said was that he had a letter for her, too, but he had been too busy. Pammachius, paying no attention to the implied apology, explained that he was engaged to go to the Lady Marcella's later in the week and would be glad of Hilary's company. The latter, only too aware of his neglect of his aunt's friends, at once agreed.

But when he went with the monk up to Marcella's house on the Aventine, all of his old misgivings returned. And they were not dispelled by his first sight of the palace of which he had heard so much. The house of Pammachius should have prepared him for it. But the atrium of Marcella's house was much larger, much more magnificent with its great pillars of red marble, and its panelling of soft gray marble, and its coffered ceilings. It held an even richer collection of busts and tablets and statuary, but these mementoes of past glory had been pushed back against the walls so that there might be room for a collection of stools and rough wooden benches which were almost entirely taken up by as extraordinary a crowd as Hilary had ever seen.

For many of them wore brown camel's hair tunics like

Pammachius's. Most of these people were thin enough, and some of them even worn-looking, but they looked far different from the wretched crowds of the catacombs. For these were obviously men and women who were accustomed to moving confidently in the world. Even the slaves carried themselves with assurance and greeted visitors with the easy cordiality of members of the family.

And then a thin little old lady with a queenly head, piled high with still dark hair, came forward. She wore a plain black sackcloth robe like a number of the other women; indeed her robe was shabbier and worn even more negligently, but there was no mistaking the air of calm and smiling authority. She greeted Hilary with casual grace, murmuring that she had known his grandmother from the time she first came to Rome on a pilgrimage, and then she turned to present him to a very coldly handsome girl, who seemed to Hilary to look quite through him with no interest whatever, her companion Principia. Then Marcella carried Pammachius off to urge some inaudible point upon him with lively gestures. Pammachius shrugged his shoulders, and Marcella beamed upon him and rushed off to see that a couple of young men who were hanging back on the edge of the crowd found seats. These latter interested Hilary, for they were clearly not monks, though they seemed to have judged it appropriate, as Hilary had, to put on their soberest clothes for the occasion.

Suddenly everybody was scrambling to his feet, and while Hilary tried to see who had come into the room to call forth this homage, the company began to sing. It was, Hilary felt sure from the attitude of the singers and from the mode of the music, a hymn, but it was in a language which he had never heard.

"It is Hebrew, the language which Our Lord spoke," whispered the monk standing next to Hilary, without looking at him. It was a startling thought. Hilary had known that Christ spoke the language of his time and place, but always when he thought of Him speaking, he heard the Latin of the Gospels in the rather dry tones of the priest Vincentius at home in

Bordeaux. It seemed to carry Christ away from everyday intimacy to think of him speaking in these harsh yet achingly solemn and impressive syllables.

Then Pammachius arose near one of the pillars, and Marcella stood beside him and announced, happily, "Our brother Pammachius has just received a letter from the Holy Land, from—" the name was lost in the exclamations of delight that came from every side. Pammachius proceeded to read the letter with as much formality as if he had been presenting a letter from the Emperor to the senate. The affectionate greeting to Pammachius and all the dear friends at the house of Marcella evoked obvious satisfaction, but the next sentences announcing the arrival of Optatus, who had apparently been sent by Pammachius to help the writer as an amanuensis, drew even keener expressions of satisfaction, for obviously he was known to many of the company.

So far the letter had been a gracious and well written one, but to Hilary, who knew none of the people involved, of slight interest. He was beginning to look around to see if he could find any familiar face in the company, when his attention was caught by a vivid phrase, "Optatus has escaped the pretentious futility of the life of fashionable Rome, and for the first time his real talents have received scope for their proper exercise." And then the still unknown writer went on to sketch with brilliant satiric detail the kind of life which Hilary had known so well in the house of Symmachus. The audience broke into laughter, and Pammachius paused, smiling a little, and then resumed his reading. It was a masterpiece of satire in the great Roman tradition. Juvenal himself might have penned that savage indictment of the pretensions of senatorial Rome. Hilary felt the blood mounting in his cheeks, and a protest forming. This was the sort of fanaticism that had driven his grandfather from Rome. Did the unknown author of such superb Latin periods really understand anything of what he was talking about? Apparently he did, for the next few sentences compared the frivolous city of today with the Rome which had mastered the world, revealing a devotion to Rome which moved Hilary and, he suspected, the rest of the company. For a deep silence fell upon the room.

The young monk next to Hilary faced him now—an ugly, hulking fellow with a surprising look of intelligence on his coarse features. "There is no one in the world who writes like Jerome," he said.

So it was Jerome, who according to the gossip in the house of Symmachus had come out of the desert and taken Christian Rome by storm so that he would have been pope if it had not been for the scandal of his friendship with the noble Paula, the mother of Pammachius' dead wife.

But now the letter had left its satire and turned into a sermon, a sermon against the life of the world and the flesh, and a panegyric of virginity. It still kept the color and the pungency of the satire, but it drove its point home so sharply that Hilary braced himself. He had been shocked enough by Pammachius' revelation, and yet he had no intention of renouncing so interesting a world when he had hardly begun to explore it. He felt a profound distaste for the unknown Optatus, who must, he was sure, be a pretentious bore. But the sharp, passionate sentences pushed him hard, with a challenge which he could not imagine himself yielding to, and yet which left him uncomfortable as if he had been arraigned by his schoolmaster for turning in a sloppy exercise.

He was therefore relieved when another speaker arose—a priest, it soon became clear—and began a formal discussion of Jerome's letter. It was clearly not the first which the group had received from Jerome; indeed, to judge from the interest with which the whole audience followed the rather flat paraphrasing of Jerome's words, these people looked to Jerome as to a master whose least word was precious. Others spoke too, but they all seemed rather colorless after Jerome's letter, though Hilary had to admit that these speakers approached religious matters with more of the decorum to which he was accustomed. He was thoroughly relieved, therefore, when the priest arose again and offered a rambling prayer that brought the exercises to a close. A happy buzz of conversation broke out all over the room.

From the talk of the young monk with a friend sitting in front of them Hilary soon learned that Optatus had accomplished what was their dearest dream, in going to the Holy Land to Jerome. But then, as one of them sighed, he was a senator's son, and could afford it. There was no envy in this conversation, only a wistfulness that reminded Hilary of Cerealis' astonishment when Patricius once spoke casually of his prospects as a Gallic landowner.

Presently, the young monk remembered Hilary.

"Are you thinking of going to the Holy Land?" he asked politely.

"No, I am going back to Gaul this spring."

The young monk looked surprised at the vigor of Hilary's response, and Hilary was surprised himself to find how clear it all seemed now. He could hardly hold himself responsible for such fanatics. And yet all these last days he had been wondering if he did not owe his grandfather some reparation for the common injury, which he, all unknowing, had aggravated so grievously. Now he was quite sure of it.

III

WHEN THE FEBRUARY RAINS DRENCHED THE chill air of Rome so that one shivered in even the snuggest winter room, Fortunatus joined the fashionable exodus and went to stay with some new friends at Baiae. He had decided that he was not going back to Gaul. "I am simply too civilized for Bordeaux," he told Hilary, "and there is no use making myself and everybody else miserable by trying to fit into that raw, provincial world again."

But Hilary had sent word to his grandfather that he was

going to start for home just as soon as the spring rains were over, and the roads could be counted on. And he set his household to preparing for the return journey. But there was still plenty of time before they would leave the city after the Easter festival. So Hilary gave only the most cursory attention to the household preparations, and spent most of his days in a freedom such as he had not known since he came to Rome, visiting the libraries of the imperial baths, and the library of Pope Damasus, picking up choice manuscripts in the shops of the booksellers' and book publishers, and looking out presents to take home in the workshops of the jewellers and the metal-workers and the silk-embroiderers. He spent hours watching the cameo-makers shave off threads of shell against their horny fingers, and the glassmakers blow and twist and clip their gleaming jewels. And on pleasant days he wandered for hours through the imperial gardens on the Quirinal and Pincian hills, and the sunny walks of the public gardens down by the river, threading his way through the restless throngs with that sense of freedom possible only to a solitary man in a crowd of strangers.

Afterward Hilary tried to remember when the rumors first began to gnaw on the fringes of his content. He must have heard some of the strangers in Rome talking uneasily about the advance of the barbarians in the east. But he had heard such rumors for months now, and had always reassured himself with the thought of the Roman legions along the Rhine. He was not sure how far the Rhine went, but doubtless there were other rivers with camps and towers warning the shadowy figures on the farther shore.

One day when he was watching a river boat unload timber down at the wharf on the Tiber, he heard two sailors talking about the vessel that had brought the timber to Ostia last fall. It had come apparently from a port to the east. But it was clear that the sailors thought that this was the last timber that would come to Rome from that region, for the roving bands of barbarians were making it too dangerous for the woodcutters in the forests.

Some days later Hilary was surprised to receive an invitation to supper from Fabius, whom he had thought to be still in the country. And when he arrived a little ahead of the other guests, he found his friend far from his usual calm self. Had Hilary heard any news of the barbarians? Hilary was about to say "No," when he remembered the sailors' gossip about the timber. To his astonishment Fabius took it seriously, and then went on to explain what had brought him back to Rome. His father had decided that one of the Campanian estates had failed to yield the crops it should during the last harvest because of a shortage of field workers. And he had sent Fabius to the slave mart south of Ostia to see if he could pick up some suitable field workers for the spring planting. So Fabius went to a slave dealer with whom his father had often dealt.

He assured Fabius he had just what he wanted, a lot of farmers from Noricum, who had fled from the barbarians swarming into their country, and who had been scooped up by some of his agents in Venetia. He would let Symmachus have them cheap, because from what he had heard from his agents the market was soon going to be flooded with refugees as well as captives. Fabius was about to strike the bargain when his steward, who had been looking over the slaves for himself, called him aside. They were a husky lot and just what they needed, but one of the men had seized upon the steward and told him that he was no proper captive but a free landholder, living within the boundaries of the empire with his name on the tax rolls of the province. The man, dirty and tattered as he was, still looked as if he might be what he said he was. The steward had decided to have him thrown out of the lot, when several other men came crowding up, protesting loudly that they were free landholders too. Of course some of them were probably snatching at any lie to save themselves from slavery, but he did not like the looks of the situation. Fabius had challenged the dealer, who had indignantly assured him that he would give him a bill of sale which would stand up in any court in Rome. But the steward was insistent that they would have trouble, and Fabius had finally yielded to the extent of coming up to Rome to see one of his father's friends who was an expert in such matters.

As Fabius was telling his story, several other guests came in. To Hilary's surprise they felt that Fabius had been foolish. Suppose they were landholders—if the barbarians had overrun their lands, what good did it do them? Everybody knew the slaves of Symmachus grew fat. Would they rather die of starvation?

Hilary protested that it might be hard for a man who had owned his own land to find himself a slave. His fellow guests rounded on him contemptuously. "Every reasonable man reckons on the instability of fortune. Men who live on the fringes of civilization cannot hope to stand when the tide of barbarism sweeps in."

But one of the guests had evidently been disquieted by Hilary's protest, for he asked what else could be done with such numbers of fugitives. In the fertile fields of Italy nobody died of hunger, and would not so long as the newcomers were put to work to raise food.

One of the older guests, the Senator Lampadius, seemed to rouse himself at that. "You young men as usual are talking theory without looking at the facts. We have to go to Africa now to get food to feed the citizens of Rome, and everybody knows what trouble we have when anything interferes with the food ships. To take in any more hungry mouths would be suicide."

It was an ugly shadow that had fallen on the security of Rome, and Hilary found that he had little appetite for the splendid supper which Fabius had prepared for his guests, and left the company early.

He found Medoc waiting for him at home, with letters from Bordeaux and, better still, with a first-hand picture of the household which he had left less than three months ago.

"Your grandfather is very proud of your letters, Hilary. And he is very proud of the letters which Symmachus and Pompeianus and other old friends have written about his heir. He has quite forgotten all his old objections."

Hilary smiled. "Perhaps he has changed his mind about my coming home."

Medoc looked startled. "Hardly. Your aunt is sure that the only thing that keeps him in this world is looking forward to your return." And then as Hilary cried out in anxiety, he shook his head. "It is nothing you can put your finger on. His doctor says he is all right physically, but he is getting old and tired. There comes a day for all of us, Hilary, when the sun has risen once too often, and a penny for Charon is all the richest man asks of this world."

There was a brazier between them, and as the warm air rose in the chill room the lamp hanging above their heads swung slowly, unsteadily fingering the shadows on Medoc's face. One of the slaves came in with a bowl of wine, and Hilary tried to rouse himself to a host's responsibilities.

"And I suppose my grandfather has settled on a wife for me?"

Medoc smiled. "No. The men you have sent with your last letters have let the household know that you have been frequenting the house of a very noble and rich Roman lady."

Hilary nearly dropped the cup in his hand. And when his hand steadied, he watched the bubbles in the pale gold of the wine break for a moment or two before he said anything.

"She would never leave Rome," he said at last.

Medoc shrugged his shoulders. "Modesty is becoming enough in a young man, Hilary, but it is folly for a lover."

Hilary, however, shook his head. A question which he had not dared to ask himself had been asked, and now he knew the answer.

Medoc shrugged his thick-set shoulders again. "I don't know what the world is coming to. Men make so much trouble for themselves when the world is full enough of real trouble." But Hilary knew that his old friend would ask no more questions.

For several minutes they drank their wine in silence, Medoc seeming to have retreated to some private world of his own. Hilary remembered seeing him do that often enough, and remembered, too, seeing him slowly return to the terrace of the house at Bordeaux with some tale of the savage mountains that wall in Spain, or the black shores of farthermost Ireland, where the seas wash in from the ends of the world. Looking at him now in the uncertain light of the swinging lamp Hilary wondered again for the hundredth time, how old Medoc really was. With that sandy hair of his one could never really be sure whether it was the sunshine or age that was turning it to the color of last summer's hay in the first spring thaw.

And then Hilary realized that there was something more which Medoc had not told him.

"I am planning to leave here after Easter," he said casually, using the commonplace to throw out a conversational bridge to those unknown regions in which his old friend had taken refuge.

For a second Medoc looked as if he had not heard, and then he seemed to come to himself sharply.

"This spring?" he asked in surprise. Hilary nodded.

"Have you heard nothing then in Rome of what is going on in the north?"

"Only rumors," and Hilary repeated the reports of the seamen and of the slave dealers, taking care to let Medoc know that he was quite aware of the unreliability of such sources of information. But Medoc rebuked him sharply. A man was wise, he said, to take a sceptical attitude toward the rumors he heard at senatorial banquets, but seamen and slave dealers were to be listened to, for their livelihood and often their very lives depended on their knowing what was going on across the frontiers of their business.

"But Noricum is a long way from Gaul," protested Hilary.

Medoc shook his head. "To you and your Roman friends travelling with large retinues. But not to frightened barbarians fleeing on their wild horses for their very lives."

"But the legions?"

"The legions!" snorted Medoc. "On the Rhine with fortifications at their back, perhaps. But here with no prepared line, yielding one position after another, with the terror of the towns undermining the ground in front of them as they fall back—" Medoc shuddered.

88

The fire in the brazier was fading out, and the dank winter night lay heavily about them with the little noises of the city underscoring the silence: the curse of a drunkard, the crying of a child, a woman's voice sharp with fright. It seemed incredible, like the ghost stories with which country folk frighten themselves in the snug warmth of their farm kitchens on winter nights.

"But they have the great mountains in their way. We saw them as we came through the passes. To the east they pile up peak on peak into the very heavens," said Hilary.

"I know," said Medoc impatiently. "But three weeks ago when I came out of the pass, I met an old friend who had just come through the mountains with some silk and jewels he wanted to get to the Gallic markets. He tells me that to the east they are pouring through the mountains with nothing to stop them. The legions have gathered around Ravenna to protect the Emperor."

"You mean," said Hilary slowly, "that the roads may be closed before we get there."

"I am sure they will be."

"But my grandfather?"

"When you read your letters you will find that I have warned him, and that he bids you wait until the picture is clearer."

"But that may be next year?"

"He understands that."

Then as Hilary thought of the months of waiting, a startling idea came to his mind. "But how did you know last fall that this was going to happen?"

Medoc shook his head deprecatingly. "I did not know that this was going to happen. But I thought it quite likely. You see, last summer at Lyons I talked with a friend of mine who the previous fall had been to Barygaza to meet the silk merchants from China. They had a story of a great kingdom to the north and east of the Caucasus that was destroyed between forty and fifty years ago."

"But that is so far away," said Hilary vaguely.

Medoc looked at him keenly, like a man who has asked a riddle and waits to see if his opponent will be clever enough to guess it.

Then he said: "You have seen the logs pile up in the spring in a forest stream until the river itself seems to be dammed. And then you have seen one of the woodsmen pry loose a single log, and the whole jam breaks free as if a volcano had erupted beneath it. It is like that with the tribes of men. Those who ruled a vast region are destroyed, and all the others are shaken from their accustomed places, and they begin to press against one another so that those who are at the edge of the lava-flow flee even to their enemies for refuge. That at least is what the silk merchants say."

"What does it mean?" asked Hilary.

Medoc looked at him thoughtfully for a few moments, and then he said slowly, "It means that these people are going to keep coming for a long time."

"I have heard nothing like this in Rome," said Hilary, drawing a long breath.

"There are a great many things in this world that you don't hear about in Rome," retorted Medoc. And then he rose and yawned. "I must start for Ostia early tomorrow."

But Hilary was uncomfortably wide-awake. "Do you think Stilicho knows this?" He searched the face of Medoc for reassurance.

Medoc blinked. "Something of it, I should say," he replied cautiously, and then, speaking slowly as if pulling his ideas together from a long distance, he went on: "But remember it is not what Stilicho knows; it is what Stilicho can convince the Emperor of, that counts. Rather," he paused, and it seemed to Hilary that Medoc was now trying to get something clear in his own mind, "it is what he dares to tell the Emperor. Look at what has happened—the first rumor of trouble and the court has sucked in all the troops in northern Italy to protect those marshes around Ravenna!"

Hilary waited, holding his breath. But Medoc went on in a low voice as if he had quite forgotten his companion: "But that isn't the worst of it. I wonder if Stilicho dares tell himself the truth." Then he seemed to become aware of Hilary's presence. "But this is beyond you and me. Only the gods know what the truth is, and what the end of it will be."

IV

AT FIRST IT SEEMED TO HILARY THAT HE HAD come to a dead end. He had no idea when he would be returning to Gaul, for Medoc had sent word from Ostia that all the merchants were having trouble reaching their agents. It was not simply that the army of Radagasius was pushing steadily to the west, but even far ahead of the threat of his hordes, those who might have organized effective resistance were removing their households and their goods to safer regions, and bandits of various descriptions were moving in. Some were runaway slaves and outlaws, moving in both directions; some were deserters from the opposing armies; some were rascals who saw their opportunity in the spreading disintegration and took it. Anybody fortunate enough to be in Rome had better stay there.

Hilary smiled wryly over that conclusion. It was March, and in another month he had thought to be on the road to Bordeaux. Now he faced the prospect of trying to find something to make the months of waiting profitable, of writing a postscript to the completed letter of his Roman experience. It was at that juncture that he received word from Fabius of his father's death on one of his Campanian estates; the troubles of the times had fallen heavily on his spirit, and forgetting that he was no longer a young man he had overtaxed his strength. Grief and pride struggled beneath the formal periods of Fabius, and Hilary felt more sympathy for his friend than ever before. But there was no use pretending that he felt any personal sense of loss. Great as was his debt to Symmachus, that period of his life was over. He at once sent a messenger to Fabius, assuring him of his readiness to help him in any way he could, but the basic problem still remained.

But Hilary had reckoned without the complacency of Rome. The traders at Ostia might anxiously match travelers' reports of the forest fire of war closing shut the Italian peninsula, the slaves might whisper of fugitives coming in from regions some of them once called home, the Roman merchants might complain of growing shortages of timber, and resin, and hides, to say nothing of more distant luxuries blocked at their little known sources, the senators might debate the anxious messages from Ravenna, and Milan, and Ticinum, and Stilicho's rare letters from villages the existence of which had been forgotten in Rome for generations, but the life of Rome went on with extraordinary composure. The fashionable fugitives from the rigors of the Roman winter had all returned. The senate had a magnificent memorial service for Symmachus; everybody from the Emperor down sent letters of condolence which Hilary helped Fabius to acknowledge properly, and everybody of importance in Rome thronged to the house of Symmachus to offer his sympathy. Fabius had always seemed to Hilary a flatter, more thinly etched image of his father, but he was unquestionably maintaining the traditional bustle of his house.

And so were the other great houses of the senatorial circle. Indeed the social life of Rome was, if anything, more active and more splendid than ever. Proba Faltonia only put the prevailing opinion in her characteristically plain-spoken fashion when she told Hilary, three places down from his hostess, at an intimate dinner of a score of guests, "We owe it to everybody to keep things going as normally as possible here in Rome."

There was a cheerful chorus of approval from the end of the table where Fortunatus and a couple of his pleasant friends from more convivial circles had been trying to tease a little humanity into Demetrias, Proba Faltonia's pale and forbiddingly shy granddaughter. Hilary had been trying to catch Fortunatus' eye, for something in the way Demetrias had looked at her quite preoccupied grandmother had reminded him of a boyhood glimpse of Blandina at her grandfather's side at some forgotten banquet, when to his astonishment he realized that his older sister was not always so sure of herself as when correcting his manners. And then Hilary became aware that Serena on the other side of Faltonius was toying with the fish on her silver plate without eating anything, and Claudian across from Hilary was trying not to watch her.

Proba Faltonia, as Hilary had already learned, for all her freedom with her friends' sensibilities, was never slow in her perceptions. Now she turned to Serena. "It's no use looking like that, Serena. Stilicho is doing marvelous things, and everybody is grateful to him, as they should be, but what good will it do for him to turn those dreadful barbarians back if we let everything go here at Rome? It is what we do here to keep Rome what it always has been that makes his victory worthwhile."

Serena smiled a too bright smile, and Hilary thought Claudian relaxed a little. Curious how tense his full face looked when he was watching Serena!

To judge from the way people behaved, most of Rome was of Proba Faltonia's opinion. Fortunatus came home later and later, and Hilary found his own days filling up with invitations to banquets and receptions and suppers and visits to the theater and to the law courts and to the senate. Occasionally he found time to go to the house of Marcella to join a little group of young people who were trying to learn the Psalms in Hebrew. He still visited Gaia whenever he could, and he enjoyed going over the day's trove of small business and gossip and discovery of human nature with her. But when he tried to talk to her of Bordeaux, she lost interest. In vain he told her of the magnificent panorama of wheatfields and vineyards and river and woods that they looked out upon from the terrace in front of his home, as if all the riches of the creation were at their feet. It was as if her mind, so wide-ranging and so acute on its home territory, lost all capacity to function once it left the world she knew.

Attis, on the other hand, who always seemed ironically elusive when he spoke of things Roman, seemed to come to life and throw off her mysterious inhibitions when he spoke of Gaul. But, like all his friends, both Gaia and Attis gave Hilary no encouragement to wonder about what was going on to the north of their sunny world. Rather they affected to see in his curiosity an impatience to be gone from their midst, and they chided him prettily for it.

Only at the house of Stilicho were the vague rumors of that confusion suffered to break through the bright surface. Serena was in constant receipt of couriers from her husband, and since she had urged Hilary to come to cheer her loneliness, he came, as the weeks passed, to hear a good deal of her news.

At first Hilary was embarrassed by her friendliness, dreading the reports that might find their way into the letters to Bordeaux. But he had had too little experience of the need for rebutting unwelcome attentions to know how to elude her invitations without discourtesy. And presently he had to admit that at the house of Stilicho he was finding something he could not find elsewhere in Rome. For often the messenger was an eye-witness of some action which had kept her husband too busy to write, and he came to give her a vivid account not only of what was happening, but of the look of the country and of the people involved. And more and more when such messengers came, Serena would send one of her slaves to Hilary's house to invite him to listen to the messenger's account again with Claudian.

More rarely, the courier brought a letter from Stilicho—a brief, but comprehensive account of his activities, which surprised Hilary by its complete objectivity. Obviously the writer of those letters was wrestling with the gravest sort of problems, lack of adequate intelligence of the movements of the enemy, lack of adequate forces and supplies, perhaps most irritating of all, lack of any effective cooperation from local authorities. And yet, so far as Hilary could tell, there was never the least suggestion of complaint or blame. And the young man wondered which it was: heroic patience, that could meet frustration at every point without resentment, or unremitting self-discipline, which never permitted itself the slightest indulgence of self-pity or self-justification. And he did not know which to admire the more.

But what, as time went on, most astonished Hilary was that, so far as he could tell, Serena shared her news with no one but Claudian and himself. The senate rose before dawn to receive with proper ceremony letters from Ravenna that contained not a tithe of the information of the letter which Serena had read to her audience of two the afternoon before. And at the houses of friends Serena listened calmly to speculations about the probable course of affairs of which the issue had been definitely stated in a letter she had received a couple of days before, and she gave no sign of knowing any more than her fellow-guests. Gossip in Rome credited Serena with ceaseless scheming to advance her husband and her children, but of the smaller vanity that would preen itself on the possession of inside information, Hilary could discover no evidence.

Once Hilary ventured to comment on this modesty of hers to Gaia. She looked thoughtfully at Hilary. "That is true. From what I have heard, she used to be less discreet. I remember my mother saying that a wise wife never admits any knowledge of her husband's business."

But Proba Faltonia quite without any suggestion from Hilary offered a suggestion that seemed to him more illuminating. Hilary in the absence of Faltonius had been escorting her home after a supper at the house of Attalus, when she asked him quite without preface as if she were giving word to her own thoughts without care for who might be overhearing, "Did you notice how quiet Serena was when they were talking about the threat to Milan tonight? They say that since the Emperor went to Ravenna she is not as close as she used to be to what is going on at court." For a moment Hilary, who remembered uncomfortably a recent letter from an old court friend of Serena's, begging her to do what she could to make her husband realize the danger to Ravenna, wondered if Proba were laying a trap for him. But she went on, quite unconcerned about his reactions, "I wonder sometimes if it isn't that she is more worried than she is willing to admit."

Hilary felt quite sure that that was not true of Serena, but as the weeks passed he began to suspect that it was true of more people in Rome than he had at first realized. For one thing, the barbarian inundation was spreading south at a rate that exceeded anything which the oldest senators could recall in all their experience. For another, it was beginning to swallow up familiar ground. Radagasius' occupation of Milan had been a peculiar shock to the many senators who had been at the court of Milan in the time of the Emperor Theodosius and had resented bitterly Stilicho's removal of the Emperor to the melancholy marsh country around Ravenna. Now some of them grudgingly admitted that Stilicho had known what he was doing. But not all; there were those who argued that if the forces known to be drawn up around Ravenna had been around Milan, this would not have happened. Then came the news that Stilicho had won a brilliant victory in the plain before Milan and had saved the city.

But the barbarians still pushed south, with the inevitable rout of refugees being invisibly thrust ahead of the dust of their wagons and racing horses. The wretched creatures, as numerous and as destructive as a swarm of locusts, were beginning to be reported on the Tuscan estates of wealthy Romans. But the senate had hardly had time to give ear to the landowners' demands for aid, when the estate managers who had complained so bitterly of the tide of refugees were themselves fleeing to Rome with tales of burned villas and looted barns and ploughed fields turned to mud by the wheels of the milling wagons that made the encampment of the barbarian hordes. And then the barbarians were at the gates of Florence, five days' riding from Rome itself. And the question of what Stilicho was doing with the armies from Gaul, that he was said to have been waiting for all these weeks, began to be heard on every hand.

And now that men had admitted their fear, the dikes of silence seemed to crumble all at once. And everybody began to give the freest rein to guesses and rumors. Some said that the armies from Gaul had mutinied at having to go so far from their families and homes. Others said that many of the Gallic armies were Goths themselves, kinsmen of the hordes of Rada-gasius, and therefore unwilling to fight against them. And still others said that the Gallic armies had refused to advance for their Roman officers, and were waiting for Stilicho himself to meet them and give them assurances that they would in due time be able to return home, for—and here the voices usually fell and everybody leaned forward to hear—they would trust only a barbarian like themselves. Indeed there were even those who in small groups of their most trusted friends were heard to murmur darkly, "What can you expect when the armies are not only made up of barbarians but commanded by a bar-barian?"

Hilary had been often enough embarrassed by the forthright-ness of Proba Faltonia, but he was grateful to her when she asked one of these complainants, Lampadius, "Where are the Roman general and the Roman army to take their place?"

Hilary often wondered how much of the gossip of Rome seeped into the quiet peristyle where Serena spent long hours writing to her husband, and where Claudian read to her and Hilary the first draft of his poem in praise of the general Stilicho.

Spring came late that year, but with its coming the tide seemed to turn. First, Florence was unexpectedly delivered from the army that had settled beneath its walls to starve it out. There was a good deal of self-congratulation in senatorial cir-cles, for it was whispered that the city officials had asked some local priests of the old faith to take the auspices in the tradi-tional manner. There were men still living who remembered when their fathers and their fathers' friends had been executed for suspicion of conspiracy against the state because they had caused the auspices to be taken. Now they whispered cautiously but triumphantly of this glorious vindication of the old religion.

But the Christians were at no loss either to draw profitable example from this sudden change in the course of events. In the palace of Pammachius a priest from Florence reported that when everything had been at its darkest, a Christian watch-man on the walls in a clear moonlit night had seen the bishop in his richest episcopal robes, carrying his staff, walk out from

97

what he had thought a locked gate near the cathedral, and start toward the camp of the barbarians. For a moment the watchman saw the bishop's face clearly in the moonlight. To his astonishment it was not the face of the bishop of Florence whom he knew perfectly well, but the face of a much older man. Then the strange bishop marched straight into the barbarians' camp—so far as the astonished watcher could tell—quite unchallenged by any of their guards. The next day the barbarians withdrew. Thereupon the watchman went with his story to the bishop who showed him a picture of the great bishop of Milan, Ambrose, who in life had visited and loved Florence, and the watchman cried out that it was the man. The delivery of Florence was clearly a victory for the Christians of that city.

Opinion was equally divided when a few weeks later the news came that the entire army of the invaders had been defeated by Stilicho at Fiesole, and the frantic Radagasius taken like a wild beast in a net.

All of Rome flocked to the house of Stilicho to congratulate Serena, and the senate framed a magniloquent message of congratulation to the Emperor at Ravenna for the triumph of his arms, and to the general Stilicho, who, everybody knew, had won the victory with very little help from anybody. But when the first outburst of exultation subsided, Hilary noticed the same division of opinion. Pagan Rome rejoiced in the vindication of the old faith's confidence in the unbroken tradition of Roman victory. Indeed there were not wanting those who said that if Symmachus had still been living, he would certainly have renewed his effort to restore the altar of Victory to the senate house.

Christian Rome, on the other hand, was no less sure that a merciful God had listened to the prayers of the martyrs for the city which they had loved in spite of its cruelty to them, and had again granted it the victory. Serena heard of the rejoicing in the house of Pammachius over this miracle of divine mercy when all human aid had failed, and for once her composure broke. After her pious guest had departed, she cried out to Claudian and Hilary that nobody was giving Stilicho his due.

It was then that Claudian, who, Hilary knew, was a cheerful eclectic and cared nothing about the issue of Providence, declared that his poem in honor of Stilicho was completed, and he would read it to all Rome. That restored Serena's poise and her good sense, for she at once said that the poem had better be read in some other house than Stilicho's. And Hilary hastened to suggest that he be allowed to speak to Attalus.

Attalus was delighted. He had been planning a banquet for some weeks now, and he had not yet been able to satisfy himself about the entertainment. But a reading by Claudian, whom everyone recognized as the greatest poet since Virgil, in honor of the hero of the hour—Attalus rubbed his hands with delight and promised Hilary that if he could secure Claudian, he would undertake to give him such an audience and such a setting as no poet had enjoyed since Virgil read to the Emperor Augustus.

Attalus was as good as his word. Rome's most distinguished, pagan and Christian alike, thronged to Attalus' palace, adorned in honor of the occasion with trophies of arms and a bust of Stilicho. There was a pretty ceremony in which a dancer representing military glory decorated the bust with a wreath of laurel, and a dance of the muses which ended with the crowning of Claudian as one of the greatest of Roman poets. And the splendid evening culminated in the reading of Claudian's tribute to Stilicho.

Never in all the readings he had attended in Rome had Hilary heard anything like Claudian's. It was not simply that he read his superb lines expertly, but that all the audience listened with a completeness of attention that Hilary had never seen before. It was as if every man and woman present felt that he was assisting at an historic occasion, and was determined to rise to its height if only with the perfection of his attention. And then the tide of Claudian's enthusiasm for his subject swept them out of all critical self-consciousness into a simple and spontaneous surrender to his genius. The tide of applause rose higher and higher as Claudian read. But Hilary noticed that when he came to the apostrophe, "Greater, thou art, O Stilicho, than all those who have saved Rome in times past," Serena

99

burst into tears, and many of the women present wept with her in tribute to her wifely devotion. And when Claudian read: "Rome only has taken her conquests to her bosom and, giving all mankind one human name, has with her citizenship made men of every race Romans," and looked up and smiled at Hilary, he, too, broke into tears, and this time he did not look round to see whether anybody else wept. It seemed to him that everything he had ever thought about Rome was gathered up into those triumphant lines. And from the shouts of applause at the conclusion of the reading Hilary was sure that everybody else felt the same way.

But when a little later Hilary was waiting in the anteroom for his slaves to come and light their torches, he overheard two men talking behind him.

"What will they say in Ravenna when they hear of that tribute?"

"Ravenna!" snorted the other, and Hilary recognized the indignant voice of Lampadius. "What can you expect of anybody when Rome swallows such nonsense about there being no difference between a Roman and a barbarian?"

Hilary could not catch the reply of the first speaker. But the other voice was as firm and clear as before: "Then it's time you did. Talk about the barbarians advancing on Rome! They are in Rome."

Hilary without waiting for his slaves plunged hurriedly into the crowd around the door.

V

BUT IN SPITE OF SUCH GRUMBLINGS THE MOOD of triumph lasted surprisingly long and eventually swallowed up even the complaints of such chronic worriers as Lampadius. At Ravenna the Emperor struck new coins in honor of Stilicho's victory, and Rome raised his statue in bronze and silver by the rostrum in the most sacred part of the forum. And in August Stilicho returned to make his triumphal procession up the Capitoline hill and to receive the formal thanks of the senate and the plaudits of all Rome.

Nor was there any evidence of real anxiety even in the letters from Gaul. Indeed, the first rumors that the legions along the Rhine had been drawn upon for the defence of Italy were received with relief at Bordeaux, because such action would result in the earlier opening of the roads for Hilary's return. And when Hilary had to write that Stilicho himself had said that the defeat of Radagasius far from making the roads safe had temporarily increased the number of vagrants and deserters to add to the confusion, his sister wrote back at once to urge him to delay a little longer that they might be quite sure of his safety. And a few weeks later a messenger came by sea to give Hilary his grandfather's reassurances about some reports of restlessness on the frontier that he feared might have reached Rome. The German tribes, Postumianus wrote, knew only too well that even if the guard opposite them had been temporarily weakened, any effort of theirs to take advantage of that fact would bring prompt reprisals as soon as Rome was at leisure to turn her attention to them.

That afternoon Hilary went to Stilicho's to wish him well on a new expedition to restore order in the recently invaded regions. He showed him his grandfather's letter, and Stilicho expressed his satisfaction that the provincial leaders were taking so sound an attitude. But Medoc who came to Rome a week later from the north, where he had met some fellow-merchants from beyond the frontiers, was less certain. Postumianus was right if it were simply the Germans on the Rhine. But there were reports of other tribes pressing in from the east, perhaps more Goths, though it was hard to imagine that there could be any more Goths in the world after the hordes that had followed Radagasius.

But Hilary still was not really worried. He told Gaia about his letters, and she was sympathetic but reassuring. Everybody knew that the Gallo-Romano population still kept plenty of its primitive vigor. She had smiled disarmingly as she said this, as if she suspected some hidden sensitiveness on Hilary's part. But then her face shadowed.

"I wish one could say as much of those cowardly officials in the Italian cities. And as for those wretched eunuchs and sycophants in Ravenna"—the fine line of her mouth tightened—"when I think of them, I can feel sorry even for Stilicho."

Indeed Gaia was feeling so depressed by the generally poor account which the empire was giving of itself these days that Hilary forgot his preoccupations with Bordeaux in his efforts to comfort her. Serena was worried too. There were reports from Ravenna of a good deal of grumbling because Stilicho had not succeeded in completely relieving them of the menace of the barbarians. Some of the Emperor's household were beginning to tell him that the barbarians in the army could not be counted on. And presently there were anonymous whispers that Stilicho was but waiting for the right moment to have the barbarians in the legions in Italy proclaim him emperor.

Again Hilary protested that nobody could fail to recognize Stilicho's devotion to Rome and to the son of his old master the Emperor Theodosius. But Serena was emphatic in her rejection of that easy comfort. "I know those wretches in the Emperor's household. They simply cannot conceive of anybody's doing what Stilicho has done for anything but his own advancement. That wretch Olympius makes such a parade of piety, and I know it's only to get the priests around Honorius to turn him against Stilicho." And when Hilary still tried to reassure her, she ended the conversation with the crushing retort that he could know nothing of what a court was like.

It was not until well into February that any more definite news came. Then Medoc came up from Ostia, where an old acquaintance of his, a trader from Dacia, had brought a report that the tribes pressing on the Germans had been identified as a group newly arrived from the east, the Vandals. To Hilary, still preoccupied with the worries of his friend Serena, this information seemed curiously remote and academic. What difference did it make what extraordinary name these remote people were known by? But Medoc was clearly concerned about something more. So Hilary roused himself from his brooding to see if he could find out what it was. Presently Medoc divulged, though with some hesitation, that his friend had gone on to say that the Vandals were reported to be cutting their way through the German tribes along the Rhine, who were not offering any effective resistance. Even then Hilary's only thought was of the added worry for the harassed general.

Soon after, Serena heard from Stilicho that a formidable leader seemed to have arisen among an obscure people who were pushing through the lands of the Germans. He was trying to find out more about their movements from some of his soldiers who came from that part of the world. Only a couple of days later some traders came from the foot of the mountains to report in the forum of Trajan that they had seen refugees coming through the passes from the towns along the upper Rhine. By night the rumor was all over the city. Fortunatus picked it up at the baths and brought it home, looking thoroughly sobered.

Hilary went at once to the house of Stilicho, but the latest news Serena had was that her husband was trying to see if he could return some of the forces he had taken from Gaul the year before at least to the upper Rhine encampments. It was still too early in the season to move any very considerable number of men very far. If Stilicho had any more exact information, he was clearly not confiding it to even a trusted messenger.

Early the next morning Hilary went to Ostia to see Medoc. He found his old friend in his warehouse, instructing an agent whom he was sending up to Placentia on the chance that he could meet a couple of other agents already in that region waiting for goods from the east. Medoc was doubtful that the pack animals would even get through the passes, but if they did, he wanted to be sure of the prospects in Gaul before he risked two of his best men, to say nothing of valuable goods.

When the man had gone, Medoc poured out a small cup of an aromatic wine from one of the Greek islands, he said, for his guest, and then summed up the situation from what he knew and could guess.

"It's the Vandals, I am sure, and I think we can take it for granted that they are all across the Rhine. Those troops Stilicho had to call into Italy made all the difference."

"Then?" said Hilary, and for the first time the possibility he had shuddered to face all night was upon him.

"I don't see how they can get very far," said Medoc slowly. "Certainly," looking at Hilary's drawn face, "not farther at most than Mayence or Treves."

"You believe that?"

"Yes," said Medoc promptly. "I do not think the towns will offer much resistance." He smiled grimly. "Between Rome and your church there is not much fight left in them. But if the country folk don't offer some resistance, then I think I shall hold your father's Martin responsible."

But only a couple of weeks later the Roman rumors had the Vandals to Rheims. Again Hilary went to Ostia, to the dimly raftered warehouse with the heavy scent of spice among chests and bales of far-come treasure.

The keenest of Hilary's anxieties Medoc soon dispelled with the help of a map on the wall of his small office. Even if the worst were true, the invaders were moving to the north, quite away from Bordeaux. The distances which rumor had given to the Vandals were simply impossible. If they were anywhere near that far, they were outriding the Huns, the swiftest-moving riders Rome had ever met. But that they were far enough into Gaul to have cut off all contact with Italy was unhappily true.

It was then that Hilary first reproached himself with having dallied in Rome until now that he might be of help to his family he was completely shut off. But Medoc rebuked him sharply. What good would it have done anybody for him to be killed or enslaved, or at best held for ransom on the northern roads?

But Hilary, when he got back to Rome, found he had little time to think of his own personal anxieties because of Serena's fresh alarm. Stilicho had written that the forces he had actually been able to get to the north had had to turn back in the face of the overwhelming numbers they found in front of them. Even as the messenger was in her house, answering her questions, Claudian had come in with the rumor heard in the baths that the barbarian troops Stilicho had sent north had mutinied.

It was only a few days later that the agony closed in on Hilary. For it was clear from the reports coming in from all sources that the Vandals were sweeping across Gaul at a pace that completely belied all Medoc's reassurances. Romans who, like Gaia, were sensitive to any attenuation of the glory of Rome listened to the reports of the Vandal advance with a deep sense of humiliation, while those who possessed Gallic estates worried about the inevitable damages of war. But most of fashionable Rome, however much it might deplore the destruction in Gaul, was clearly relieved that the Vandals had chosen to go west instead of turning to the south.

Indeed, in a curious fashion one worry seemed to cancel out another. There had been a report from Britain of a Roman general whose troops had raised him on their shields and proclaimed him emperor. There had been a good deal of amusement when it was learned that the upstart Caesar on the strength of his name had claimed descent from Constantine. And then had come the news that the adventurer had crossed the Channel into northern Gaul. After all, he was a Roman; so now men began to hope that perhaps Constantine would yet vindicate Roman arms.

But in the middle of March word came that some of the Vandals had suddenly turned south, to Paris. Then they were at Tours. And presently all Rome was talking of the destruction of Bordeaux as an accomplished fact. It was impossible any longer to check the stories—they were coming from everywhere. Hilary asked Medoc if he did not think they had better start north at once to find out the possibilities of going farther. But Medoc reminded him that his family would certainly take the first chance of sending him word, and urged him to wait for it. He would himself send a freedman of his, who was accustomed to finding his way in uncertain country, up to Milan to see what he could pick up.

There was nothing for Hilary to do but to wait at least until some more certain news arrived. It was not long in coming. Less than a week after his talk with Medoc, in the early evening, one of Hilary's slaves came to tell him that a messenger from Gaul was at the door; at least, he said he was from Gaul, though the doorkeeper whom Hilary had acquired with his Roman lodgings gave it as his opinion that the man looked more like a shipwrecked seaman if not a runaway slave.

Hilary went at once to the anteroom where he found the stranger slumped over on a bench, seemingly exhausted. Sending the slave for some strong Italian wine, Hilary greeted the man, and he raised his head. It was Cerealis. With a cry he staggered to his feet and flung his arms about Hilary, clinging to him as if indeed he were his one hope in shipwreck, and sobbing incoherently. Hilary, half dragging, half carrying the emaciated form of his once stocky brother-in-law to the atrium, shouted for his slaves to hurry with food and drink. And he made Cerealis drink the wine before he tried to speak. But when the slaves brought food, Cerealis waved it aside.

"Has nobody come?" he asked when he had recovered a little of his strength. "I sent two men by different roads."

Hilary shook his head, feeling his heart chill at the agony in Cerealis' eyes as he groped for words, and then he asked the commonplace question, "How are they all?"

Cerealis made a great effort and steadied his voice. "As Christians, we can only say, 'It is well with them.'" And then as Hilary stared at the formal piety, so unlike the usual matter-of-fact reticence of his brother-in-law, Cerealis broke down. "Hilary, they are all dead, dead!" And as that cry rang through the house, a couple of slaves rushed in. And now it was Cerealis who caught at Hilary and held the wine cup to his lips. And while the world reeled around Hilary, Cerealis ate wolfishly of the bread and meat on the table.

But after half a dozen mouthfuls he pushed the food away, and taking Hilary's hand, with something of his wonted competence, he told his story. All the household was clustered now at the end of the atrium, but he seemed completely unaware of anybody but Hilary. They had not really been afraid until the Vandals were reported at Poitiers. Even then they had not believed Bordeaux was in any danger. Cerealis had suggested that they go to the house of friends in Bordeaux, but Postumianus disliked the idea of facing the crowds and confusion of the city. But the women were worried. So they had all decided that Cerealis should ride across country through the woods to the north, and see if he could find out something about the direction the Vandals were taking, and form his own opinion about the situation. He had left his most reliable man, old Sertorius, in charge of his mistresses with instructions to stay close to them on the very unlikely chance that bandits might take 'advantage of the uncertainties of the time. And he had armed the most dependable of his men and set them to guard the house in his absence.

"They all thought I was worrying unnecessarily, and so did I, Hilary," he added pitifully.

Cerealis was still not entirely sure what had happened, but he was inclined to think that the Vandals were making a feint of by-passing Bordeaux, which everybody knew had strengthened its fortifications, and had sent a small portion of their forces to the south. These men had obviously decided to turn the pretended diversion to their own account for a little looting, and so had passed through a corner of the estate toward the villa itself. On the way they had come upon a storehouse full of wine, and had stopped for a while, long enough for a message to reach the men at the house. Then while the main body of the group set the wine to flowing, a few of the more impatient ones pushed up to the house. They met a prepared resistance at the gate below, and two were killed, but a couple escaped to bring up reinforcements.

Then things began to go wrong. The shock of the news that the enemy was at the gate had been too much for Postumianus, who collapsed. That had claimed everybody's attention, and even the men at the gate had apparently been too upset by the news to keep proper watch, or perhaps they had thought that they had saved the day. At any rate the Vandals, when they returned with more men, both drunk and enraged at the resistance, penetrated to the house without much difficulty.

At the sight of Hilary's sick face, Cerealis shook his head. "In some ways it was better than you might think." And then he went on to explain that a few of the slaves had succeeded in hiding, and with their story and what he found when he returned himself several days later with a party of woodsmen who had gone out to find him at the first news of the attack, he had pieced together what must have happened. Apparently, the family were gathered in his grandfather's room when the Vandals arrived at the house. The first of them penetrated to the door of the room without being stopped. There the Lady Claudia met them and commanded them to go away. They hesitated; somebody cried out in the room, and they struck her down.

"She died instantly," Cerealis reassured Hilary. Then they broke into the room. Old Sertorius drew his dagger, and then seeing that there was no hope of resistance, he plunged it into the heart of Blandina where she sat beside her grandfather's bed. She fell dead across the old man's body, and the slave boy who leaped from a window in the excitement a moment afterward was positive that the old man made no sound, made no movement.

The children's nurse was with them on the terrace. As the Vandals broke out of the house in pursuit of some of the slaves, she grabbed the children and climbed up on the balustrade and leaped to the rocks below. The children must have died instantly, and she very little after. Then the Vandals set fire to everything. Some of the slaves they tossed into the fire; others, particularly the young women and boys, they took with them. Then apparently messengers from their commanders must have summoned them to the attack on Bordeaux. There were only a couple of sleeping drunkards by the smouldering ruins when Cerealis and his aids reached there a few days later.

"We found them all," said Cerealis in a voice between despair and reassurance, "and we buried them. The priest was dead; so we said a few prayers ourselves, and we marked the spot." And as Hilary began to weep again, Cerealis tried awkwardly to comfort him, saying over and over again, "They are safe. They are safe." And when Hilary was a little calmer, Cerealis explained that in all the desolate days since, he had never ceased to give thanks that they had not lived to be carried off into slavery. And Hilary remembered that Cerealis' grandfather had been a slave.

It was with the greatest difficulty that Hilary could draw from Cerealis any information as to what had happened to him after that. Obviously, it seemed to him of no importance. But gradually Hilary got the salient facts. A few days after the burial, one of the slaves who had escaped came back with word that the Vandals had burned and looted Bordeaux and were turning south again. Cerealis had hidden in the woods, and there he began to think of how he could reach Hilary. He had sent two freedmen separately, and then he had started for the port of Narbonne. There he had fallen in with a merchant from whom he used to buy supplies, and the latter had helped him to a boat. They had been wrecked, and his friend had perished, but Cerealis had made the shore and found his way to Rome. But none of that seemed worth mentioning now. He had accomplished the only purpose that remained to him. Even as he talked, he fell asleep from sheer exhaustion.

VI

ALL OF HILARY'S ROMAN FRIENDS, PAGAN AND Christian alike, thronged to his house and were kind to his grief. He bowed gravely when he was reminded of the inscrutable ways of fortune, and of the mysteries of Providence alike. He murmured something vaguely polite when Attalus said that only the gods could tell whether those who had been cut off early had been cheated of the gifts of life or spared further suffering. And he agreed quite as vaguely when Laeta said that, since God had let it happen, it must be for the best. But he stared when Pammachius, in the dusty monk's robe in which he had hurried up from his hospital at Ostia to offer his sympathy and the promise of his prayers, observed thoughtfully, as if speaking to himself and not to Hilary, that he would find that grief is a low door through which the proud spirit stoops to its freedom.

He spent long hours reading and answering the formal letters of condolence that all his grandfather's old friends sent to him. And he spent even longer hours at the bedside of Cerealis, who lay for days, with eyes shut or staring blankly at the ceiling of Hilary's bedchamber. And over and over again until his voice lost, it seemed to him, all power of conviction, he assured Cerealis that it would have made no difference if he had stayed at the villa that day. How could all the men on the estate, even if armed and drawn up, have withstood such a horde? It might only have prolonged the agony for all concerned.

But Hilary had his own questions too. When the rattle of the heavy wagons from the country and from the wharves along the river broke the darkness of night, and Hilary lay tossing until the first ravellings of dawn sifted through the closed shutters, all his consciousness writhed with the same questions over and over again. If only he had started for home when the first reports came! If only he had been content to stay in Bordeaux and never had coveted the brittle splendor of Rome! Sometimes he fell asleep again and dreamed unquietly of things that had happened long ago—like losing on the rocks beneath the terrace a child's toy, a little wooden chariot drawn by two tiny wooden horses. And then slowly he awoke to the inexorable burden of another day.

Gaia, in particular, was kinder than he had ever thought possible. When at the end of a fortnight after Cerealis' arrival he had still not thought of going to see her, she had sent a messenger, inviting him to a private supper. And he had been astonished to learn that she had cancelled her plans for a trip to her villa in the Alban hills on the chance that he might want to see her. He felt sharply rebuked for his self-absorption, and he apologized and thanked her warmly. But with a humility unusual for her she seemed to guess that he had gone into a land where it had not occurred to him to think of her for help, and she looked crestfallen. So he redoubled his expressions of appreciation, and she, reassured, began to ask him about Bordeaux with a warmth of interest she had never displayed before. But where he had once tried to interest her in his home with all his powers of description, he found now that he could not bear to answer the simplest, most objective question. He saw that she still looked baffled as he took his leave, but he had neither the strength nor the will even to try to say anything more.

But the next night he slept until the first thin but incredibly fresh rays of the sunlight seeped through the shutters. He had been dreaming that he was back in Bordeaux, sitting in the late afternoon sunlight on the terrace, and they were all there, his grandfather, and his brother, and his aunt, and his sister, talking serenely about some trifle, and somewhere in the background he could hear the voices of the children. He woke with a sense of sweetness, and he clung to the dream for a minute as warm and sunny as the terrace itself. And then as he woke more fully to the world around him and watched the light of the morning fraying around the edges of the shutters and sifting lightly over the bronze-bound chest beneath the window, he remembered that he had not known such content for a long time, that, outside the warm sweetness fading fast in his awakening consciousness, there was something even the unremembered shadow of which chilled—and then he was dully and fully awake to the trouble that filled every crevice of his being.

But that day Cerealis seemed suddenly to have recovered his strength. He had been sitting in the garden behind Hilary's apartment for a day or two, astonishingly indifferent to the coming and going of the household around him. Now he wanted to go out. Hilary gave orders for his slaves to prepare a litter for the two of them. And then he asked Cerealis where he wanted to go—the imperial fora, St. Peter's, and then, struck afresh by the wretched thinness of Cerealis' face and the gauntness of his arms, almost as white as his tunic, Hilary suggested the tombs of the martyrs in the catacombs. To his surprise, Cerealis seized upon that suggestion with the closest approach to interest that he had shown since his collapse.

As they swung along the Appian Way past all the magnificent pagan tombs, Hilary was reminded sharply of his earlier visit. There were not so many people on the road today, for, as they reached the highway, Hilary had heard the cheers of the crowd within the Circus, and been astonished at how completely he had lost track of what was going on in Rome.

But when they drew near the basilica of Saint Sebastian, the road began to fill with pilgrims on foot. It was as dirty, as crippled, as pinched a looking lot of humanity as Hilary remembered, but now it seemed to him only fitting that he should be in this company. For he soon discovered that Cerealis had no desire to see the wonders of the catacombs, but only to go down to the graves of the martyrs and to pray for his dead. The galleries were crowded as they had been before, and they had to walk some distance before they could find room for two to kneel together. And when finally they found a clear space in a shallow chapel, Hilary was surprised to find himself standing once more before the tomb of Pope Cornelius. But this time he had no trouble in finding what he should say in his prayer to the martyred pope.

As they regained the upper air of the church, Hilary reflected that though everything was as he had remembered it, yet everything seemed different. He thought of the sentence of Pammachius about grief's low door, but there was no freedom in this. It was simply that in these wretched ranks he who had been so proudly assured had at last found his proper place.

He looked at Cerealis, and was astonished to see that he had recovered some of his usual businesslike assurance.

"I want to see one of the priests to have a proper requiem sung," he said, "at that altar down there."

The priest was obviously accustomed to all sorts of petitions, for when Cerealis said it was for some people who had been killed by the barbarians and buried without the rites Christians should have, he asked no further questions. Only when Hilary gave him the offering for the poor which he had brought, the priest, surprised at its size from two plainly dressed men who came alone, asked what names he should give the beneficiaries of their generosity for their prayers. Hilary hesitated, but Cerealis answered firmly that they should be asked only to pray for all the dead in Gaul to whom it had not been possible to give the proper rites. It was a long way, he said with a sigh, but he thought the saints would not be troubled by that.

And when a few days later the requiem had been sung, and the first of the gifts had been distributed to the crowding poor and their blessings heard, Cerealis began to talk to Hilary of the things that must be done.

"Do you think," he asked as they were carried back to the city, "that you could take care of the Campanian estates for now?"

Hilary for a moment stared without comprehending, and then in a flash he saw that the time had come when he could no longer draw the money he needed without thought of where it came from. So he suggested that they go together.

It was now Cerealis' turn to look surprised. "I must go back to Gaul."

"But not now. It is not safe."

"Safe!" Then Cerealis seemed to take compassion on his companion. "Not now perhaps, but the roads will be open shortly, at least to the merchants."

"Then I shall go with you."

But Cerealis shook his head with an authority Hilary had never before seen in him. "Hilary, the bird that flies low can take refuge now and then in the brush. No one would think me worth robbing, but even in rags you would suggest a ransom."

Besides, he argued, there would be trouble on the Campanian estates if the rumor reached them that the whole family had vanished in Gaul. It was asking too much of human nature to expect the estate managers to spend themselves for masters they might never hear from again.

"Then, at least, you shall go back as the master to the Bordeaux estate," said Hilary. But Cerealis refused. This was no time to make any changes in the family inheritance.

Later Hilary appealed to Medoc, but the old merchant, who had taken very hard the disaster that had befallen his friends, supported Cerealis at every point. He would send a good man he had been keeping in reserve at Ostia north with Cerealis, and there he would put him in touch with agents who could advise him of the possibilities ahead.

But Hilary still tried to keep Cerealis a little longer. Fortunatus had at last received word from his family in Gaul. Their estates had lain just off the line of the Vandal advance, and had not been molested. But his older brother had been killed while out hunting in the woods shortly after—whether by the slaves who fled or by some straggler, no one could tell. Fortunatus looked soberly at the prospect. He did not pretend to be inconsolable for the loss of the brother whose superior claims to attention had from earliest memory been dinned into the younger brother by the lowliest slave on the estate. But he was awed by the sudden change in fortune.

"I suppose it is what your pious friends would call providential," he said to Hilary. On one point, however, he had no uncertainty. His father had roused himself enough from his grief to suggest that, when a proper time had elapsed, the heiress who had been promised to his brother might accept the obvious substitute.

"No lapse of time, proper or improper, can make Bassula anything but the dullest girl in Gaul," said Fortunatus. If Hilary could manage now without him, he was going to Baiae to see what he could do with a young widow whose society he had enjoyed there. So Hilary urged Cerealis to remain with him until Easter at least. But Cerealis declined. The sooner he got some idea of what was going on in the north, the better. One could hail the Resurrection at Florence or Milan as well as at Rome.

So Hilary found himself once more alone. But as Cerealis must have foreseen, he had recovered his breath. He still awoke in the gray dawn with a reluctance that sharpened with returning consciousness into a dull pain which formed the ground of all his day's awareness. Every memory of the estate at Bordeaux, every chance reminder of his family, came to him with a vividness and a tenderness that he found unbearable. It seemed as if the anguish of the end stained all the colors of the past a deeper dye, and he could not bear to remember even the simplest commonplace of that life or those relations.

Once in the thrashing of the pre-dawn gray he remembered the terror of his old illness. For weeks he had lain helpless in the shadows of his darkened room with all the household whispering, "It is the fever that lamed his sister." And when the priest had bidden him ask only that the will of God might be fulfilled in him, he had shuddered to think that the mysterious purposes of Providence might very well be realized without him. And when the household had rejoiced piously in his recovery, the thought had come to him perversely that perhaps he had been allowed to escape this time only to be caught later. Now the bitter thought came that his old distrust had been justified, that it was for this that he had been spared. But some instinct of justice deep within his spirit asked if he really wished he were dead. And the very ache of his pain answered that question for him. And justice probed even deeper. It was not God trapping him; it was his letting the good things he had slip through his fingers without really valuing them.

It was then that he decided that this year at least he would try to make some real preparation for Easter, that he would forget the debate over what God had given, and that he would for once take the gift of the moment and use it in the season's confession of the human failure, of his particular failure.

Once he tried to tell Gaia something of this, indirectly and obliquely offering her a little of the trust she had been seeking of him these last weeks. But she had looked frightened at the very suggestion that one did not know the good one had in one's hands. "That is what is so morbid of you Christians, all

115

this sense of guilt of yours. What is done is done. Not even the gods themselves can change that."

It had never before occurred to Hilary to try to argue religious ideas with Gaia. Perhaps because they had threatened to erect a barrier where he most wanted none, perhaps even because they had not seemed so important to him then. Now he tried to explain to her the Christian idea of the forgiveness of sins, of the restoration of the soul's possibilities. But to her it obviously seemed a poor business. It would be all right for those miserable creatures whom one saw creeping down the Appian Way, perhaps even for her ancestor, who certainly looked as if he had had some unease of conscience in that old picture. But to suggest that a man of position, rich, well-born, intelligent, should turn his thoughts from the intellectual interests of the cultivated Roman citizen to such brooding about himself seemed to her nothing but a maudlin undermining of his own integrity. Uncomfortably, Hilary felt some shadow of justice in her rebuke; he had perhaps been thinking too much about himself of late.

He thought of it again, incongruously enough, during the Easter Mass when the restless shifting of the crowd gave him a momentary glimpse of the Pope sitting on his throne, his golden robes and his white hair standing out firmly against the scarlet hanging behind his gilded chair. There were many pilgrims in the great church, and they kept pressing for a glimpse of the high altar blazing with its golden candelabra, and of the Pope on his throne. Hilary had seen the Pope a number of times since he had come to Rome, and he had been a little disappointed.

Innocent seemed to him to look exactly like what he was, a member of the bustling equestrian class, shrewd, curious, cautiously enterprising, but with no talent for grace or magnificence. Physically even, he was unimpressive, of medium height, of medium complexion, with a quiet voice and a quiet manner, distinguished only by a certain neatness and painstakingness, even fussiness of demeanor. Rather surprisingly—report said—though he was sparing of speech, he listened with uncommon alertness to whatever men said to him, and sometimes put extraordinarily acute questions on matters about which he could not be expected to know much. All this came to Hilary's mind now as he gazed at the quiet figure, completely absorbed in what was going on at the altar. Abashed, Hilary tried to focus his own thoughts on the distant mumble of the chant, so steady, so swift, echoed by the louder, more ragged responses of the huge congregation thronging the aisles of the vast basilica. Once again Hilary caught a glimpse of the Pope, now standing with his hands clasped before him, but with the same look of calm and complete concentration investing the white figure standing so still in front of the scarlet hanging. It seemed as if that figure gathered up the whole prayer of the congregation standing before the altar. Perhaps, Hilary thought, that was what a pope should do.

Afterward Hilary, when he knelt down to put his personal petition into his Communion prayer, found that even the memory of the dead seemed a calmer thing, as if what had happened had been gathered up into some larger fabric of which he could not yet make out the pattern. And then his thoughts swung out, and he began to pray for the Pope and the congregation gathered here, and all the congregations in the universal Church. Only when he lifted his head to catch the opening words of the last Gospel, did he remember that he had not said anything of himself. And then the great words swept him off: "That was the true light, which enlightens every man that comes into the world."

VII

HILARY THOUGHT OF THOSE WORDS AGAIN AS HE came out in the great courtyard of Saint Peter's and saw the monk standing at the side of Pammachius in one of the porticoes, acknowledging the greetings of many of the stragglers, who like Hilary had lingered for a final prayer at the first pope's tomb. For the light from that shining face transformed the thin figure in the dusty monk's cloak and seemed to cast a radiance about the whole circle of shining faces thronging about him.

"It is Paulinus!" exclaimed a middle-aged man next to Hilary, and flung his arms wide for an embrace. Even Pammachius, standing smiling at the stranger's side, seemed to have caught something of his warmth. And Hilary looked curiously at this man of whom he had heard all his life. For Paulinus had come from Hilary's country, and Postumianus had bought some of Paulinus' wheatfields when he sold his Gallic estates and went to Rome never to return. Even in the house of Symmachus men had still asked Hilary if he knew Paulinus, and told him of the splendor of his consulship. It had not been difficult from their reminiscences to conjure up that radiant figure of youthful beauty and strength riding in the consular chariot up the Capitoline to the plaudits of all Rome. For an hour Rome had recovered its ancient glory in that magnificent procession which Gallic wealth returned to its imperial source. And even the pagan senators could relish the drama of the sequel to that brilliant morning when Paulinus came back to Rome alone, on foot, in a dusty pilgrim's cloak, and nobody recognized him at the gate of the city but a beggar to whom he had flung an alms from the consular chariot.

It was not a young face any longer, Hilary saw, looking closer. The skin was pulled tightly over the finely moulded bones, and time and the weather had blanched and thinned the curly golden hair of the legend and turned the ivory of the skin to a pale honey color, but the light in the large brown eyes and the full laughing mouth shone through the transparent flesh like the soft radiance of the burning oil in an alabaster lamp. Hilary listened to the slightly muted richness of the voice, warm and easy in greeting, and he remembered how in the house of Pammachius men said that Paulinus had written verses as fine as anything of Claudian. Then Pammachius caught sight of Hilary.

"I remember your grandfather well," said Paulinus, when Pammachius had presented Hilary to him. "He told me what he thought of my throwing my land away, but he offered me full value for what he wanted, and paid promptly for it. An honest pagan who would not cheat even a fool," Paulinus laughed, and then he sobered. "I prayed Saint Felix for him when I heard of his end."

Now he went on to ask Hilary if he did not have some lands in the neighborhood of Nola which he should look after. And when Hilary said that he had waited only for Easter before setting out, Pammachius at once suggested they should travel together. Paulinus must have caught the young man's involuntary drawing-back, for he laughed sympathetically. "A young landlord visiting his estates goes a different pace from an old monk returning to his monastery. But when you have finished your visitation, and done everything you can and still found it too little, then come to us, and we'll make you forget your troubles."

"They say Nola is heaven on earth," said Pammachius wistfully.

"Then why do you never come to heaven?" Paulinus rounded on his friend with a mock severity that made everybody laugh.

"Perhaps because I have not earned it?"

The monk made a graceful gesture of despair with his slender hands. "You are as bad as Severus."

That reminded Pammachius to tell his friend that Hilary had seen Severus just before he left Gaul. And Paulinus behaved quite as Pammachius had, staring at Hilary as if he thought to find still on this stranger some lingering ray of his friend's presence. Again Hilary was mortified to realize how little account he had taken of Severus. Only now in the presence of Paulinus the cheerfulness of Severus seemed somehow less irrational.

In the following weeks Hilary often thought of the radiant face of Paulinus, particularly at night when, too exhausted to fall asleep, he tried to shake his mind free of the accumulating frustrations of his days. Medoc had tried to prepare him for what he would find on his Campanian estates by reminding him that what he had known at Bordeaux, where the family lived on their lands, was the ideal situation. One would find very few landowners as astute as his grandfather, very few estate managers as devoted as Cerealis.

"After all," said Medoc dryly, "few estate managers are working for the profit of their own family."

But Hilary felt much less confident than Medoc assumed, that he would remember how the effect of the Bordeaux estate was achieved. He thought of haying from the boy's pleasure in riding the hay cart home and tumbling in the sweet fragrance of the haymow afterward, but he had no idea of the generalship that marshalled the slaves and the farmers at the right moment, that cast the odds between another day of ripening sun and the feathering of clouds in the west. And still more did he own himself over his depth when he tried to remember all the processes that intervened between plucking the grapes off the vines and getting the famous wine on the road to Rome in great straw-wrapped amphoras.

He tried to get Cerealis before he left Rome, to give him some notion of what he should look for, but the latter would only say, "You will learn fast enough when you get there." Once he had added with a smile, "You were always a lot cleverer than I, Hilary."

But the latter had protested, "Perhaps I was cleverer at reading about it in the *Georgics,* Cerealis, but you learned it in the fields, and that is what counts now."

So when, after the departure of Cerealis, Fabius offered to go with him, Hilary thankfully accepted his friend's offer. Fabius was no Cerealis, but he would have his experience of his father's estates.

In the beginning Fabius was certainly of the greatest help to Hilary, for he gave him confidence in his own judgment. At the first of the Campanian estates he confirmed Hilary's suspicion of the too-genial, too-talkative manager, who had arranged for Hilary's arrival a rural festival that seemed to bring Theocritus to life, and had followed it the next day with a banquet for which he had produced Greek wines that Hilary knew from his Roman housekeeping must have taken both care and expense to obtain, particularly here off the main highway in the depths of the country. Before he left Rome, Hilary's Roman agents had told him that the yield of this estate had been falling unaccountably in spite of the manager's reputation for competence. Now, during the banquet which only a couple of the estate officials sat down to, the man talked much and amusingly of the unreliability of the free farmers on the fringes of the estate, who were always complaining of non-existent abuses and claiming quite unheard-of privileges. Fabius' agreement that the fellow looked and sounded like an unctuous rascal encouraged Hilary to insist the next day on going over the estate at leisure.

And now Hilary noticed that the best-kept and fullest barns and storehouses were those closest to the farmhouse. Farther off, especially on the small stream that served as a main outlet for the farm, the storehouses were much less carefully kept and certainly not as well stocked. This the manager at once admitted, explaining that the farmers were so unreliable that, except when there was a boat actually at the river landing, he tried to keep things under his own eye. But while Fabius asked the man about the yields of various crops, Hilary took the chance to talk with a couple of the farmers who had been fishing in the stream, and who, in spite of the manager's orders to take themselves off, had persisted in hanging around in an open-mouthed, foolish-looking way.

Now they came to the point fast enough, telling Hilary that the manager kept open house for the merchants, who repaid his hospitality with all sorts of gifts of wine and spices that never appeared, they were sure, in the accounts of the estate. So Hilary asked for another look at the storerooms in the farmhouse courtyard, and found there a wine cellar that in quality if not in quantity would compare very favorably with the notable wine cellars of Postumianus at Bordeaux.

The manager met Hilary's observations by asking rather sneeringly if Gallic landowners acted as their own bailiffs. And when Hilary asked if he might see the accounts of the estate, the manager declared that on such a big farm as this no one had time to do much fussing with accounts. At that, Fabius protested that his father had always had the most detailed accounts sent up to Rome from all his estates. And when the manager, turning ugly, threatened to leave the fields at the moment when they obviously needed attention, Fabius advised Hilary to take the man at his word and promised to lend him an experienced bailiff from one of his estates only a day's journey away.

But there were other cases where it seemed to Hilary that Fabius only confused him. There was one huge farm given over to cattle and the grains needed for their fattening that troubled Hilary greatly. The manager was clearly conscientious, and the cattle were well-cared for, but it seemed to Hilary that the slaves on the estate were a sulky-looking lot. Even in the evening when the day's work was done, there was no sound of laughter and singing in their barracks, such as had often drawn him in his boyhood to forbidden territory. The next day, when the slaves were all in the fields, Hilary announced that he was going down to their quarters, low brick buildings set around a slate-paved court. The manager shrugged his shoulders.

Even in the summer sunshine the narrow cells were dark and dirty with the foul straw that seemed to be their only furnishing, giving off a stench half of moulding vegetable matter, half of rotting flesh. Shocked, Hilary directed that the cells be cleaned out and provided with fresh straw. The manager looked startled, and then rather sullenly nodded agreement. But when as an after-thought Hilary suggested that the cells might be white-washed, he exploded: "My lord, the hay will be ready to cut in a day or two! Do you want to lose the hay crop for coddling barbarians who will not know the difference?"

And when Hilary curtly bade him buy more slaves, the man grew impudent and asked him where. He had even bought some of the new crop of barbarians that the slave dealers had brought in, paid a good price, too. Half a dozen had run away, and when he had had them brought back and put in irons, two of them had sharpened some dull knives, and cut their throats. But Hilary stood his ground. Was that all? Had he not had them beaten? The overseer spat on the ground in disgust. "Of course, I had them beaten. How much work do you think I could get done with half the slaves running away when they liked?" And Fabius backed the man up. He said he would be glad to hire him if Hilary gave him the chance, for the man obviously knew his business. One had only to look at the cattle to tell that.

On the next estate, however, the slave barracks seemed clean, but many of the slaves looked thin and listless, with a grayish tinge to the weather-beaten brownness of the field-worker. Hilary tried to ask some of them how they were faring, but the manager dogged his footsteps so that the men only mumbled something noncommital about a man's having to take what the gods sent. This estate had a good reputation with Hilary's Roman agents, for the dependability of its yields; so Hilary could not be sure whether the manager's close attendance meant anything more than unusual conscientiousness.

Hilary took the chance of a few minutes alone in the farm-house kitchen to ask the housekeeper, a stalwart peasant woman whose air of independent self-confidence had caught Hilary's eye as soon as he entered the smoky room, why the slaves did not look healthier. The woman looked startled at his question; then she came over to where he sat on a low stool, and leaned over him so that her linen coif brushed his cheek. "What can you expect when you try to get oil from even the fallen olives, and leave nothing but the hard green ones to the slaves?" At that moment the manager came back into the kitchen; so the woman had time only to mutter, "I told him he'd have trouble." But a little later when Hilary asked the man about the diet of the slaves, he answered casually enough: "The usual thing, the broken wheat, the fallen olives, the vegetables we can't sell, and fish from the brook. Of course, they complain. Slaves never think of anything but their bellies and their backs."

"But so many of them look sick and ill fed," said Hilary.

The overseer for the first time looked troubled. "They were

a poor buy, that last lot. Cheap enough, but always getting sick. You think they are only pretending, and then they die on you."

"Wouldn't more oil with their bread help?" asked Hilary.

"Perhaps, but even poor-grade oil brings a good price these days."

Hilary insisted on the added ration of oil, but when the manager protested that he would not be able to keep his contracts with the Roman agents, Fabius reminded Hilary that he had the best men in Rome, and they could hardly be expected to work with much enthusiasm in his interest if he cut the ground from under their feet in the country.

In the literary circles of Bordeaux it had been the opinion that though money was a useful thing, any preoccupation with the means of its acquisition was destructive of the liberal spirit. Grimly Hilary reflected that he had never realized before how destructive it was. For the night he completed his visitation of his last estate, only a day's journey from Nola, he dreamed that he sat at the farmhouse gate, and that a long line of people came down the highroad, and each of them gave him a penny. They were men of all sorts: bailiffs, woodsmen, shepherds, farmers, house slaves; each of them gave him a penny. When it seemed to him that the road must be empty, he turned and looked up the road, and the line stretched out as far as he could see. And when he awoke, he found that his right hand was cramped beneath his body.

VIII

SO GRATEFUL AS HILARY WAS TO FABIUS FOR HIS help, he was relieved when his friend said that he really must return to his own Roman house to get on with the editing of his father's letters. And Hilary took the chance of giving his friend a proper escort to reduce his own retinue. So with only a couple of grooms to take care of the horses and a couple of body servants Hilary started on the last lap of the journey to Nola.

It was, he told himself, a courtesy due to a distinguished countryman, but he was beginning to wonder if perhaps there were not something owing to his father, too.

On either side of the Appian Way golden fields, with the deep grass shimmering in the breeze, stretched to the low vine-clad hills to the east. Several times they passed groups of workers in the distance, too far away to take any notice of the road. Then they came upon a little group sitting in a cleared patch of meadow just off the highway.

"They're having their midday lunch," said one of the slaves hungrily. As they paused to look, Hilary noticed that one of the men was in monk's dress. So assuring his companions that they must have reached Paulinus' lands, he rode up to the little company, and told them where they were going. There was a joyous shout from the whole group, and the monk smilingly bade them welcome to one of the farms of Nola. Then two of his companions took the horses, and the monk produced food from a reed basket.

"We always bring something extra on the chance of visitors," he said, offering sections of black bread dripping with olive oil and stuffed with herbs and lumps of goat's cheese. The food was excellent, and Hilary accused the monk of keeping his best for his guests, but he denied it, and the plump and smiling faces of his companions bore him out.

Indeed, one of them, a brawny young fellow obviously still growing out of his canvas tunic, very seriously explained to Hilary that at Nola the best food went into the fields.

"Thank God," said the monk, "we have plenty. But when we do run short in the spring, we fast in the choir. It is easier to push a pen than a plough on an empty stomach."

Then he told Hilary he would go along with them to show them the way. When he was mounted on one of the spare horses, he admitted that it was really quite unnecessary, but he never could resist a chance to ride a good horse.

Even as he spoke, there came over the fields the sound of a

distant bell, swinging slowly on the late summer air as if its sweetness were but another shimmer of the brightness of earth and sky.

"It is the bell which Paulinus had the bronze workers cast for our church so that, wherever we are, we may join in the prayers in the choir," said the monk, slipping from his horse to kneel in the dusty grass at the roadside. And Hilary noticed that, as he and his company followed his example, the workers in the field stopped singing and knelt in the high grass.

So they came to Nola, and its pretty, brightly painted houses with balconies spilling flowering vines like festal wreaths above their heads. And then they rode up a little rise of ground above the town toward the majestic pile of the church, with its towers and its domed apse and floating wings of porticoes and colonnades, stretching away from a great hollow square of marble pavement.

"You should see it at Easter," said the monk as Hilary reined in his horse and paused to stare in admiration at the beauty of the gleaming marbles against the blue sky, which somehow in that setting of radiant newness seemed young and fresh itself. "All the countryside comes to the tomb of Saint Felix then, and pilgrims from all over Italy and from Africa and Greece and Syria, even. They fill every inch of the church."

But even as he spoke, a little group of country folk came straggling into the open square in front of the church. Some of them still clutched the reed baskets and the large linen squares with tied corners from which they had doubtless been dining on the way. Others carried fat babies in too short shirts. There were a couple of cripples leaning on their sticks, and a blind man with his hand on a little girl's shoulder. It looked very much as if the whole parish had walked here, each keeping his own pace and slowly converging on the court before the great church, laughing and chatting gayly.

As Hilary started forward, the monk put his hand on his bridle, "Wait a moment." And then Hilary saw a single man come round a corner as if from a side door of the church, carrying a standard with a bronze cross wreathed in bronze flowers at the top. In a moment the cross had been lifted, and as if a magnet had been held to a spray of iron filings, the aimless sprawl of humanity was galvanized into an orderly, purposive pattern, as the company lined up in pairs behind the cross. Somebody raised a low dirge-like note, and the whole procession began to sing a hymn in praise of Saint Felix and to move forward with great dignity through the bronze doors, which had opened at their approach.

"A beautiful sight, isn't it?" said a familiar voice, and Hilary turned to find Paulinus standing behind him in one of the arches of the colonnade. And then when he had made Hilary welcome, Paulinus pointed to the end of the procession, disappearing in the church. "It was that that converted me. Of course, I had been here when I was a boy, and I liked to watch the crowd that came to the shrine of Saint Felix, especially on his feast day. And I suppose, being the kind of little donkey I was," the bishop went on with an amused glance back at that remote self, "I liked distributing my father's silver coins to them, and hearing myself praised as a generous little lord."

A subtle undertone of mockery came into the rich voice at the last phrase, and Hilary thought of Laeta on the steps of Saint Peter's.

"Some of us never grow up, you know," he said musingly, and the bishop looked more sharply at him.

"Oh, it was no credit to me," he protested. "I had a good deal of help. It was after the consulship, and I suppose I had begun to get a little tired of all the fuss. Then I came here, and I saw all the pilgrims, not like these solid peasants, but wretches from poor fishing villages and farms where there had been a drought the preceding season, and slaves from the big estates." Even at the memory the smile died away on the mobile lips. "It was raining hard that day, and as I watched them coming with so much faith to Saint Felix to ask for help with their hard lives, I felt ashamed that I who had been given so much had borne so little fruit. It was then I began to repair the shrine, and to build the first"—and he pointed to one of the colonnades—"of those shelters." And then as he caught the admiration on his guest's face, he apologized, "And now here I am like an old woman running on about the past, when you are tired and hungry."

Hilary hastened to assure his host that he had already eaten his bread and found it good.

"Then let us go and give thanks that somebody from Aquitaine has at last found his way here," said Paulinus, leading the way to the side door from which the cross had emerged. But when they came into the great cool space of the church, blinking a little from the loss of the sun in the square outside, Hilary was astounded to find that the church was ringing with a very different sort of hymn from that which he had heard outside. This was a triumphant song of praise, and it was rising from the crowd of villagers, now standing clustered about some invisible center down at the bottom of the nave of the church.

"To Thee, O God, we lift our praise,
We give glory unto Thee, O Lord."

rang through the high vault. And then the hymn broke off suddenly and started again as if some invisible choirmaster were giving the signal.

Paulinus smiled, "It is Nicetas. They told me he had gone to the church. I knew then he would be teaching the pilgrims his new song."

This time the pilgrims finished their hymn, and it must have satisfied their leader, for they broke into loud cheers and then turned to straggle around the church, in the same untidy fashion in which they had come into the square. As they fell apart, Hilary saw the monk standing with his back to the altar rail, talking earnestly with a couple of young farmers. It was a very arresting figure, the firmly moulded head with a tension to it, rather like a coiled spring, Hilary thought. Then the monk turned toward them and smiled. He was older than Hilary had at first thought, with the durable look of a man who has lived outdoors in all kinds of weather.

He greeted Hilary cordially but briefly, and then he turned to his host: "You ought to give more thought to your music,

Paulinus. These people have an inborn sense of rhythm and a feeling for tone and pitch that my Dacians are years away from. You could have a congregation singing here that would put most of the choirs in Christendom to shame. It's all that is lacking to this church of yours."

Paulinus put his hand on his friend's shoulder. "Give me a little time, Nicetas. I have just got the paintings finished."

Nicetas patted his friend's hand briefly, and then in the same brisk, even harsh, but curiously vibrant voice, he laughingly tossed the plea aside. "The nearest thing to perfection on this troubled earth, and you ask for time for the one thing that would make it really perfect. But come, the light is just right for these new paintings of yours, and you know I have had no time to see them yet."

And then Hilary saw the great apse above the high altar, with a breath-taking Christ in glory sitting crowned and throned in the midst of a garden. The garden was a radiant place of flowers and blossoming trees and shrubs and vines, in bright yet muted colors, as if the painter had wanted to suggest that all the natural world's beauty pales before the majesty of the supernatural. For the face of Christ was shining with a light of understanding and compassion that made Hilary wonder what sort of man had had that superlative vision. Then as the piercing eyes of Nicetas went speculatively to his friend's face, Hilary saw that although the painter had made his Christ the epitome of youthful beauty and strength, he had taken the expression on the face from the more worn features of Paulinus.

But clearly that idea had never occurred to Paulinus, who was pointing out the beauties of the figure and the garden as if it were all indeed a vision from heaven and not a thing of human contrivance at all. And especially he pointed to the four rivers running foaming from the base of the little mound on which the throned figure sat, to the outer curve of the apse. And then they turned from that bright vision to the paintings on the walls on either side of the apse and down the sides of the church, paintings depicting the four empires of the world's history, with one whole wall given to the triumph of Christianity in Rome from Saint Peter to Constantine. Beautifully done as these wall paintings were, they yet seemed crude, and even a little garish compared with the painting on the apse. And Paulinus at once agreed with their verdict.

"These are the work of local artists, good men too," he explained. "But that," pointing to the apse, "was done by a stranger. He was shipwrecked, and he was in bad shape. So a friend of mine in the town told me about him when he came up from the port. He said he was a Christian, and he thought from something the man said he was from Constantinople. So I told him to send him up to us. We put him in the infirmary, and he recovered. Then when the weather got warmer in the spring, he began to go into the church and to talk to the workmen. And they said it was clear that he knew something about churches. Finally, he asked me if I had thought of painting the apse, and I said I had but I had not found the artist. Then he asked me if he might try his hand. He asked only one thing, that the whole apse be shut off with curtains."

Paulinus smiled. "Of course there was a lot of talk, and there were those who asked what I would do if the picture were quite impossible, but I thought the man looked as if he knew what he was doing. He painted all summer and fall, and just before Christmas he asked me to go to the church with him—in the night, with a lantern, and when he held the lantern up so as to show that head"—Paulinus' voice shook a little and then steadied—"I simply fell on my knees. When I got up"—again the voice shook—"there was nobody there. And nobody has seen him from that day to this."

"In my part of the world," said Nicetas dryly, "we would say that it was an angel."

But Paulinus was alarmed. "No. He was a man. We all knew him. But I have had one or two visitors who have thought that they had seen a figure like it in Constantinople; only the face was different."

"There have been a lot of people in Constantinople who have found it wise to run away during these last years," said Nicetas.

"He may have been afraid somebody would recognize his style. I only hope he has gone to Remesiana."

"Remesiana," said Hilary thoughtfully.

"My cathedral city, a fortress on the edge of the Dacian wilderness."

"Dacia!" said Hilary, catching his breath. But Nicetas went on, quite unaware of the interruption. "It's a grim stone church that might be the citadel. At that I am lucky. Three of my priests have log churches, and the rest tents. That is why I promote congregational singing. It uses the raw materials we have, and requires nothing we do not have."

Trying to hold his excitement at arm's length, Hilary looked around the beautiful church, now aglow in the softening light of the afternoon. "You must find it hard to leave this."

Again, that curious huskiness came into the voice of Nicetas. "It would be except that each time I tell myself that I am a couple of years nearer heaven, and this is what heaven will be like."

But Paulinus had flushed with tenderness and pleasure, and, Hilary thought, a little fear. "Hilary, you must not take that too seriously. There is nothing here at Nola that begins to compare with what Nicetas is doing at Remesiana. He is winning whole tribes—"

But Nicetas lifted his hand authoritatively, and Paulinus stopped. Then Nicetas smiled a thin, matter-of-fact smile that Hilary found oddly moving. "Every man to his job. And now, young man"—he turned his penetrating glance for the first time on Hilary—"why, when I look at you, do I think of a priest of mine, Desiderius?"

"He is my father," said Hilary simply, taking up the challenge of a lifetime. Then he proceeded to tell how he had gone to the caves on the Dordogne where his father had been last reported and there learned from Severus that he had gone to the Dacian frontier. Only at that moment did Hilary remember that it was there that he had heard the name of Nicetas of Remesiana that had been teasing him so with its inexplicable sense of familiarity.

Nicetas, however, for the first time seemed to be at a loss as to what to say. Then Hilary remembered something else that Severus had said about his father. "Desiderius was never the man to settle down as most happy men do. He was always the first to know when the wind had changed on our height here."

He must have stiffened against the expected revelation of further vagrancy of his father, for a look of compassion came into the face of Nicetas.

"He is dead," he said softly.

For a moment Hilary said nothing, his mind caught in the vise of shock. As his thoughts began to break the surface of confusion, he said only, "So he knows about Patricius—and the rest." And then the full measure of his desolation overwhelmed him.

Nicetas misunderstood his silence. "He died a martyr if ever man did." And with his wonted enthusiasm kindling afresh he went on to tell how Desiderius had made friends with a company of wandering Goths and set up church in a tent. That was all Nicetas had known until just before he left Remesiana. Then another of his missionaries came in with the story of how some Huns had fallen on Desiderius' Goths, and Desiderius had stayed behind to pick up the wounded. His Goths could not believe he was dead, and still insisted that he would presently come riding up with his tent. But the missionary had talked with one of the Goths who had found the torn body of the monk and had buried it.

Aware at last of the distress on the face of Paulinus, Hilary roused himself. "I never knew my father," he said flatly. "He," carefully he reached for the neutral word, "went away before I was born."

But Nicetas was looking at him thoughtfully. "You know," he said at last, "you have a great look of him."

Paulinus must have misinterpreted Hilary's start of surprise, for he put a hand on the arm of the missionary bishop. "Nicetas, none of your recruiting tricks here. I shall consider it—"

But Nicetas only shrugged his shoulders and, with the dry

smile that had first awakened Hilary's interest, said, "It does not matter. He will find his own way."

But that, Hilary decided, was the one thing he was not likely to have a chance to do. For when he went to the guest house a little later, a messenger from Rome was waiting for him with a packet of letters which Medoc had been at pains to gather. Medoc's own was the most urgent. It looked as if it would be possible for the merchants to move into Gaul, and Cerealis had gone with them. Now there were certain plans Medoc would like to talk over with Hilary. There was a letter, too, from Gaia. She had not realized how much she was going to miss him: things were coming to such a pass in Rome that a reasonable man, pagan or Christian, was the hardest thing to come by.

Finally, there was a letter from Serena telling him that Claudian had gone back to Egypt to get married, and she was desperately in need of someone whom she could trust. Hilary thought of Stilicho's appeal of now nearly two years ago; it had not seemed his affair then.

Paulinus was disappointed when Hilary told him the next morning that business he could not deny in times such as these had called him back to Rome. He promised Paulinus that he would come again, if only to be reminded of what heaven on earth might be like. But when he turned to Nicetas to take leave of him, the Dacian bishop took his hand. "Remember the four rivers of Paradise still carry the waters of God's grace to the ends of the earth."

III
THE FALL OF
THE CITY

I

As HILARY RODE BACK TO ROME THOSE
pleasant autumn days, he thought a good deal of what he had
seen in Campania. When he contrasted Nola with what he had
found on his own estates, he wondered if perhaps the best thing
he could do might not be to settle down in the middle of them
to see if he could not make a happier world there in ordinary
lay terms. He even wondered if Gaia would find that kind of
country life thinkable. Perhaps if she could spend part of every
year in Rome—

But as always when his thoughts took that direction, he found
himself brought up short by the remembrance of the actual
world in which he lived. And he rebuked himself that in his
thoughts he was running away from that world as definitely as if
he had stayed in Campania. For whatever he might want to do
later, two things were clear. The first was his family duty, that
the inheritance of his ancestors should not be lost because of
the weakness of the one surviving member of the family. And
the second was his public duty, that whatever he could do to
make his infinitesimal contribution to the defence of the
empire against the barbarians that he owed to Rome and to
the faith which, please God, would some time transform Rome.
Sometimes he thought uncomfortably of Stilicho's rejected invitation. It still seemed to him that there was nothing he could
do to help a general. And yet he had to admit that Stilicho was
the only person he knew who was really doing anything for

Rome's defense. He thought of the serene brow and the level glance of the great barbarian general, and the reflection that here at least was a sure and steadfast judgment gave him something of the assurance for the empire, which he had found at Nola for his estates.

But even before he reached Rome, that confidence was to be troubled. It was when he stopped to spend the night with Fabius at his estate near Tusculum. Fabius was busy with his labors on his father's letters, but although he had no hope of taking his father's place in the leadership of the senatorial circle, he conscientiously maintained his father's habit of keeping in touch with Rome.

To begin with, there were rumors of the continued restlessness of Alaric, hanging always like a cloud over the approaches to Italy.

And then there was all the talk in Rome about the barbarians in the legions. And still worse, there was the misunderstanding between Honorius and his brother Arcadius, the Emperor of the East. Men said it might come to war yet. In short, the only news that came out of Rome these days was of trouble. Yet Hilary could not avoid a feeling that Fabius was leaving most of it unsaid. And that was puzzling, for the son of Symmachus usually took it for granted that any man of his own social position would see things as he did. And he was always a little incredulous when he finally realized that Hilary did not. But tonight Hilary was conscious of some deeper awareness of possible difference that was distressing Fabius' very real kindness.

It seemed to Hilary that something of the same cloud had fallen over a number of the friends he went to visit in Rome. Gaia welcomed him warmly and asked him about his visit to his estates with an interest that made his day-dreaming in the Campanian fields seem not so impossible. And when he spoke of the general state of his properties and the efficiency or inefficiency of bailiffs and managers, she listened with real interest. But when he began to tell her of his anxieties about the slaves and the tenants, she looked almost bored, and when he went on to Paulinus and Nola, it seemed to him that he could feel a wall rising between them. So he began to ask her about Rome, but here she seemed to withdraw even farther from him. She repeated some of the reports which Fabius had mentioned, but she seemed even more uncomfortable, as if he were forcing her to violate her own standards of courtesy. She sighed when Hilary said he must go, but he felt sure that she was relieved even if she must guess where his next call would be.

But when he reached Serena's house, he found there a still more puzzling situation. He had expected Serena to be sober, for Fabius had told him that the old rumors of something odd about the death of the Empress Maria had been circulating in Rome again, nobody knew why. But he had never expected anything like the alteration he found in the woman who now greeted him. He had always seen Serena poised and cheerful, recognizing problems that must be faced with an obvious confidence that she could manage any difficulty. But now she suddenly appeared harassed and uncertain. And to his surprise she began to talk as if she had not had a chance to talk for a long time. "They are saying those dreadful things again about Honorius and poor Maria."

Hilary tried to remember the gossip he had heard when he first came to Rome, something about Serena's protecting the too young bride with a potion that stole the bridegroom's manhood —an old wives' tale that had astonished him in the house of Symmachus. Now with a little catch in her voice she told him, "They say Honorius had her done away with."

"But how?"

Something of the old look of sure intelligence came into Serena's eyes. "Poison, perhaps. There are all sorts of ways, you know. But," and here a passionate earnestness that Hilary had never seen in her broke forth, "that would make him a monster! And I have known Honorius all his life. It was I who carried him across the Alps in winter when his father was dying. Besides," she added more gently, "he was grief-stricken when he came here to bury her. All Rome talked of the pearls and gems he heaped on her for her burial. And what is more important, he has now sent word that he will never remarry unless he can have a bride as like her as possible. He has asked for Thermantia."

Hilary's astonishment must have appeared in his face. For Serena seemed to gather her forces as if the implied challenge had steadied her. "You need not look so shocked. Honorius is a Christian, too, and he has his priests to advise him."

A little color had come into her face with the spark of defiance. "Yes, you are wondering what Stilicho thinks of it. He is completely opposed."

"Then," said Hilary slowly, "that settles it, I suppose."

But Serena shook her head with a speculative look in her eyes. "Stilicho has never denied Honorius anything he asked of him."

When a few days later Hilary came again to see Serena, he found her calmer. At first, she talked casually enough like any hostess, expressing her gratitude to a considerate friend. Stilicho, she told him, was at Ravenna, seeing the Emperor. The anxiety deepened in her face, but she went on easily enough to say how much she missed Claudian, who had been such a comfort to her in times past when Stilicho was in the field. It had been such a joy to listen to his poetry—it seemed to bridge the chasm of absence.

And Hilary, glad to encourage her return to her more habitual temper, murmured that of course there was the inevitable anxiety of the soldier's wife; but this she denied emphatically. She had always had too much confidence in her general's soldiership for that. And then the anxiety came back.

"With a man like Stilicho, it is not his failure that one fears. It is the envy of lesser men. What they cannot emulate they seek to destroy," she said with a touch of quite uncharacteristic bitterness. And then she went on to tell of how her uncle, the great Theodosius, had told her, when he asked her if she would like Stilicho for her husband, that of all the young men he had ever known, this was the ablest and the finest. And when he knew he was going to die, he had entrusted his two sons to him. And from that day to this Stilicho had never put any personal interest ahead of that duty, not even the interest of Eucherius, his own son.

It was then that she lifted another corner of her half hidden worry. Stilicho had taken Eucherius with him. He was anxious about the boy. He had been spending his time with some of the young pagans, and they had been flattering him. And when he had said careless things about religion, as young men often do, they had made much of him, and said they would have him free of all that Christian nonsense yet.

The few times Hilary had seen Eucherius in the company of his parents he had wondered, if, like Fabius, he were finding it difficult to rise to the expectations of his father's son. Eucherius, with his reddish-brown hair and his clear skin, seemed a fairer version of the bookish Fabius, and a more lively and quick-witted one, but still not likely, so far as one could tell from appearance, to turn out the man his father was.

But that was not what was troubling Serena. "It is Galla, I think, who is spreading those stories about Eucherius turning pagan."

But now it seemed to Hilary that Serena had let her anxiety undermine her usual good judgment. "But why on earth should she?"

And then Serena explained that long ago she and Honorius had planned that Galla should marry Eucherius. It had seemed the least the family could do for Stilicho after all that he had done. But Galla had been sulky and then, it seemed to Serena, simply perverse. She had always been difficult, Serena sighed, seeming to resent Serena's position in the family as if the long-ago favor of the dead Theodosius had somehow robbed her, and she had always affected to see in Stilicho only an upstart who had married his master's daughter. But now Galla's resentment of Eucherius' pretensions had turned to hatred.

And yet Hilary felt sure that even this was not the real core of Serena's worry, for disappointed as she was in Galla's attitude toward Eucherius, she still was sure Stilicho could keep Eucherius out of trouble. Indeed, it was some time before Hilary was able to discover what was really troubling her so much. He had arrived at her house one day well into fall to find her engaged with a messenger from Stilicho, but Thermantia who had been reading in a corner of the peristyle urged him to wait. For a moment Hilary thought she was not going to say any more, for hitherto when Hilary had seen her, always in her mother's presence, she had seemed abnormally shy and withdrawn.

He was startled, therefore, when she said quite without preamble, with a directness that reminded him of her mother when he first saw her, "I am going to be married to the Emperor." So surprised was Hilary, not so much at her news as at her manner, that for a moment he forgot to congratulate her. She seemed to notice his hesitation, and he thought from a gleam in her eye to be amused by it. But when he wished her much happiness, she said only, "That is as God wills." Then she added, as if she expected him to see that it explained anything that might puzzle him, "It ought to put things right."

But before Hilary could make any comment on this surprising remark, Serena came in, followed at a respectful distance by a courier. She still seemed haggard and tense, but, it seemed to Hilary, no longer confused. Rather she looked as if she had reached a not easy decision and in doing so had found unexpected relief. Thermantia lifted up her manuscript and began to unroll it again.

"I am sorry to have wasted your time, Hilary," said Serena, a little breathlessly, "but it was something that could not wait." And then she went on to explain: "You have heard of all the trouble there has been over the Empress and the Archbishop John of Constantinople. Somebody persuaded Honorius to send a protest to his brother Arcadius, and Arcadius refused to receive the mission. Of course it was an insult, but you know the kind of ministers Arcadius has had. If only he had paid attention to his father, and let Stilicho advise him!"

She paused, and Hilary saw that Thermantia was looking keenly at her mother. Hilary guessed that the memory of an old disappointment was sharpening present anxiety. Serena seemed to admit as much when she shrugged her shoulders and said,

"But that is past remedy. It's this present scheme of Stilicho's, going off with that Gothic firebrand Alaric, to take Illyricum from Arcadius."

"But what good would that do?" asked Hilary in astonishment.

Serena looked encouraged by his reaction. "That is what I asked." And then she leaned forward, and for the first time Hilary noticed that her hands were twisting nervously in her lap. "But you know how statesmen are. They always have lots of reasons. It would strengthen the west; it would give Alaric, who is simply spoiling for action, something to do—you know how they talk in a council. And the one thing they never think of is what will happen afterward. That I can tell you. It would be war, the worst kind of war, war between brother and brother —one son of Theodosius against the other."

She began to cry a little, and Thermantia laid her manuscript down and came and stood beside her mother. But Serena put down the hand that had been laid timidly on her shoulder, and with a little laugh, half of defiance, half of triumph, she said, "But that is what I have just written to Stilicho."

For a moment Hilary had a curious feeling of alarm, as if he should do something to avert disaster. But the messenger was gone. And then he told himself that surely Stilicho would know how to deal with his wife's hysterical fears. Curiously enough, when Hilary came to take his leave, Serena was looking much more like her usual composed and confident self.

II

ONE OF THE THINGS ABOUT ROME THAT HAD most fascinated Hilary in these last months was the ebb and flow of rumor and its effect on the minds of the Roman public. And now as the winter deepened, with men putting their heads together over the brazier as they warmed their hands, it seemed to him that the whole process accelerated.

The journey of Serena and Thermantia to Ravenna for the wedding to Honorius was one example. As Thermantia had predicted, it was impossible now for even the Roman gossips to say anything about the death of Maria or the Emperor's relations to Stilicho. And the reports that came from Ravenna of the magnificence of the Emperor's gifts to his bride whetted the public appetite for display, and satisfied the more sentimental among the Roman ladies. But to those who thought about the course of affairs, especially in senatorial circles, the marriage gave no satisfaction. To Gaia and Lampadius and Pompeianus it was impossible to forget that the Emperor's new bride was, even if the grandniece of Theodosius, still the daughter of a barbarian. To Marcella and Pammachius the marriage of the Emperor to his dead wife's sister was a scandal. And even to less exacting Christians like Laeta and Proba Faltonia it seemed of doubtful taste.

But even more teasing to Rome were the political and military reports that drifted in from time to time, particularly from the east. The struggle between the Archbishop John and the Emperor in Constantinople roused very little interest in pagan Rome. The Empress Eudoxia, daughter of a barbarian and choice of a hated eunuch minister, made little appeal to senatorial sympathies, but the thunderings of the archbishop, who had arraigned so contemptuously her luxury and display, made even less, and men asked what could you expect of a city so overrun with monks. But Christian Rome of the more serious persuasion saw in John Chrysostom a new John the Baptist, and repeated with delight the sentence he had hurled at Eudoxia from the pulpit of Santa Sophia, "Herodias dances again, and again she asks for the head of John on a platter." But when Honorius rebuked his brother for his treatment of the Church, both pagan and Christian Rome rejoiced that the true Rome, even though hiding behind the marshes of Ravenna, had finally taken a stand against the upstart Rome of the east.

But the old grumbling stirred again when the news of the expedition to Illyricum began to be bruited about. The expedition itself gave general satisfaction. It was doing something at last, always encouraging to those who sit safely behind the walls. But the news that Stilicho was doing it with one of the most persistent threats to the frontier, the Goth Alaric, met a much more mixed reception.

There were those who could not forget the terrors of his advance six years before, though they were perhaps counterbalanced by those who pointed out that this time Alaric would be marching away from Rome rather than toward it. To others this partnership with Alaric aggravated the growing resentment of barbarian domination in the army. There were some, among them Pompeianus, who divined Stilicho's strategy and said that it was a good thing to keep Alaric busy, and busy under his eye. But they were few, military strategy being on the whole a subject of limited appeal to the determinedly non-military mind. Much more popular, because more understandable, was the rumor that came seemingly from nowhere, that Stilicho was really going to the east to depose Arcadius and to set his son on the throne of Constantinople. And then the old rumors about Serena's weakening of Honorius crept out again from their holes, and men said that this was what Serena and Stilicho had been aiming at all the time.

It was well into the winter before the news came from Ravenna which was to shake Rome like a boulder from a catapult that has missed the citadel of a beleaguered city and landed in a farmyard. "If the cackling of geese were all that Rome needed," said Lampadius one day that winter, "Rome would be safe for ever." It was the news that Stilicho had abandoned the expedition to the east. He had lingered in Ravenna for weeks, making preparations for his expedition, and there had been some wonder if he were not growing cautious. But it was a shock to hear in a letter from the Emperor to the senate that the expedition to the east had been called off. The Emperor had given only the explanation that it was in the interest of peace within the empire.

There was no question of the disappointment in Rome. Men might pay lip-service to peace; in fact, some eloquent tributes to peace were now delivered in the senate house. But in the forum, and the baths and the circus, and even at the senatorial levees, there was a chill air of slackening of interest and vitality. Something of great importance had been going forward, and now nothing was going to happen. Pious men in the house of Pammachius rejoiced at the escape from civil war, which would have done religion no good in either the west or the east. And thoughtful men in the house of Symmachus observed that they were, after all, where they were when the whole business started, but Lampadius held them up sharply, "That is where you never are. You have either gone forward or backward," and the acidulous tone in which he spoke left no doubt as to where he thought they were. But Rome soon roused itself to the congenial enterprise of finding reasons for what had happened. Some of the older senators were inclined to believe that Honorius had drawn back from the prospect of civil war because he felt doubtful of his ability to win quickly. But more took pleasure in the thought that Stilicho had lost his nerve and given up for the time being his project of putting his son on the eastern throne. Curiously enough, nobody suggested that Alaric might have lost enthusiasm for the plan. His eagerness for cooperation was simply taken for granted.

And so far as Hilary ever heard, only one person in all Rome seemed to have wondered what Alaric would think of the change of plan. That was the Pope. Pammachius had gone to see him about some monks who had arrived at his hospital in Ostia in the wake of the troubles in Constantinople. And in the course of their conversation Pammachius himself, so he told a little group of friends afterward, had mentioned his relief at the dropping of Stilicho's expedition. The Pope had nodded his agreement as Pammachius took it for granted he would, and then to his visitor's astonishment he had asked, "What do you think Alaric thinks of it?" The question had astonished Pammachius and, Hilary gathered, shocked him.

For he said thoughtfully, "It was as if he were trying to see it from Alaric's point of view."

That, as it turned out, was what all Rome was trying to do only a few weeks later. The new Empress had returned to Rome for Easter, and her father and mother had come with her. This distinguished visit coming on top of the mingled relief and boredom that had followed the news of peace was a boon to Roman society, which Christian and pagan alike proceeded to make the most of.

"It is such a pleasure to have an empress who looks if not like an empress at least like a competent human being," said Gaia at a banquet which Attalus gave in honor of Thermantia. And everybody agreed that she had developed poise and confidence to an extraordinary degree. For the first time people began to say that it was easy to see that she was her mother's daughter even if she would probably never have her mother's beauty or charm.

But Attis, who consented to make one of her very rare appearances in honor of the occasion, was not so sure. "She looks to me as if she knows that she must take a firm hand," she told Hilary the next day.

But while Rome gossiped and played, Stilicho worried. Hilary found him alone one afternoon soon after his arrival in Rome. He thanked Hilary for his kindness to Serena, and then he confessed that he was waiting for a messenger from Alaric. Startled, Hilary repeated the Pope's question, "What does Alaric think of it all?"

"What do you think? I have been trying to tell them in Ravenna for weeks now that Alaric is a human being. When I proposed that plan, I told the Emperor that it would mean money and supplies to Alaric. He agreed. So I promised Alaric both. And he went ahead as I did. Then"—he hesitated—"when the plan was dropped, they were very quick at Ravenna to say that they would be delighted to have the extra forces which I had assembled, for the defence of the Emperor. But they turned a deaf ear to my reminders of the promise to Alaric."

"And Alaric?" But at that moment the messenger was announced, and with an apology Stilicho left the room.

The next day brought the answer, with the news that the senate had been summoned to hear Stilicho's report. But long before the senate began to assemble, all Rome knew that Alaric was back. He had crossed the Julian Alps, and was waiting only for one last appeal to Stilicho before marching south.

Fabius who had brought the news to Hilary asked his company to the senate house. The sum which the Emperor's letter had given for Alaric's demands was a staggering one, but Stilicho had pronounced it fair.

"Of course," Fabius said, "they are saying that Stilicho is sympathetic to Alaric because he is a barbarian too."

Again Hilary felt a chill in the pit of his stomach, but Fabius went on placidly, "I think they ought to remember that without Stilicho Alaric might not be giving us this second chance," and Hilary was profoundly grateful.

He thought of Fabius' generosity again as, waiting for his friend in a little room off the speaker's platform of the senate chamber, he listened to Stilicho addressing the senate. It was Stilicho at his best, his lofty brow serene under his white hair, his eyes clear and sure as they swept the senate. With great candor he told of the projected expedition with Alaric, reading the Emperor's letter of approval and the transcript of the promises he had made to Alaric. Then with a stiffening of the neck and shoulders but with no change in voice he went on to tell of Serena's letter and of the impression it had made on the Emperor. And now the first note of pleading came into his voice: "I need not remind you of what you all know, that my wife was brought up as a daughter in the house of the Emperor Theodosius, and her love for the two Emperors is as a mother's love for her sons."

There was a great stillness in the senate house as Stilicho spoke. Of the propriety of Serena's scruples no man there would make any question, but of their effect on her husband? For as Stilicho spoke, Hilary saw that, whatever the conventions or the fictions, the senate knew that it was listening to the real ruler of

148

the empire. Then as the faces lengthened in front of him, Stilicho told the senate that Alaric was once again in Italy and had threatened to march on Rome unless his demands were met. And he gave the figure of the demands, and declared it reasonable. Hilary saw all the faces close to the platform stiffen at the precise figure, and now he knew the issue was joined.

But Stilicho was ready for the questions. No, he saw little chance of repeating his victory against Radagasius. There were reserves then which had been called in, with what disastrous results for Gaul everybody knew. If he called in all the troops from Italy, he might have a chance, but they could not leave Ravenna exposed. There were also, and here his firm voice grew cautious, variations in the quality and experience and dependability of their forces. He thought they would understand. They did. The difficulties between Roman and barbarian in the legions were not a new story, but they had been growing acute. Every man in the senate house knew that Stilicho did not dare to count on holding his barbarian auxiliaries in the face of Alaric, and that without the barbarian troops the Roman legions would never hold. In sum, Stilicho gave it as his opinion that their best course was to pay Alaric and to try to find a place for him in the defense of the frontier.

It was a bitter pill. Lampadius leaped to his feet, his usually dry voice shaking with anger and humiliation, "We are lost if we start buying off this barbarian brigand."

But Stilicho patiently repeated his explanation of the bargain.

Then Attalus suggested that Alaric had probably no choice himself but to appease his followers or lose his command of them. Stilicho agreed with him gratefully. It was his experience that the barbarian leaders could not count on the discipline that a Roman general took for granted, and the barbarian leader had nothing like the claims on the devotion of his followers that the Emperor had. Then Faltonius asked whether there was any hope of money from Ravenna, and Stilicho said carefully that Ravenna had heavy obligations already and must think of the defence of the Emperor.

Hilary saw several of the senators look at each other as if this was what they had expected. But no one pursued that topic any farther. Stilicho would have exhausted all the possibilities there, everybody knew. As they sat silently facing the prospects, Attalus rose again and reminded his colleagues that whatever the difficulty of raising the sum Alaric demanded, it was, as they all knew, but a fraction of the damage which his last raid into Italy had cost. As for the next, Attalus shuddered. The debate was over. Only Lampadius voted against the payment of Alaric, and when he saw that he was alone, he leaped to his feet again and, in a ringing voice as if the years had fallen away in this final despair, shouted, "Fools, you have sold yourselves into slavery."

But there was no triumph in Stilicho's face as he turned to leave the senate house, and no one came up to him to congratulate him on perhaps the finest speech of his career. But quite alone, he went home.

III

MUCH OF THAT NIGHT HILARY LAY AWAKE thinking of Stilicho's rejected invitation and of his own resolution in Campania. But when he reached the house of Stilicho in the morning, he was startled to find the usually quiet street crowded with soldiers and servants coming and going through the open gate. And when he reached the doorkeeper, he learned that the general was busy with the preparation of letters for the waiting messengers. And the Lady Serena? She had gone to take her leave of the Empress, who was departing that day for Ravenna.

Even as Hilary stood there talking with the doorkeeper, Fabius and Faltonius came out of Stilicho's house, and waited for Hilary to join them.

"Did he say that Stilicho is leaving the city?" asked Faltonius. Hilary nodded. "In a week."

"It is just as well," Faltonius said in a low voice. "When people hear what has happened to the city treasury, Lampadius will not be the only indiscreet babbler."

But Fabius for the first time in Hilary's acquaintance with him turned hotly on his companion. "What else can we do with Alaric hanging over us?" Faltonius shrugged his shoulders, and Hilary was startled to see how miserable his usually debonair friend looked. And Hilary, unable to bear the reflection of his own anxiety in the faces of his friends, took his leave of them when they came to the street that led to Gaia's house.

But Gaia was too sick with the common shame even to want to talk. Listlessly she sent one of her maids for wine, and began to pick some dead leaves from the shrub near which she stood. A cheer came in the open window of the anteroom beyond; Hilary guessed, from a group of young men hurrying off to the races. Gaia shuddered, and bade a slave close the shutters. "That is all the Roman rabble cares about these days, the betting on the chariot jockeys!" And neither the wine nor Hilary's best efforts could rouse her from her despair.

So Hilary took his way to the house of Pammachius. The monk-senator would feel the humiliation of the city as keenly as anyone, he knew, but he felt sure that in Pammachius at least there would be none of the resentment gnawing at the vitals of personal pride that was devastating his pagan friends. But to his surprise he found that the great hall of Pammachius' house was crowded not with his usual shabby clients from the Suburra, but with friends of his own rank from the soberer circles of Christian society.

Pammachius received him, with his usual grave courtesy, but seemed preoccupied. When, however, Hilary was about to withdraw from the little group to which Pammachius had been especially talking, he gestured to him to stay. And then to his astonishment Hilary discovered that Pammachius was as troubled as his pagan friends. Only what concerned him was the reports which his friends had been bringing him from all over

Rome; that the pagans were saying that if only the city had continued the public worship of the gods that had given it its greatness, this humiliation would never have befallen it.

"It is as if Symmachus were beginning his agitation for the return of the altar to Victory all over again," said Pammachius with the first signs of weariness Hilary had ever seen in that serene face.

So it went all over Rome. Only one of Hilary's friends seemed to have escaped the prevailing depression, and that was Attis. When a couple of days later Hilary gave up trying to break into the preoccupations of Stilicho, he decided to fill in a little spare time before the bath hour with a visit to the dancer. She greeted him with a gleaming light-heartedness that he found incredible, and rallied him on his downcast looks. But when he asked her how any one in Rome above the level of the thoughtless rabble yelling their heads off in the circus could be anything but depressed these days, the smile faded. And the look of ageless gravity that had first fascinated him came into her face. "Are you as big a fool as the rest of them to think that you of all men shall never know the common lot?"

It was at this time that Fortunatus chose to return to Rome with the news that his lady at Baiae had accepted him. His first question was whether Hilary had had any word from Cerealis as to the possibilities of sending the news to his family. Hilary who had just received a cheerful letter from Claudian, full of the praise of wedded bliss in Egypt, groaned inwardly again at the Olympian self-absorption of all lovers and proceeded to give Fortunatus the latest news about Alaric.

That broke into his cheerful complacency, and he gazed thoughtfully at his friend. "Look here," he said, "you have been taking Rome too hard. Come down to Baiae with me and we can make our plans, with my beautiful Artemia to cheer us up."

And when Hilary told Fortunatus why he must stay in Rome, Fortunatus stared at him. "You are certainly asking for trouble," he said. "If half of what you tell me is true, Stilicho is beaten before he starts."

But Fortunatus, like the rest of Rome, had underestimated Stilicho. When at length Hilary did find him at home without messengers thronging the anteroom, he was amazed to find the general his usual calm and alert self. Indeed, for the first time since Hilary had known Stilicho, he understood how Claudian's lines about the terror of the great Vandal's glance were more than a flattering figure of speech. For the glance which Stilicho turned on Hilary was one that would make even a friend quail.

But he was soon gracious in his acknowledgment of Hilary's offer of help, and then the tense look of resolve returned to his strongly moulded face. "It is good of you, but there is nothing you can do for me but give Serena a little company now and then." And then he unbent a little to explain briefly that he had just had word from Honorius at Bologna to ask his help with the barbarians in his troops there. They had mutinied, and their officers were not sure that they could be responsible for the Emperor's safety. His glance darkened as he spoke, but Hilary saw that he was no longer confused and uncertain. This was something he could understand. He had sent a messenger to Bologna to tell Honorius that he was coming at once to take the necessary measures. He spoke now with all his old assurance.

Somehow, before he left, he succeeded in communicating this confidence to Serena, and even to the Roman officials who came to see him about the negotiations with Alaric. Indeed, so strongly did he impress all those who saw him in those last hours at Rome with the old sense of his power that when the reports of the seriousness of the disaffection in the legions began to seep through the city, there were those who complained about his leaving Rome unprotected. And when, presently, the news came that he had quelled the mutiny with the threat of the old Roman punishment of decimation, the relief was so great that there were not wanting those, even among the pagans, who felt that he had been too severe.

And when a little later the news of the sudden death of Arcadius came to Rome, there was much talk in senatorial circles that now was the time for Honorius to take possession of Constantinople and its infant emperor, his nephew Theodosius, and restore the unity of the empire. Not since the advent of Radagasius had Rome known such an upsurge of confidence.

In the middle of June Stilicho wrote to Serena from Bologna to report that he had reached a complete understanding with Honorius. He had persuaded him that an expedition to the east which Honorius had contemplated making himself to settle the confusion attendant upon the death of Arcadius and the accession of his infant son, Theodosius, was impossible. Ravenna lacked the resources to equip such an expedition with proper provision for either the Emperor's dignity or his security, and he had succeeded in convincing Honorius and his advisers that they should let him go to Constantinople instead to see what he could do. Stilicho wrote with characteristic objectivity, but at this point Serena who was reading the letter aloud to Hilary put it down, and laughed with some of her old humor, "It was not too hard to accomplish, I think." It was the first time Hilary could remember that she had given any sign of sharing the current Roman opinion of the Emperor's competence. But the humor changed quickly to triumph when Stilicho went on to report that Honorius, although still refusing to give Alaric the title of Master of the Imperial Forces which he craved, had agreed to let Alaric take his barbarians west to see if he could not recover Gaul from the upstart Caesar from Britain.

"It is a complete victory," said Serena triumphantly.

And her triumph was made complete when the next month Stilicho wrote still from Bologna that Honorius had undertaken to go up to Ticinum to strengthen the loyalty of the Gothic and Roman troops, who were mobilizing there for Gaul, while he himself would go on to Ravenna to make ready for his expedition to Constantinople. But he would wait at Bologna for her to come and take leave of him before he left for the east. With the letter came another for Hilary asking the favor of his escort for Serena.

But long before they reached Bologna, Serena's party began to hear that there was trouble at Ticinum. At first it was vague, simply trouble with the troops. Then as they began to run into travellers from that direction, the rumors grew more precise. It had been a revolt of the legions against the severity of Stilicho's discipline. Then came the word that it was a revolt of Roman against barbarian. And since this came from some barbarian auxiliaries who had overtaken them on the road, Serena became alarmed. And her anxiety received no relief when an escort which Stilicho had sent out from Bologna found them on the road and insisted on joining them.

The commander of the escort was Probinus, a young aide of Stilicho's whom Hilary had met in Rome. Now he was clearly evasive when Serena tried to find out what the situation was at Ticinum. And when she asked how her husband was, he would say nothing more about what he was doing than that he had things well in hand. But it seemed to Hilary that there could be no question that an unusual number of military parties were on the road, and that, to judge from their appearance, they were mostly barbarians.

Presently the leader of one of these parties was requesting the opportunity to pay his respects to the Lady Serena. And in spite of the warning of the young aide to say nothing that would worry her, the barbarian general, a direct and plain-spoken veteran, obviously incapable of dissimulation, was soon replying to Serena's questions that Stilicho had summoned to Bologna all the leaders of the barbarian troops within reach. And he confirmed her worst fears that, however it had started, the revolt at Ticinum had become an affair of Roman against barbarian.

The combination of the rigors of their hurried journey in the summer heat and of her anxieties had so exhausted Serena that when she reached Bologna she offered no resistance to Stilicho's insistence that she let her women put her to bed. Indeed, Hilary suspected that the culmination of her anxiety had been the appearance of Stilicho himself as he met them in the crowded antechamber of the praetorial palace at Bologna. It was not simply that his face was almost as white as his famous hair, and cavernous from lack of sleep. It was rather the expression on it—the calm that comes to a strong man who has looked

ultimate and complete disaster in the face and found that its
sight has not destroyed him. Serena must have read that expression, too, as she stumbled into his arms, for she made no
protest when he told her tenderly that her only thought for
tonight must be sleep, and put her in the hands of her women.

IV

BUT WHEN SERENA HAD LEFT THE ROOM,
Stilicho turned to Hilary and smiled bleakly. "When you have
had a little food, join us." And he directed Hilary to a small
chamber where already a slave was setting out food. Hilary had
hardly begun to eat when Probinus came in. Hilary, as he
looked up now and then to see the young man eating wolfishly,
and between bites covertly scrutinizing him, tried to remember
what he had heard about him in the small change of Roman
gossip. He was, Hilary felt sure, a scion of a senatorial house
that had lost its fortune, and so its place in the world of Rome.
There was something more that he ought to remember, Hilary
thought, as he caught the young man looking away again. And
then he remembered it. The grandfather of the young Probinus
had been fantastically honest. He had spent what he might have
saved, paying his debts, and then he had killed himself. His son
had disappeared into the country, and his grandson had re-
appeared in Rome in the service of Stilicho. There were those
in Rome who affected to see in his action a betrayal of the
honor of an ancient line, but most of those who knew his story
simply regarded it as fresh proof of what the world was coming
to in these confused days.

Feeling sure, therefore, that his companion would not open
the conversation, Hilary came straight to the point, "Exactly
what has happened?"

For a moment Probinus looked at him, and Hilary felt an

even greater dismay, for in the thin, dark face he glimpsed the fear of the young man who has seen the ramparts of his world crumbling around him, and deep within his own being Hilary felt the nerves of an old fear quiver. Then Probinus seemed to make up his mind.

"You'll know in a few minutes anyway, for they're all meeting in there." He nodded in the direction in which Stilicho had gone.

"Who are they?" asked Hilary, seeing the man hesitate as if from some sudden access of delicacy.

"Stilicho has summoned all the commanders of the barbarian forces within reach."

"I gathered that from what I heard on the road. What has happened at Ticinum?"

The young man's distress deepened, and a little color came into the wan face. "The Roman legions have revolted against their barbarian leaders."

Hilary must have looked puzzled, for he added, "Some of the Gallic commanders came in to Ticinum. They were driven out by the British troops of Constantine, you remember."

"But everybody knows it was not their fault. Stilicho had to weaken their forces to stop Radagasius."

Probinus shrugged his shoulders, and Hilary saw that in some indirect fashion which he could not fully understand his companion had recovered a little personal confidence in the midst of the larger confusion.

"It does not matter. They say that the barbarian generals are betraying the empire to their kinsmen. The reports are confused, but they all agree that a number of the generals have been killed, and even the Emperor is in danger."

But at that moment another aid came in to bring them to Stilicho.

The conference was being held in the great hall of the praetorial palace. It was a fairly large room, but it was well filled. As they entered, there was a sudden quiet and all eyes turned in their direction. Then all over the room the low rumble of deep and anxious talk rose again, and for a minute or two Hilary, finding a bench modestly against the wall, had a chance to look at the company.

Oddly enough, they looked very little like the barbarians of whom he had heard all his life. A few of them were chestnut-haired, with clear blue eyes and ruddy complexions, but most of them would have been indistinguishable from the Roman senate, except that they were larger, more sinewy, more weather-beaten, hardier-looking than present-day senators. In their broad military belts and straight woolen tunics they looked like men who were accustomed to call the turn of events. There was excitement now in their deep voices, but they looked angry rather than frightened, it seemed to Hilary.

Suddenly there was a hush, and everybody turned at once to the door through which Hilary and Probinus had come. So instantaneous was the silence that some of the broken-off conversations seemed to hang in the air.

Stilicho appeared more composed and more resolved than he had earlier, and he lost no time in addressing the company. "The Tribune Brictio, whom many of you know, has just come in and collapsed. But he tells us that not only are the generals dead, but before he fled there was a rumor that the Emperor himself had been murdered."

He paused as if to let the low gasp of astonishment exhale from the assembled multitude, and then he said quietly, "I have sent two of my best men out toward Ticinum to see if they can pick up any more information on the road. Somebody we can trust is sure to be coming in soon."

Again there was a gasp, and a little flush of uncertainty came into Stilicho's pale face. Then before he could begin to explain what he was doing, a large, powerfully built man with russet hair seemingly standing on end in wrath and with blue eyes flashing rose to his feet, shouting, "What are we waiting for? We know that Limerius and Chariobaudes and half a dozen of our most celebrated comrades are dead. We have heard that the Emperor is dead. We know, every man of us, that if this is not stopped we shall be dead, too. What are we waiting for?"

Stilicho's face froze into something rock-like, and Hilary saw the faces in front of him sober. The great general's voice was harsh but perfectly controlled as he replied, "We shall not do anything, nobody will do anything, until we know whether the report about the Emperor is true. Sarus, you of all men should know that we cannot."

The giant had started to his feet, but all over the room men were muttering: "He is right. We must wait." And Hilary thought he saw Stilicho relax a little now that he was satisfied that he yet held in control the forces he had summoned. But there was a watchfulness in the look he cast around the room as if he were quite aware that he might not be able to maintain that control much longer. The low mumble of conversation had broken out again, and Stilicho sat down near Sarus and began to talk to him.

But before he could have said half a dozen words, one of Stilicho's aides appeared in the doorway, half thrusting forward, half supporting a messenger. As he felt Stilicho's eyes upon him, the man, obviously a soldier in spite of his coarse slave's tunic, stiffened and Stilicho went to him. After a few whispered words Stilicho said aloud, "Speak up so all can hear."

"I saw," said the man, breathing hard, "the Emperor, without any insignia of rank, being dragged through the streets and begging the rioters to go back to their barracks. Then I saw him go down as if his horse had stumbled, and there was a great shouting. And then somebody said, 'The Emperor is dead.' But when I went forward to see what was going on, I heard somebody in the crowd say"—the man gulped and his voice dropped —"'There is a spy of that traitor Stilicho,' and I fled. But from the roar, I have no doubt he is dead."

There was an awed silence in the room as if, now that certainty had come, men did not know what to do. Only Sarus, flailing his huge arms, started to his feet. But before he could say anything, Stilicho said very quietly, "That settles it." A cheer rose, but Stilicho raised his hand, and went on: "Before we do anything, we must know what we are doing. So long as the Emperor lived, for us to march on Ticinum unbidden was, whatever our intentions, mutiny. But now that the rebels at

Ticinum have slain the Emperor, we shall arrive as avengers of the sanctity of the empire, and"—he paused for a moment—"it does not matter whom we find ourselves fighting."

A great cheer rose from all over the room, and from every side strong men began to tug at their belts and straighten their tunics. The tension of a few minutes ago had broken into excited talk and even some laughter. Probinus whispered to Hilary, "When they get there, the auxiliaries will hoist Stilicho on their shields and make him emperor."

Only Stilicho stood still by the doorway. That was why he and Hilary, who was watching him, were the only ones to see the third messenger arrive. At first, Hilary thought it was one of the prefect's servants, and then he noticed how dusty the man was, and how he lingered there as if he were stupefied by the shouting throng. Then the man saw Stilicho and came to him. Something in his movement attracted the attention of those standing nearest to them, and they quieted to watch. In a moment the silence was spreading, and when Stilicho's voice rang out in the room, everybody heard it. "The Emperor is alive!" he shouted, and there was no mistaking his relief. Nor the shock to the crowd in the suddenly sobered room. And then he motioned to the messenger to speak. "I have seen the Emperor," the man began dramatically. "And when I told him that the general was worried over the reports coming from Ticinum, he assured me that he was quite safe, and that Olympius had firm control of the situation. And he gave me this letter for Stilicho."

From all over the room came a groan, "Olympius!" But Stilicho broke the seal of the letter and, with the eyes of the whole room upon him, he read it aloud. It was very brief. "Peace is restored. You may start for the east without worry. Honorius."

Again there was silence, but this time it was of consternation. Hilary saw the men around him look at each other. And while Stilicho dismissed the messenger, the silence deepened. Then Stilicho turned to face them, and the look of relief on his face clouded over.

But before he could speak, Sarus was on his feet again, now ominously calm. "What are you going to do?" he asked.

The whole room hung on the answer. The cloud on Stilicho's face deepened, as he began to speak in a firm, low voice, "I am going to ask you to return to your posts and assure the stability of your commands." There was a low growl of protest, but he paid no attention to it, still talking as quietly as ever. "I am starting for the east directly." He had been holding up his right hand, rather unnecessarily, for attention. Now that he had said what he had to say, it fell as if from exhaustion.

Again, all over the room the voices broke out, and now something high-pitched, even shrill had come into the harsh tones. But the anger of Sarus had reached the point of explosion. "Do you mean to say," he fairly shouted, "that we are to go back as if nothing had happened? That we are to leave our slaughtered comrades lying there in the dust and do nothing about it?"

For the first time Stilicho winced. Then he spoke with his usual quiet reasonableness. "No man grieves more than I for the murder of our comrades. But it is the Emperor's province and not ours to do them justice."

"Justice!" shouted Sarus. And for a moment the word rang out in a chorus all over the room. But in his indignation the voice of Sarus rose above the others, "Do you think the Emperor will make any attempt to bring those murderers to justice?"

"We must put our trust in the Emperor."

But Sarus fairly shrieked, "Do you think for a moment that the Emperor will ever punish Romans for murdering barbarians?" The company must now have begun to sense, however dimly, what Hilary had realized when Sarus' voice rose, that within him the dams of years of disciplined habit of thought and feeling had broken. For all the other voices had died away, as men now turned to Stilicho.

Something tense and drawn had come into his face, and Hilary suddenly noticed that he had no arms, not even a javelin in his belt. But his voice was perfectly firm as he faced Sarus, and it rang coldly through the room: "What you are asking me to do is to march barbarians against Romans, to do what our enemies have falsely accused us of doing, and betray Rome from within. That by the oath I have taken to defend Rome I will never do."

Sarus started to speak, and then he looked at the face of Stilicho, firm and implacable. With a gesture of despair he flung his arms over his head and rushed from the room as if he did not trust himself to stay there any longer. More deliberately the others followed. Most of them saluted Stilicho, but not one of them stopped to talk. In a couple of minutes only Hilary and Probinus were left in the room, staring at Stilicho standing alone on an island of desolation that seemed to Hilary to defy any approach. But when they started to follow the others, Stilicho seemed to rouse himself and gestured to them to stop.

"In the morning," he said to Hilary as if coming back from a great distance to try to focus his attention on his present company, "tell Serena I have judged it wise to go at once to Ravenna." He spoke very quietly as if this were a routine decision. And then his voice sharpened, "And take her back to Rome as fast as you can." With a nod he dismissed Hilary, and began to talk in a low voice to Probinus.

V

AS SOON AS IT WAS DAWN THE NEXT MORNING, Hilary went to the apartment in the praetorial palace which had been assigned to Serena. There he found her dressed and waiting, still haggard from the anxieties of the journey but clearly in possession of herself.

She listened without speaking to Hilary's brief summary of what had happened the night before. And he admired afresh the calm way in which she seemed to weigh the implications of the night's events. Only when he came to Stilicho's departure without waiting to see her, did she give the first sign of alarm. He hastened to reassure her as best he could, though he suspected that she appeared to accept his explanation only out of consideration for his anxiety. But when he repeated Stilicho's injunction that he should take her straight back to Rome, she protested indignantly. She was no base-born camp-follower to flee at the first approach of danger. Indeed, she would make every effort to overtake him on the road to Ravenna, and if Hilary would not give her the small company Stilicho had given him to escort her, she would go alone with her own servants.

It was a problem beyond Hilary's experience, and he was considering the possibility of a compromise that would at least keep her in Bologna until a messenger could return from Stilicho, when a dishevelled soldier burst into the room, followed by the protesting doorkeeper. As the man flung himself at the feet of Serena, Hilary recognized one of Stilicho's aides whom he had often seen at his house in Rome.

"Sarus"—he choked for a moment—"Sarus attacked Stilicho's tent last night, and burned it, killing everybody in it."

For a moment Serena looked as if she would faint, and then the man realized what he had done and hastened to reassure her, "Stilicho had gone a couple of hours before, and he is now well away from Bologna."

"But where is Sarus?" asked Hilary, remembering how surprisingly noisy the small city of Bologna had seemed before dawn.

The man looked surprised at the question. "He has gone to join Alaric. That is what they are all doing."

At the news of Stilicho's escape Serena had recovered her look of weary composure, but now her eyes darkened with horror. The soldier seemed unaware of this, however, for he went on eagerly as if he had just been reminded of something he had undertaken to do. "My lady, that is the only safety for any of us. I will gather an escort for you, too."

But this Serena rejected with indignation. And as if there had never been any question of what she would do, she turned to Hilary. "What are we waiting for? Let us start at once for Rome." And then she explained to the bewildered soldier, "That is the command of my husband, and I shall lose no time in obeying it."

But she had reckoned without the effect of this last shock on strength already depleted by the exertions and anxieties of the journey. It was several days before she was able to travel, and then only slowly with long halts for rest.

For Hilary that journey was a nightmare of rumor and anxiety. The roads were full of wandering troops, and only the fact that Stilicho had chosen Serena's escort out of legionaries whose loyalty he had tested in many a battle saved them. But Serena's confidence returned as she rode along. Stilicho had escaped the madness of Sarus and was on his way. That was the only thing that really mattered, she told Hilary.

And when they began to meet various generals of the auxiliaries hurrying to regain their commands, she told Hilary that as usual the first reports had been exaggerated. Only a few of the barbarian officers had followed Sarus to Alaric. Most of them had stayed loyal and vindicated Stilicho.

Yet there were still curious reports from the direction of Ticinum. Olympius, who owed his first advance in the Emperor's household to Stilicho, was said to have inspired the riots in that city, inflaming the Roman troops against the barbarian leaders. At first Hilary tried to keep that rumor from her, but she saw him talking to the soldiers who had straggled up when they stopped by the roadside for food, and she insisted on knowing what was being said. To Hilary's surprise she did not seem especially alarmed when he told her.

"I never did like that Olympius," she said, thoughtfully. "Too pious for my taste." And then seeing his surprise she added hastily, "Hilary, I don't mean piety like yours, or even your friend Pammachius', though I think he overdoes it. What I mean is"—she hesitated—"he makes such a fuss of it."

She seemed to be lost in the rather detached contemplation of Olympius. And when she saw that Hilary still looked worried, she hastened to reassure him. "Thermantia will not let anyone turn her husband against her father. There will be some word from her when we get to Rome."

That thought seemed to steady her. Not even the report that Alaric with the barbarian deserters was again turning toward Rome troubled her, though it made Hilary redouble his efforts to get to the city before the roads should be closed, and before panic should have awakened in the summer-burned streets of Rome.

"We'll have word from Thermantia when we get home," she said as if that were the answer to all their problems.

But when they did reach Rome, there was no word from Thermantia. Hilary hoped that Serena had not heard the questions which some of the guards at the city gate had flung at him as he rode up to clear the way for the women. After they had ridden by, he had gone back to find out what the guards knew, but all they could tell was what some travellers had reported, that there had been rioting at Ravenna. They were simply curious about that, not really alarmed, as they were about the persistent reports that Alaric was again marching south.

When they reached the house of Stilicho, they found a knot of curious idlers about the gates. Some of them raised a cheer, some hissed, most stared with greedy eyes as they went in. But there was no word from Thermantia. Serena staggered to a couch and assured Hilary that he need not stay with her. She was going to bed. And when Hilary insisted on talking to her steward, she roused herself enough to jeer at him, "Don't be absurd, Hilary. This is Rome."

Even so he lingered after she had retired with her women. He had something to eat in the pretty honey-colored dining room which had always seemed to him the most elegant room in the rather bare house. And as he ate, the steward talked. He was an old man who had been in the household of the Emperor Theodosius when he brought his favorite niece, a precociously bright and pretty child, home to cheer his cowed household. Magnus had had a difficult time, keeping his staff to their duties with all the gossip flying around Rome, and he had done his best to discount all the reports and to minimize the alarms. But he was so worried that it was a relief to talk to somebody who would not panic if he admitted it.

"It's quite all over Rome," the old man said, "in the markets, in the courts, in the baths. They say the Romans in the legions are convinced there is no hope of turning the barbarians back when they have control of everything in Rome itself. Rome will never be safe until all the barbarian commanders are killed like the generals at Ticinum."

Talking there in the peace and security of the pleasant little dining room, softly lighted with oil lamps, to a young nobleman who listened with respect and sympathy was suddenly too much for the faithful servant. He burst into tears, the thin, convulsive tears of age. Hilary comforted him as well as he could and told him to see if he could not get a little rest. He would talk to the captain of Stilicho's escort. And then smiling a little at himself he repeated Serena's jeer, "After all, this is Rome, you know."

So Hilary went to talk to the centurion in charge of the escort. A guard at the gates for a night or two might not be amiss. He could always tell his general that he had lingered to give his men a rest. Then Hilary went out to talk to the doorkeeper, dozing by the shut gates. The country carts were beginning to roll into the city in their nightly fashion, the heavy iron-bound wheels clanging on the stone pavements. It was then that he heard the knocking at the gate, and the low voice calling so anxiously. It was Probinus.

"Thank the gods, you are here," he said, lurching wearily against Hilary. And then he said nothing more until the sleepy doorkeeper had been left behind to close the gates, and Hilary had taken him to the bright little dining room and given him some of the wine still standing on the table. Probinus drank and ate the remnants of bread and meat on the table ravenously, shivering like some hunted animal who has for a moment found cover. Then he looked at Hilary, and whatever Hilary had ever thought of his being a dull and commonplace young man faded as he gazed into the dark tarns of horror that his eyes had become.

"Stilicho is dead," he said very calmly, putting the horror on the little bronze and marble table between them. Three mermaids with curling fish tails for the pedestal and wind-blown curls to support the marble top, the ruby glass of the wine bowl sparkling in the soft candlelight—and there lay the horror between them.

166

"Dead!" Hilary repeated in the same low voice.

"Killed by Honorius' order!"

For some moments the two young men stared at each other with the growing terror of the young who have seen all the mature and adult strength on which they had counted melt before their eyes, and who, looking to each other for comfort, see only the reflection of their own terror. The swearing of some carters in the street outside broke incredibly into the room. And Hilary wondered irrelevantly whether he had ever before known such desolation as this. It was that shifting of the ground of shock that gave him strength to say, "What happened?"

Clearly, Probinus felt he could not tell, but once his shaking voice had begun to give sound and shape to the agony within, he found unexpected relief, and his husky voice steadied and grew clearer. The first part Hilary knew. Stilicho had left Bologna, feeling that his life's work was shaking under his weary feet, but he still had no doubt that with Thermantia's help Honorius would understand.

"Honorius understand!" repeated Hilary with bitter scorn.

But Probinus, who had had many lonely hours on the road to ponder this, thought he could explain it. Stilicho had always seen Honorius as a man sees his son. The youth may disappoint him today with his foolishness, but his father never ceases to believe that tomorrow he will be wiser. And he counted on Thermantia. And for the first time breaking the shackles of his agony, Probius deviated into irrelevance, "Have you noticed how wise Thermantia is for one so young?"

But when he saw that Hilary had no interest in Thermantia, he went back to his story. "We were well on the road out of Bologna when a soldier from the tent next to Stilicho's overtook us. He had heard Sarus shouting in the night that Stilicho was a traitor to his own blood. And he had heard the screams of the men in the tent, and he had seen the flames, and then he had fled."

"It can't have surprised Stilicho after what Sarus had said in the praetorial palace hall," said Hilary.

"You forget—when Sarus lost faith in Alaric, Stilicho took him into his service. Sarus always seemed so grateful."

And quite without patronage Hilary saw that disaster had already begun to work its accustomed alchemy in the imagination of Probinus, giving him a sensitiveness and an insight that he had never had before.

"But even so, Stilicho did not think of himself. He thought only of Rome." And then Probinus went on to tell how he changed his route to Ravenna so that he might pass through some of the towns where the hostages that Alaric had given in the last years were held, and everywhere he told the commanders that if the barbarians should come there, they were on no account to release them. And he told them that the safety of all Italy depended on their obeying his orders.

So he had come to Ravenna, where a large number of his troops were waiting for him, as well as the imperial garrison.

"We were barely in the city when they came," said Probinus, his exhaustion returning, as if the weariness of that arrival had returned to redouble the weariness of the present, "that wretched creature of Olympius, Heraclianus, with some guards. He came up to us as we were crossing the main square of the city, and he saluted us, smirking as if nothing were wrong, and said he had a message for the general. He read it to us. It was an order from Olympius to that tool of his to arrest Stilicho in the Emperor's name!"

Again Probinus stopped, overpowered with shame, and rage at his helplessness, and grief all at once. Then as Hilary reached out and touched his hand, he braced himself afresh.

"Heraclianus and his creatures just stood there grinning, but before they could move, Stilicho spurred his horse and rode up to the door of the cathedral and went in. I followed him, and I found him kneeling before the altar. He told me to get the bishop, but the bishop had heard the uproar as those scoundrels broke in, and he came out to see what it was."

Again Probinus paused, as if he found it difficult to sort out all his recollections, as if the only thing left for him to do now was to get the tragic facts as straight as possible. "You know the bishop, handsome and easy-going looking. He was all right this time. He made Stilicho rise up and stand beside him, and then he asked those creatures what it was all about." Probinus shut his lips firmly until they made a very straight line, and then he went on, with a cold indignation astonishing in one so young, "Heraclianus showed him the letter of Olympius, and he swore that they had no other intention but to take Stilicho into custody for questioning on the barbarian disorders."

Probinus' voice shook, and then steadied again. "The bishop looked at Stilicho as if to ask him what he could object to in that, and Stilicho without saying anything followed those scoundrels out of the church. By now there was a great crowd outside, both citizens and soldiers, and I am sure that most of the soldiers were Stilicho's. For there was a great stillness as we appeared. I have thought since that those wretches must have misunderstood that stillness. They thought that the soldiers were frightened to see their general in the hands of the court officials. For as soon as they reached the square, Heraclianus produced another letter, this one bearing the seal of the Emperor, and read it. It commanded the immediate execution of Stilicho as a threat to the safety of the state. And before Stilicho could speak, Heraclianus drew his sword. It was then that the crowd realized what was going on. From all over that square there went up a roar of anger, and somebody shouted the soldier's cry, 'To the rescue.' But Stilicho raised his hand and fixed on all that mob that glance of his, 'like lightning under his white hair' as Claudian once said, and everybody hushed so that you could hear him to the edge of the crowd.

"All he said was, 'Soldiers of Rome, you and I have sworn fealty to the Emperor and to Rome. I have kept that oath till now, and I shall keep it as long as I live. And I do not intend to let you break your oath because of me.' And with that he leaned over and said something to Heraclianus, who put his hand on him. But at that there went up a groan from all over the square, and somebody standing next to Stilicho pulled out his sword and thrust it between Heraclianus and Stilicho so that the man jumped back in fright, dropping his own sword. All over the square men reached for their weapons, but before they could draw them, Stilicho took the sword from the hands of the soldier who had drawn, and thrust it into Heraclianus' hands. And they all waited in astonishment, and the whole place was so still that I heard Stilicho say to that executioner, 'Do your duty before it is too late, and the peace is broken.' And he cried aloud, 'Rome!' and bowed his neck. With one stroke Heraclianus struck off his head, and it fell to the pavement with the lips still moving as if he were praying. And all over the square there was a gasp of horror, and then a great sob."

Probinus stopped. A couple of drunken voices singing came in on the heavy night air. Hilary roused himself as if from a spell and looked at his companion, who added, "There was nothing more I could do; so I came away to bring the news to— Rome," and he pronounced that sacred name with indescribable bitterness.

VI

PROBINUS HAD WANTED TO BREAK THE NEWS TO Serena at once, but Hilary had insisted that she must have the night's sleep to face what nothing could now help. It seemed to Hilary only a few minutes later that he was startled by a shouting outside the window. For a moment he thought he was in the square at Ravenna. Then he heard a mocking chant, "The traitor Stilicho is dead! The traitor Stilicho is dead! The traitor Stilicho is dead!"

He flung the shutters open. The shout was coming from the crowd outside the high wall of the garden at the rear of the house. He turned back, and he saw that Probinus was sitting up, but he was not looking at Hilary. He was staring at the doorway where Serena stood motionless.

"They woke me up," she whispered, and then she came in and sat down. And now that the worst had happened, Serena astonished her two young friends by the calmness with which she listened to Probinus' story. There was quite as much pride as grief in her face as it drew to a close. And Hilary marveled to see dawn in its weariness something of the ageless peace of the newly dead. Only once did she speak, and that was at the end, when Sextus told of Stilicho's dying with the name of Rome on his lips, "He was always a great lover of his country." And Hilary wondered if she remembered that she was quoting the sentence which the aged Augustus had pronounced on Cicero whom he had caused to be slain in his youth.

And then she asked if he had heard anything of her son Eucherius, but Sextus could tell her nothing. And then with a sigh she said it was strange that no word had come from Thermantia.

But that afternoon a messenger arrived from Ticinum to tell her that the Emperor had repudiated his Empress and had sent her back to her mother.

"That explains it," said Serena, in a final calmness of despair, and then she turned again to the messenger, "Are you sure she is alive?" The look of shock on the man's face reassured her, and she shrugged her shoulders as if there were not much more in this world that could surprise her.

But here as so often, Hilary reflected, she had underestimated the possibilities of life. For as the late summer sun was setting, red as blood, another messenger came to tell her that Eucherius was dead. She did not wait to ask how or where, but fell to the floor in a faint. Only after she had been carried out to her chamber, and Hilary and Probinus had assured the frightened soldier that he had nothing to blame himself for, did they learn that some creatures of Olympius had dragged Eucherius from the church in which he had taken refuge under pretext of taking him with the deposed Empress to his mother in Rome, and then just before they were to meet the Empress' escort, they had strangled him where he stood in the dust of the road.

The news must have seeped out into Rome somehow, for the next morning there were no taunts in the dawn. And when.

a few days later, the repudiated Empress arrived, weary and travel-stained, even the crowd of curious at the city gates fell back as if they were afraid of any closer contact with so much misfortune.

By the next day fashionable Rome began to rally a little from the shock of the downfall of Stilicho's family. Fabius came alone to call on Hilary, who had remained in the house at Thermantia's request, and to ask if he might present his sympathy to the Lady Serena. Attalus followed with a couple of friends, and Pompeianus, more cautious, sent a message by a freedman. And so did Gaia, who had always thought Serena arrogant. But Proba Faltonia made a great point of coming in person, telling everybody that, whatever they might think of her husband, nobody had ever accused Serena of treason. But however they came, Thermantia received them all, very quiet and very self-possessed, and took them back to the peristyle, where Serena sat in a basket chair with a shawl over her knees. And everybody, having mustered courage to say a few unrepeatable nothings to the courteously bowing but apparently uncomprehending old woman, went away, looking relieved and satisfied with himself.

But there was one visit that was an exception to this cautious decency. After several of the leading members of the senatorial circle had paid their respects, and people had begun to whisper about who had stood by Serena and who had not, the Princess Galla Placidia came to call, looking very beautiful and very self-possessed. But she seemed to be moved unexpectedly by the sight of her cousin sitting hunched over in her chair, for she put out her delicate hands, sparkling with gems, in a very pretty gesture of affectionate compassion. Hilary was about to retreat from this affecting family scene, when he heard the voice of Serena ring out sharply, "Keep your hands away from me, Galla. They are dripping with the blood of Eucherius." And Galla Placidia's face flamed the color of the rubies on her hands as she swept out of the room.

At an imploring look from Thermantia Hilary followed her, but the young princess only tossed her head, "She never thought of anybody but that brat of hers anyway," and stalked from the house.

Hilary was still standing looking after her, when Thermantia came up to him, looking startlingly mature.

"Will you and Probinus see if you can find us a modest apartment in a poorer district? We have been flying too close to the sun long enough."

All Hilary was able to find, even with the help of Fabius, was a small apartment in a shabby section down by the river. But Thermantia insisted it was eminently satisfactory. It had a little balcony above the street where her mother could get some air, and it was near the parish church where she herself could pray for their dead.

"We shall take three or four of our most dependable servants," she said, "and then I pray God that Rome will forget that we ever lived."

For a few weeks it seemed as if she might have her wish, for Rome had plenty to think of as the reports came piling in of the march south of Alaric and his army. At first Hilary, shocked and exhausted himself now that he had settled his friends in their humble refuge, paid little attention to the rumors.

"It is the same old story," he said uninterestedly to Gaia, who had insisted that he forget the family of Stilicho long enough to visit an old friend.

She looked at him as if she did not believe he could mean what he said. And then when she realized that he did, she remonstrated with him sharply, "But this time it is serious."

And she proceeded to tell the story of the revolt of the Roman army against the barbarian commanders.

"A shoddy piece of palace intrigue," he said, glad to speak out at last after all the forced discretions of the house of Stilicho.

To his surprise she not only agreed with him, but pronounced the pious cloak which the conspirators had tried to throw about the whole affair a sheer travesty on patriotism. And then she proceeded to tell Hilary that once Stilicho was out of the way, the troops had not rested content with the murder of the barbarian generals, who were probably no more innocent than generals usually are, but had invaded the towns where the barbarian hostages were held—women and children, who were certainly guiltless of any political scheming—and had slaughtered them without mercy. And that she held a disgrace to the name of Rome. One could hardly be surprised that the husbands and fathers of those victims had despaired of Rome's justice and fled to Alaric. Now, as Alaric advanced, the barbarian slaves and freedmen were everywhere running away to join his army.

"You know they would not dare to do that if they did not believe Alaric were going to win," she concluded.

But he was firm. "There is nothing you and I can do. It is up to Ravenna now."

"Ravenna!" she repeated with ineffable scorn.

But he soon discovered that it was going to concern him. For with astonishing speed Alaric advanced straight on Rome, gathering up as he went fresh reinforcements of slaves and deserters. Rome was frightened before the vanguard of his troops was reported in Picenum, and in a panic when the first of his watch-fires could be seen at night from the Janiculum. The senate met and elected a deputation to go to the Emperor at Ravenna, and Fabius, who had been asked to accompany it, tried to get Hilary's advice. But Hilary refused to be interested. "What can the Emperor do? He can no longer send Stilicho. Do you want Olympius?" But before Fabius could reply to that taunt, a messenger came from the city prefect Pompeianus, asking Fabius to come to see him before he left the city. And Hilary accepted his invitation to go with him to the house of Pompeianus. For he knew now only too well that it was not every young senator who would choose to appear in public with a known friend of Stilicho.

But Pompeianus only nodded to Hilary in a preoccupied fashion, and plunged into his worries, "Alaric has closed every road into Rome. You know what that means for food."

"But," said Fabius, "there are the river boats."

"Alaric has thrown a bridge of boats across the river above the city as well as below."

The praetor relaxed as he saw that his visitors had comprehended the gravity of the situation, and then he insisted rather gratuitously, "You know what that means."

In the weeks that followed, all Rome found out, too. First, there was the obvious shortage of food, the cutting of the ration of bread by a third and a half and then two-thirds. For the first time in remembered history Rome woke in the night to unbroken quiet, for no carts came in from the country to bring fresh meat and vegetables, and no boats came up the river with the wheat from Africa. Once the storehouses along the river were emptied, there was no wine and no oil, either. Pammachius and Marcella distributed bread to the starving and medicines to the ill, and then even they had to give up as the jostling mobs threatened to tear down their walls when their supplies ran out. In the circus the crowd chanted, "Put a price on human flesh," when Pompeianus appeared in the praetorial box, and that cry passed like a shudder across Rome, and Hilary's cook swore to him that the strange-smelling meat on his plate was really rat, roasted and seasoned with his best skill.

But that was only the beginning. Men died that fall of 408 as men have always died, but no one could take them to the tombs outside the city, because Alaric's troops were at the very gates. And the unburied dead took their revenge in the autumn heat, and the fever ran through the crowded apartment houses of Rome and stalked its victims through the teeming circus and the empty markets. Hilary helped Pammachius organize burial squads to bury some of the dead quite illegally in some of the great gardens of the city, but there were too many dead, and the gardens were too few. The Pope said Mass for the doomed city in Saint Peter's, and men and women sickened as they prayed.

But still the measure of Rome's humiliation was not complete. For in the night, when not a farmer could bring a basket of food into the city, the barbarian slaves found ways to get over the walls and across the river, and Alaric's men made them welcome and gave them arms. It was that that made the reason of Rome finally reel. All over the city the terror of betrayal from within spread, so that men predicted with confidence that tonight the slaves would force open the gates and let Alaric in.

175

It was then that someone (Proba Faltonia swore it was Galla Placidia) remembered that the wife of the traitor Stilicho was still in the city. The reminder went, like all the rumors, across the city, from the barracks of the gladiators near the Flavian amphitheater and the brothels of the Suburra to the senatorial houses on the Aventine and the Caelian. Hilary heard it at the house of Fabius, where he had gone one day, for sheer distraction, to help with the letters of Symmachus.

At first Hilary shrugged his shoulders. Nobody who had seen the grief-stricken Serena sitting so patiently hour after hour on the little balcony above the teeming street, seeing and hearing nothing of all the flood of life below her, could believe that anybody would pay attention to such a story. And then as he started back to his own house and heard the gaunt and apathetic crowds in the street taking new life of their fright as they talked of Serena's plot to betray the city, he grew alarmed. His first thought was to take his own servants over to Serena's apartment and post a guard. And then he reflected that that might precipitate the very trouble he feared. So he went to the house of the praetor, Pompeianus.

Pompeianus was getting ready for the meeting of the senate that was to take place shortly, his servant informed him. But at a second glance at Hilary's face he admitted him to his master.

Hilary saw at once that the praetor had heard the rumor, although he made Hilary repeat the reports that had alarmed him. Then he asked him what he feared. And when Hilary said that he feared the mob, Pompeianus looked thoughtful and said that he would send some guards to Serena's house at once. Asking Hilary to wait, he went out and gave the order, and then he came back and invited Hilary to go along with him to the senate house.

But when they neared the forum and heard the assembling senators on every side talking in high, excited voices of the plot to betray the city, Hilary became alarmed afresh, and, excusing himself, hurried to Serena's house. And as he went along, he blamed himself that he had not gone there at once, for it seemed to him now that Pompeianus had been deliberately holding him off.

When he reached Serena's house, there was a crowd before it, pointing to the balcony, and when he went up the stairway, he found one of the praetor's servants, a man he had often seen with Pompeianus, sitting at the top of the stairs. Seeing Hilary, the man rose hastily and told him that the apartment was empty and sealed. Nobody could go in. At first he professed to know nothing of the whereabouts of the ladies, but finally, taking compassion on Hilary's distress, he admitted that Pompeianus had sent his guards to remove them to his house for safekeeping.

Reassured, Hilary was starting back up the Caelian hill when a fresh uneasiness made him pause. Pompeianus had said nothing of bringing them to his house. So Hilary turned back. On the way he passed a corner of the forum from where he caught sight of what seemed to be an enormous crowd around the senate house. Perhaps there was some message from Ravenna. But he was too worried to linger to satisfy his curiosity. So he bade the servant who had accompanied him go over to the senate house to see what was going on, and then to join him at the praetor's house, where he would wait for him.

At the praetor's house Hilary had no trouble learning that the Lady Thermantia was there, but the lady Serena was not. No, he could not see the Lady Thermantia. Nobody could. It was for her protection. No, the doorkeeper had no idea where the Lady Serena was. As they talked, another of the praetor's servants came in, a man whom Hilary had often seen waiting for his master. He looked frightened when he saw Hilary, but he escorted him in silence to the gates. There he told Hilary that the Lady Serena had been taken to the old prison by the senate house. More than that he could not or would not say.

Hilary was debating whether he should wait for the praetor to return from the senate or should go directly to the prison, when his servant came up the street. The man had been running, but it was not that that had blanched his face with horror. When finally he could find breath, he came close to his master and whispered, "The senate has condemned the Lady Serena to death—and they have done it!"

"They can't have!" cried Hilary, but the man insisted. He

had heard the crowd talking, and they were saying that the curse of the vestal had come true.

"The curse of the vestal?"

"You remember the story. When they were putting down the worship of the old gods, the Princess Serena went into the house of the Vestal Virgins and took the necklace from the goddess Rhea and put it about her own neck. And when the old vestal who was the last there protested the sacrilege, she laughed. And the old vestal said that the necklace would choke her."

"That is pagan superstition," said Hilary sharply. "A Christian should know better than to believe it."

But a stubborn look came into his servant's face, "But that is how she died, my lord, strangled by the neck."

At that moment Pompeianus came up to the gate, and his servants tried to thrust Hilary aside. But as he protested, Pompeianus heard his voice.

Apparently exhausted, he sank into a chair. "Don't ask me what happened. I never saw anything like it. Nobody would listen to reason. I tried. Pammachius tried. Then they began to shout that we were traitors, too."

"But is it true?" Hilary insisted.

Pompeianus nodded miserably, and then he lifted his head as a tumult of shouting broke in from the street, "Rome is saved from Alaric! Rome is saved!" And as the yelling mob moved on, the supreme judicial officer of Rome broke into hysterical laughter.

VII

BUT THE HURRICANE OF HATE AND SUSPICION that had destroyed Serena seemed to have exhausted itself as quickly as it had arisen. In a few weeks Pompeianus agreed to release Thermantia and to send her under escort to any place

Hilary chose. But Thermantia herself insisted on returning to the refuge that had proved so inadequate. And when Hilary protested, she rebuked him, "All life is a borrowed thing, Hilary, and a Christian should know better than to squander it on fear."

And when he had settled her with a couple of slaves who still clung to her, in the apartment with the empty balcony, he asked her what she would do now. "Pray," she responded, and then seeing his hurt, she smiled with a faint afterglow of her dead mother's charm; "Hilary, there are many kinds of idolatry. In the battle between Christian and pagan my father and my mother held to the Christian side, but the god to whom they sacrificed everything was Rome."

So for a while Hilary kept anxious watch over Thermantia without intruding on the solitude she had asked. Sometimes he sent a slave to watch; sometimes he went himself. And then one day he had an inspiration.

The ground floor of the great apartment house was a veritable hive of little shops in which modest craftsmen of all sorts plied their arts from dawn to dusk, with the fruits of their obscure industry hanging on the walls behind them or spread on the counters that edged the street. From time to time he had caught sight of a bright head or two in the cavernous shadows of the little shops, and he wondered if perhaps there might not be some veteran of Stilicho's armies here who would take pity on his old leader's daughter. It was, he knew, a fantastic thought, but he reminded himself that a Christian should not always expect the worst of chance.

At first, he thought the weaver's shop empty, and he was going on when he heard a woman's voice singing. It was a small sound in all the noise of the shops, and he would not have heard it at all but for a faint, stirring sense of familiarity about it, like a familiar odor caught in a strange place. He paused. The woman was singing a lullaby, a little almost meaningless song which he had heard the nurse sing to his sisters' children in that incredible tear-glistening world of the past. And then he knew the voice.

"Rhodope!" he cried, and he stood in the narrow gateway

between the counter and the wall of the shop. A slim figure rose from beside a basket in the back of the shop and picked its way between the looms, and then drew itself up. For a moment she stood listening as if she feared for her senses. And with a flash of his old imaginative truancy Hilary thought that thus Eurydice must have looked, when Orpheus first caught sight of her in the depths of hell.

Then she knew him in a sudden cry of unreflecting delight, "Hilary!" But when he put his arms out to her, she moved back, and when he started to speak, she put a finger to her lips and gestured toward the basket. Silently Hilary went over and looked down at the sleeping child, a little creature with a thin fuzz of reddish hair on its small head. Across the humble cradle Hilary looked for a moment at Rhodope.

"Who is the father?" he asked. And he thought a shadow of anxiety crossed her face, as she beckoned to the front of the shop, where she leaned against the counter. Now Hilary could see her face more plainly, and he was shocked to see how thin and worn it had become.

Then as if bracing herself against something more than the counter, she replied. "You remember Dagridus, whom the other men in the shop used to call the Red?" Hilary remembered the young Saxon weaver, whom he had liked for his gentleness, surprising in one so burly-looking.

"Is he good to you?" he asked, looking into her large eyes.

"The best husband woman ever had," she said, and a touch of pride came into her face. And then anxiety. "You must go now. I will not have him worried."

"But," said Hilary, suddenly feeling unjustly rebuked, "I want to know what has happened to you both."

"That is simple," she said quietly. "We fled ahead of the armies until we came here last spring." And then sadly, "We were doing very well until the armies came again." And then as if ashamed, "But we are so fortunate really when you think of all those others."

Hilary looked around the little shop with its ladderlike stair in the corner twisting up to the single low room with its one window that constituted, he knew, the home of the owner of such a shop. She must have guessed his thought, for she said, "No," very firmly. "We used the dowry for the shop in Bordeaux, and we had enough to start here. Anything now he would consider a dishonor. I will not have him worried," she repeated with a touch of fierceness that awed Hilary.

Then he remembered his errand. Rhodope was all sympathy at once, and when he repeated Thermantia's remark about flying near the sun, she shook her head vigorously. "She is right," she said. "The poor are safer, from the envy of men and gods at least."

"That is precisely what I am worried about," Hilary said. "You know how her mother died."

But again, looking surprisingly old and wise, she said firmly, "You need not worry. The poor know their own. She is safer here."

He had to be content with that. In this very tired, very patient woman who stood before him the girl whom he had once known and loved seemed to be fading before his eyes. Perhaps she guessed what he was thinking, for she said to him very gently, almost as if she were speaking to a child, "Do not be so troubled. It is the common lot. Who are we to think we should escape it?" And Hilary left the shop, groping his way through the crowd in the street, blinded with tears.

So completely absorbed was he in the contemplation of this sudden revelation of all the losses of the last years that he had almost reached the senate house before he saw that the senate had been meeting, and the senators were coming out. For a moment he turned to flee the sight of the men he had thought he could never bear to see again. But before he could do so, he caught the tone of the voices coming down the steps. They were sullen, he thought, even angry, but puzzled and frightened, too. This time it was hardly murder. He was turning away when he heard his name called.

It was a servant of Pompeianus. Hot with shame, Hilary waited. It seemed a disloyalty to Serena to be seen in the forum with the man who, whatever excuses he made, had given her up to her murderers. And yet to refuse to wait might confirm the old suspicions—but Pompeianus was simply asking Hilary to meet him at his house in an hour. Slowly and painfully Hilary forced his mind to reach outside of its own iron circle of personal preoccupation. Some new crisis—some new dying in a dead world!

But he had no time to think of himself when he returned to the praetor's house an hour later. For Pompeianus, usually so blandly confident, looked as frightened and confused as any of the senators whose voices Hilary had heard in the forum.

"It's religion again," he began bitterly. "As if Alaric were not enough!"

Religion—Hilary tried to recall the old fights between Christian and pagan of which Symmachus used to talk—the statue of Victory? Pompeianus seemed to recollect himself.

"Of course, you have had your hands full"—Pompeianus had the grace to look embarrassed—"but everybody else in Rome is thinking of nothing but Alaric's terms. We have food now, but he is stripping us clean of everything else. Some of those senators would listen to the devil himself if he offered them a way of saving something from their fortunes." Pompeianus paused, arrested at last by Hilary's indifference. "Look here," he pleaded, "you are a friend of Pammachius, aren't you?"

Hilary tried to focus his mind on the thought of friends, living friends. "Yes," he said slowly.

"Won't you say something to him then about seeing the Pope?"

"About what?"

Pompeianus put his hands to his head, the sort of head Hilary had once told himself would look very fine in a bust on a column in the forum, and suddenly he felt sorry for any man on whom the ends of these days had come. Pompeianus saw his sympathy, for he relaxed a little, "I am making no more sense than the rest of them. Do you remember what happened at Narnia a few weeks back?"

Hilary shook his head uncertainly. And Pompeianus went on. "The town on the rock up on the Nar? Alaric's army reached there just before sunset, and they were ready to attack it, when suddenly there came a terrific thunder storm, and the lightning struck, and the whole town seemed ablaze? And Alaric's men were so frightened at the portent that they fled down the road?"

In spite of himself Hilary remembered the picture of the town on the rock blazing against the storm-darkened sky. And then he remembered something else. "Oh, and some pagan augurs or others tried to pretend that they had raised the storm?"

"Tuscan augurs! They are here in Rome now. And they say that if we will let them perform their rites in the old places, they will turn Alaric back from Rome right now. And they will do it for a thousandth of what Alaric has asked."

"But that is preposterous superstition," said Hilary incredulously.

"Call it what you like." Pompeianus shrugged his shoulders. "Half the pagans in Rome are clamoring to give them a chance, and the other half when they hear about it will make an even louder noise."

"But surely the senate—"

"The senate!" Pompeianus almost spat out the word and then recovered himself. "That is not the point. It happens to be against the law. But the pagans think that if the Christians would overlook it, they could do it. And if the Christians refuse, the pagans will say that they do not care what happens to Rome, that they are traitors like the barbarians."

For a moment there was silence between the two men. Then Hilary said coldly, "But as a Christian you cannot have anything to do with such superstition."

"You are as bad as Pammachius. But I am the praetor of Rome, of all Rome, pagan and Christian alike." Hilary wondered how seriously the praetor took his faith, and then reminded himself that he was hardly the man to ask. Pompeianus was quick to catch the moment's hesitation.

"And if the Pope would tell the Christians not to stand in the way, then the pagans could try it, and if it failed, at least they could not blame the Christians." A note of pleading came into Pompeianus' voice.

"If it failed!"

"Just for the sake of argument."

Mentally, Hilary conjured up two faces he had once seen close together at Saint Peter's. "I think I should sooner try to persuade the Pope himself than Pammachius to consider that line of argument."

"Perhaps you are right," Pompeianus said slowly. "Will you come with me then?"

Hilary stared at the praetor.

"To see the Pope? It would be an impertinence for me."

But Pompeianus insisted that he must have some Christian companion, and Hilary finally decided that there was a point where modesty crossed the line and became pride. For such a futile piece of folly it was hard to say which it was.

But when the next day the Pope received them in a bare little room in the Lateran palace, Hilary discovered that he had been mistaken. Pompeianus had simply wanted a good exordium, for he opened his plea by saying that it was Hilary who had suggested that he appeal directly to the Pope himself.

Hilary felt the clear eyes of Innocent on his own burning cheek, and then he gave all his attention to Pompeianus' speech. The Pope did not interrupt him, except once to make sure that he had heard correctly. Not until the end, when Pompeianus, obviously impressed by his own eloquence, concluded with a little flourish, did he speak.

And then he came briskly to the point with a matter-of-factness that startled Hilary. "I am a Roman, too. But there are some things that a Christian cannot do for any reason, and taking part in heathen rites is one of them. If the pagans perform those rites, they must do it in private. I at least will raise no objection to that under the present circumstances."

"But," protested Pompeianus, "they say to be effective, they must be done in the old way by the whole city."

"That," said the Pope quietly, "is impossible. Now tell me what your latest news from Alaric is."

184

Groaning, Pompeianus retailed the terms: the gold, the silks, the dyed hides, the spices. Again, Pompeianus groaned, "It will take everything we have."

The Pope smiled grimly. "I have heard that Alaric is being taunted by his women that he has nothing to show for all his victories. But is that all?"

"All!" repeated Pompeianus bitterly, and then more thoughtfully as if he were checking up Alaric's terms afresh, he added, "And that matter of the appointment as Master of the Forces. That the Emperor has refused, of course."

But the Pope's voice cut into the official's complacency like the crack of a whip. "But that is the most important of all! Has no one told the Emperor what that means to Alaric?"

Pompeianus, bewildered, stared at the quiet face, now so taut. "We sent an embassy to the Emperor, but he said no man of Alaric's blood had ever held such a post."

Hilary gasped, and the Pope looked at him thoughtfully. Then he said with a slight but surprisingly attractive smile, "There are some things that they understand better at Bordeaux, aren't there, than at Ravenna?"

In his bewilderment Pompeianus saw a straw and snatched at it, "But would your Holiness go to Ravenna yourself to tell the Emperor?"

"I would indeed," was the quiet answer. "Get your senate to approve another embassy, and make it ready, and let Alaric know. And the sooner, the better."

Then Innocent turned to Hilary, and his whole manner softened. "Thermantia's pastor, the priest Liberius, was here this morning. He was telling me about you. Will you come with me on this embassy, young man?"

Temptation? Suddenly Hilary knew that he had deceived himself, when he had thought of himself as one dead. With quite unfeigned humility he thanked the Pope for the honor he had done him.

But when that evening he went to Gaia's house to tell her of the embassy and to take leave of her, she looked alarmed. "I did not know it was that bad," she said, and then at his obvious puzzlement she added, "Of course, I have been worried, but I thought people were getting over the hysteria and beginning to face the facts."

"Worried! Then why don't you go to the country now while you can?"

"I? What have I to be afraid of?" She sounded genuinely surprised. Then she smiled, "Isn't your friend Thermantia staying?"

But before he could say anything, she changed the subject. "You will find your friend Fortunatus ahead of you at Ravenna. He was here today looking for you. He says"—her lips tightened—"Rome ended long ago. It is the empire that counts; so he has gone to Ravenna."

He stared at her, and she shrugged her shoulders. "You are wasting your time, and you will say you can't help it." And she refused to talk any more about politics. For how could they hope to see eye to eye when they came out of such different worlds?

Only when he rose to go, did her manner soften, and she held his hand for a moment and assured him that, whatever she thought of some of his friends, she had never doubted his love for Rome. With that he had to be content.

VIII

"IT WILL BE SIX WEEKS TO TWO MONTHS AT most," said Hilary to Lupicinus, his Roman steward, when he took leave of him at the Flaminian gate. But now as the papal party reined in their horses on the turn of the road from which Hilary had first beheld Rome, he wondered if again he had been too arrogantly sure. It was still winter, and as they turned to look back, Rome seemed as beautiful as it had been that first winter day. But there was death in those teeming streets, and hate and murder and festering heartbreak beneath those gleaming roofs, and these things stretched between that day and this broader than the shining river which Alaric's men had dammed. But Rome was still beautiful—"And the devil took him up into a high place and showed him all the kingdoms of the world, and the glory of them."

He murmured it softly to himself, but the Pope just in front of him heard. For he turned swiftly, and looked at Hilary, "I suppose that is what a young man should think of." He spoke so impersonally that Hilary stared at him with frank curiosity, and the Pope smiled, "While I never turn here without thinking of Christ weeping over Jerusalem."

And he turned his horse from the magnificent view and started down the road, as if he were looking for a traveller who had failed to put in an appearance. Hilary overheard him ask his secretary, "Do you think there was any difficulty with the message, Rusticius?"

"No," said the man, a quite dependable-looking middle-aged priest with "trusted official" written all over him. "When Pompeianus asked for the safe-conduct, a message was arranged for Maximius, too."

But even as they talked, a mule appeared, coming up a path from below the road, with his rider crouched low in a brown robe and hood that made him look as if he were a part of the creature. The rider, as he caught sight of the group waiting for him on the highway, threw his hood back, and urged his mule forward. But to the amusement of the onlookers, the mule stopped and refused to move. The rider gave up the struggle, slipping to the ground and dragging the useless mount after him.

He was a sandy little man, Hilary saw, as he came nearer, with a certain casualness of manner that brought him to the Pope's feet as quickly and neatly as he had disposed of his balky mount. Now as he faced the Pope, Hilary saw that there was a look of quiet alertness in the brown eyes that looked so directly out of the weather-tanned face.

The cortege formed again, the newcomer riding beside the

Pope on one of the spare horses. At his command Hilary rode close behind, to hear the news of Gaul and the monastery on the Dordogne.

"The barbarians did not reach us," the monk was explaining as Hilary rode up, "but there were a lot of refugees of all sorts. Severus thought we should know more about what was going on in the world, though. And he said we could go to the Holy Land to see Jerome while we were about it. Only Brother Gerontius died of the fever at Narnia, and I had to bury him there at the foot of the cliff. It seemed so far from Rome," he added with unexpected wistfulness.

"The angels of the resurrection will find him as easily on the Nar as on the Dordogne, you know," said the Pope gently.

"I know," said Maximius, "a monk on his superior's errand is in his cell, but it's a long way for this life."

"Now for Alaric. Was it just chance?" The Pope looked shrewdly at his companion.

The latter laughed. "Your Holiness already sounds like Severus. But I assure you that I never look for adventure. Only—" he paused, and Hilary thought he looked embarrassed.

"But you never run away from it, Maximius?"

"Well," said the monk, obviously undecided between embarrassment and making a clean breast of it to so unexpectedly sympathetic an auditor, "if I were to get some idea of what is likely to happen in the world, I thought what Alaric is thinking would be as important as anything."

"I am delighted to find somebody with sense enough to realize that," said the Pope dryly. "Now begin at the beginning. It was in a field near Narnia that you met him?"

"Yes," said the monk. "After I had buried Gerontius and said the prayers in the thunderstorm. I was crossing the field away from the town, thinking I might find a dry spot in the rocks down below. It was then that I met a little group of the barbarians, who had been left behind by their comrades and were looking for a place for the night. So I told them of my plan, and they came with me."

The monk was obviously afraid of boring his audience with unnecessary detail, and Hilary realized with sudden envy that though he was awed by the presence of the Pope, he had no thought of impressing him. But Innocent insisted that he wanted every detail of the meeting; that he had never had any chance to see Alaric himself, and he wanted to take advantage of his companion's good luck. So encouraged, Maximius expanded his narration a little to include his own impressions. He explained that he had no idea at first that the tall, formidable-looking man who was obviously the most important person in their company was Alaric. Anyway he seemed badly upset, not so much frightened as puzzled.

To Hilary's surprise, the Pope seemed to follow Maximius completely, and the latter went on with more confidence. It was not until they had eaten and lighted a fire in their cave that Alaric really said much of anything, and Maximius was astonished to find out who his companion was. Apparently they had talked for quite a while then, with the rest of the company falling asleep around the fire.

"He wanted especially to know if I thought the old gods had put the wall of thunder and lightning about the town because the inhabitants had invoked them with the proper rites. Of course, I told him that was nonsense. But he looked queer at that, and he said that, though he is a Christian like any civilized man, he had had some odd experiences himself. And then he told me about seeing Athena on the walls of Athens when he was there. That was why he decided to spare the city."

Rusticius laughed. "What an extraordinary thing for a barbarian to imagine!" And the Pope looked at the monk sceptically.

But Maximius went on steadily, "He has a great veneration for Rome, too."

At that Rusticius seemed to lose all patience. "Then why, in heaven's name?"

"He feels that he is driven to it," answered Maximius. "He spoke several times of a voice that says to him, 'You will go into the city.' He thinks he was born for the destruction of Rome, for a great and a terrible destiny from which he would escape if he could."

"I should think it would be simple enough," sniffed Rusticius, exasperated at folly humored so inexplicably by authority.

But Maximius insisted that it was not so simple. Alaric had his obligation to his people. They had followed his leadership, and they had gained nothing by it. The wives of his warriors had taunted their husbands, "What kind of victories are these that bring us no gold, and no slaves, and not even the lands and the arms we were promised?" It was to pay his obligation to them that Alaric wanted the wealth of Rome, Maximius insisted, and not for himself.

But what then did Alaric want for himself? Surprisingly, several of the little company asked the question at once. Maximius was quite sure of the answer. Alaric wanted to be recognized as an ally of Rome. He wanted to become a master of the Emperor's forces as Stilicho had been.

At the mention of Stilicho's name there was an uncomfortable silence. Political talk would have to be governed by discretion at the Lateran palace, Hilary reflected. Finally Rusticius took the plunge. "Stilicho, whatever his origin, was at least a Roman citizen."

The monk looked puzzled. "But Alaric assured me that he would be proud to become a Roman citizen and take his oath to protect Rome."

"His oath!"

The little monk turned to Rusticius appealingly, "I think he would take his oath seriously. He is a Christian, even if an Arian. I know he spoke very bitterly of the promises that had been made to him and broken."

"It is impudence for a barbarian or anybody else to talk of broken promises when the Emperor has said that he could not imagine confiding the defence of the empire to a barbarian, to a Goth." Outrage vibrated in the thin voice of Rusticius.

Maximius looked from the secretary to the Pope, who still listened to all that was being said without giving any hint of his own opinion. Then the little monk turned to the secretary and said very simply, "But to a Christian is there such a difference between a barbarian and a Roman?"

It was at that point that the Pope ended the conversation by inquiring if the villa on the horizon were not the place agreed on for their midday halt. And then he turned to the monk and asked him if he would go with him to Ravenna. "I want the Emperor to have a chance to hear you."

When they took the road again, the Pope seemed to have lost interest in Alaric, for he began to question Hilary about Bordeaux. And for the first time since the news of its destruction Hilary found that he could bear to talk about his home to this surprisingly interested and sympathetic listener. And in that discovery he began to feel a confidence in the success of their journey. But when he ventured to mention that to the Pope, the latter rebuked him, "We can make the effort, but the issue is not ours."

Hilary thought of those words some weeks later when, after various delays due to the unsettled state of the land, they finally reached the gloomy marsh country of Ravenna, now shadowed doubly for Hilary with the memory of last summer's horror. Early that morning the Pope left Hilary with most of his party in the bishop's palace, and with his host and Maximius for company followed the splendid escort the Emperor had sent for him to the imperial palace.

In the middle of the long day somebody came from the imperial palace and asked for Hilary. It was Fortunatus, whom Hilary found quite magnificent in gold-bordered robes, sitting very much at his ease in the bishop's own reception room. It was some time since Hilary had seen his old comrade, and he was startled by the change in his appearance. He was still the same brilliant young man, but the old carelessness had gone as if something long fluid had suddenly hardened.

"You always were on the edge of being a fool, Hilary," Fortunatus began without preamble. "I was sure you had at last gone quite over the edge when I heard whom you had come with to Ravenna."

"Never mind that," replied Hilary, curious about the new

look on his old friend's face. "Tell me what you are doing here."

Fortunatus shrugged his shoulders. "It's all the same thing. A cousin of my wife is here, and he spoke to the right people about me."

Hilary stared at his old friend. Nothing seemed to have survived of his old light-hearted cynicism, as he said flatly, "Rome is finished. Here is the center of the world."

"Ravenna!" Horror and contempt sharpened Hilary's voice.

Fortunatus flushed. "What do you think the Pope cares about? Nothing but religion!"

"Beside the court of Ravenna," began Hilary, but something dangerous had come into the face of Fortunatus.

"You are a fool!" he exploded, jumping to his feet.

Hilary had plenty of time to wonder whether he could not have made more of an effort to detain Fortunatus and find out what he thought he was doing. For the night fell without any word from the Pope, and the rest of the Pope's company accepted the bishop's hospitality and went to bed. Hilary was about to follow their example when one of the Pope's servants came for him.

He found Innocent alone with Maximius in an elegant little reception room which the bishop had placed at his disposal. But in contrast to the splendor of their surroundings, both men looked unmistakably dejected. The monk was sitting down, but his eyes were fixed on the figure of the Pope pacing the little room restlessly. When the latter caught sight of Hilary, he lifted his hands in a gesture of bewilderment.

Then he sat down in a low chair and began to tick off the points on his fingers. "The Emperor has no money or troops to send to Rome. The Emperor is astonished that anybody should presume to dictate his choice of generals to defend the safety of the empire. The Emperor is profoundly aware of the sacred trust he has received from God to defend the empire, and he has no intention of jeopardizing it by turning it over to barbarians. He will not under any circumstances make Alaric his general or his ally." The low voice had risen, and Hilary was startled by the passion under its dry surface. Then a wry smile broke on the Pope's grim face. "In justice to the Emperor I should add that he professed the deepest devotion to the see of Peter and declared his intention of coming to Rome and expressing publicly his high personal regard for the head of the Church as soon as possible."

Hilary looked at Maximius, but Maximius was still staring as if fascinated at the Pope.

"Then he did not believe you?" said Hilary compassionately.

Maximius shrugged his shoulders, and the Pope spoke more quietly, "God in his mysterious providence has given the empire to Honorius." And then recovering something of his accustomed matter-of-fact calm, he sat down beside Hilary. "In a few days we shall start back for Rome. No man can guess what we shall find there, or how long it will last. As for you," and now his voice rose more surely, "you have done your part. So now I think you should go along with Maximius here. In a few weeks you will be able to find a ship to Palestine. I will give you a letter to Jerome which I have been wanting to send for some time, and you may say you are my messenger to anybody who tries to stop you."

At first Hilary made the obvious objections. He had his obligations to his household in Rome, to Thermantia, to Cerealis if he should succeed in sending him word, to Medoc if he should return. The Pope met all his objections with his characteristic directness. "These things will wait. You came from Bordeaux to see Rome. You have seen Rome. It is time that you saw that not even Rome is the whole of God's world."

Then Hilary protested that he had very little money with him and no attendance. The Pope promised letters to his own agents in the port, and reminded him that he could hardly find better attendance than that of the monk who had in a few months' space talked with the barbarian conqueror and the Pope and the Emperor. But when Hilary at last asked why they could not wait until summer and do things properly, the Pope finally came to the point: "They have been dismissing all the officials whom Stilicho appointed here and in Rome. They have begun to imprison and even to torture some of those suspected of being in his confidence. How far that will go no man can tell. But at best you have seen enough of the fall of princes; at worst, you have it in you, I think, to pay God a better death than to fall a victim to some frenzy of spite or fear."

The realization that in all his care for Rome Innocent should yet find some corner of thought to give to one young man so overwhelmed Hilary that he could only stammer, "I am not worthy all your—"

But the Pope interrupted him with his customary briskness, "That is settled then," and as Hilary knelt to take his leave, the Pope smiled, "And don't forget that God will find his workman when He is ready for him."

IV
TO THE ENDS OF
THE EARTH

J

But the disturbances of the times had complicated every aspect of life and most of all the possibilities of travel. It was fall, therefore, before Maximius and Hilary reached Bethlehem. The monk was still full of the enthusiasm of the pilgrim, to whom a windless day at sea was a chance for reading the Scriptures, and a report of bandits on the road ahead a chance for another visit to village shrine and church. But Hilary was weary, weary of travel, weary of rumors of war, weary of endless uncertainty.

Now as they came slowly up the western hill of Bethlehem on their tired asses, it seemed as if the very earth were exhausted. In the fields that fell away in terraces on either side of the road the vines were blackening, the bare stubble of the grain was shrinking into the dun stones, and the olive trees above were turning to smoke. And beyond, the autumn mists were blurring the harsh lines of the hills. In front of them the gray stones of the ancient town piled heavily against the tired light of the autumn sky. And Hilary thought of the weariness of those other travellers, four centuries ago.

But into the exhaustion of the end of the journey came something grimmer when they reached the foot of the hill, with their first sight of the fortress at the top piled against the now fading light of the east. High walls of rectangular stone blocks, with low doors and narrow windows like slots under the flat roofs, made Hilary feel as if here the sorely beset world had drawn itself up to make its last stand against the tempest of its troubles.

And Jerome, whom they found in front of the guest hostel just above the highway, seemed the very embodiment of their embattled age, with the leashed passion of the Gothic warrior and the serene dignity of the Roman general at once in his very stance. He was an old man, Hilary saw, but he had as yet made few of the usual surrenders to age. Only his thick white hair, and his darkly shadowed eyes, and his strongly knotted hands betrayed him. A fighter, and for all the scars of a lifetime of fighting, a formidable one—awed, Hilary signaled to his companion to explain their errand.

Maximius, who seemed to have the gift of keeping his head in the presence of the mighty, proceeded to explain their business with his usual directness. But at the first mention of the name of Severus, the volcanic look on the face of the old warrior melted into a radiant smile, and exclaiming, "Do you really come from Severus?" Jerome flung his arms around his fellow monk.

"Are you from Severus, too?" he asked, looking a little uncertainly at the plain travel-stained tunic and cloak of Hilary, hardly to be distinguished from the habit of his companion. Hilary shook his head, and said simply, "From the Pope and Rome."

"From the Pope and Rome!" and his voice rose on that last magic word.

But he was a perfect host, seeing that his guests had a chance to bathe and take food before he would hear a word more of their travels. And then he led them into a small, bare chapel that carried Hilary's thoughts a world away to a chapel in Gaul, to give thanks for their safe arrival.

But when body and spirit had been thus fortified, he plunged with the eagerness of youth into the news which his visitors could give him. He was, Hilary soon decided, quite as good a listener as the Pope, though in a very different way. For Jerome plunged into his guests' narrative with so lively an interest and so insatiable a curiosity that presently he seemed to Hilary to be a part of it all. He asked endless questions about the cells on the Dordogne, about their devotions, about their work in the surrounding countryside. He asked about the invasion of the barbarians with an obvious dread that surprised Hilary. But he caught Hilary's reaction immediately, and stopped to explain in his husky but still movingly vibrant voice, "It isn't just Gaul. It is all over," and as if he had forgotten his visitors, his voice fell, "I tried to make Rome see years ago, but she has been proud with the pride of Babylon, and her children have given themselves to the fleshpots of Egypt." Suddenly, however, his face brightened, "But a few have seen the handwriting on the wall, and fled from destruction." Then he remembered that he had interrupted Maximius in the middle of his story.

So Maximius recounted the adventures of his journey from Primuliacum. It was the first time Hilary had heard this part of his story, and he listened quite as fascinated as Jerome while Maximius told of how he and his companion picked their way across the path of the invading armies, which he described as like the wake of a forest fire, of how presently they had to dodge fresh invaders, and of how finally they had stumbled at Narnia into the very midst of war.

But he was clearly much less sympathetic with Maximius' interest in Alaric. For Jerome, Alaric was the embodiment of all that threatened civilization—the greed, the ignorance, the envy, the violence of the barbarian world. When Maximius managed to suggest, without putting it into words, the deep interest which the Pope had taken in Alaric's state of mind, Jerome looked astonished. But though he condemned those who had misled Alaric with false promises for their failure to face their problems as men should, he was inclined to agree with the Emperor. He had thought the reliance on Stilicho, and here he spoke with caution, obviously mindful of something which the Pope had written in his introduction of Hilary, badly placed. He caught the flush on Hilary's face, and he hastened to add that he had been impressed by the antique flavor of Stilicho's death, and he had prayed for him.

And then he began to talk of Rome as he remembered it,

and Maximius and Hilary settled back to listen, breaking the radiant monologue only when now and then he asked a direct question. For Jerome's conversation had the sparkling quality of his letters. As he talked, he went way back even to his first days as a student at Rome, when he met Pammachius and was filled with admiration for the high-minded young nobleman who eschewed the pleasures of patrician Rome for his studies. And then he moved on to Milan, the Milan of Theodosius and of Ambrose.

"There were giants in the earth in those days," he said; "men still talked of Ambrose standing at the door of the cathedral in Milan like Christ come to Judgment, and the Emperor slinking away in shame to do penance for the thousands his anger had slain at Thessalonica."

Then he told of his return to Rome after the desert, and Hilary was not sure whether he took it for granted that any man who would take the trouble to come to Jerusalem would know of his desert experience, or whether tonight only Rome was relevant to this golden truce of memory in the life of the old warrior. That had been his first entrance on the stage of the larger world, and as he spoke of it, the old excitement came back to him. He described, too, the wonders of the library of Pope Damasus where he spent many of his free hours turning over ancient manuscripts, with the Pope coming in now and then to enjoy his discoveries. And he recalled the meetings of the pious Christians of the senatorial circle in the palace of Marcella to read Scripture with him and to listen to his exposition of it. It had been a golden time, he said finally, and though no man had ever spoken more sharply than he of the sins of Rome, no man had ever had better reason to hope for the saving of Rome. And now—with a charming apology he asked their forgiveness for his forgetfulness of their fatigue and himself took them to their beds.

But he roused them early the next morning, telling them that the fine autumn weather would not last, and he wanted the pleasure of showing them at least something of the immediate

neighborhood before the winter made the outdoors too diffi-
cut for his stiffening limbs.

So they began with the farthest site, the Field of the Shepherds, and this gave them a chance to become acquainted with
the life of the countryside, now relaxing a little after the long
labors of the fields and the vineyards.

To Maximius every step of the way was clearly an old dream
come true, but to Hilary it was more of a revelation, sometimes
a disconcerting revelation. For when he had thought of the
Holy Land as something different from Bordeaux and the
Bordeaux countryside, he had thought of it as perpetually bathed
in a haze of antique memory and supernatural awe.

So while Maximius exclaimed with delight over finding the
Field of the Shepherds as he imagined it, Hilary was reduced
to silence with astonishment that it looked so different from
what he had expected. Seen now on a sunny morning, it was
brighter than any landscape he had ever seen, with a clearer,
sharper color so that everything stood out more rawly, both the
familiar things and the new. Even the sky seemed a little
brighter in its strange blue. And finally there were the shepherds, not the shepherds of the great story, beings half way between men and angels, but very grubby, strongly fashioned men
in squalid clothing, who were too busy with the prosaic business of sheep-watching, to be listening for any angel songs. That
the Son of God had walked a very poor and humble world
Hilary had learned from the first Christmas sermon he ever
listened to, but it had never occurred to him that it was such
an actual and even in its own strange way commonplace a one.

Suddenly Hilary realized that both of his companions were
looking at him curiously. He hastened to apologize for being
lost in his thoughts, and the puzzled challenge in the face of
Jerome yielded to a smile of pleased recognition.

"You remind me of Paula," he said, "when she first came to
this blessed land." A note of tenderness came into his enthusiasm. "She told me that when she knelt down in the field here,
she could see the light of the star waking the sleeping shepherds,
even though it was noonday when we came here. And though

we were talking all around her, she said she could hear nothing but the shepherds' cries of surprise, and the song of the angels. It was that way everywhere we went."

Hilary had of course heard of Paula in the houses of her son-in-law Pammachius and her old friend Marcella, a bright legendary figure whose very name brought a light to the faces of those who remembered her. There had been some gossip, too, but Jerome might never have heard of it, to judge from the quite unself-conscious fashion in which he spoke of Paula. "I never knew anybody who brought such a fullness of heart to everything she undertook. There was more brightness in her weeping than in most people's laughter," he said as he took them to the Virgin's Inn, and showed where Paula had knelt on the doorstep and wept that there had been no shelter for that most precious of mothers.

"It was then," said Jerome, "that she vowed that she would build a hostel for strangers and pilgrims that never again would anyone be houseless in Bethlehem."

When the next day Jerome invited them to go over to the women's convent to visit Eustochium, Hilary welcomed the idea, for now his vision of Paula would be brought to earth with the actuality of her daughter's presence. But there was nothing of the Paula of yesterday to be discerned in the first appearance of the austere young woman in a dark nun's dress who knelt with such completely unconscious grace for Jerome's blessing. Rather as she rose and waited for Jerome to present his guests, she made him think once more of Gaia. A less surely beautiful Gaia perhaps, certainly a much more haggard and self-disciplined and even self-effacing one, but still with the high dignity and nobility of Gaia.

With surprising sweetness she welcomed Jerome's guests, looking very frankly but briefly at Hilary. And there he decided she was very different from Gaia, for there was nothing speculative in the brief glance she gave him. Rather, Hilary decided, it was like the quick graciousness of the happily married young matron who looks with casual and disinterested kindness on all the human race. But while she answered all their questions readily enough, Hilary noticed a certain look of anxiety that now and then came into her clear face.

Jerome must have perceived Hilary's curiosity, for as they returned to the men's convent, he complained that in the confusion of the times one could no longer be sure of even the pilgrims who came to their gates. And as he spoke, a surprising touch of humility came into his manner.

II

THAT AFTERNOON JEROME TOOK HIS GUESTS away from the main convent buildings to a ridge of bare gray limestone rock, in which a doorway and a window had been cut.

"This," he said, pushing open the door, "is my Paradise." And he led them into a cell hewn out of the living rock. At first sight it seemed completely filled with bookshelves and cupboards and tables heaped high with manuscripts, and ink pots and reed pens, and all the tools of literature.

Then Hilary became aware that scattered among the books and manuscripts were several people, who looked up as they came in, among them a young monk apparently copying a book on a roll of clean yellow-brown paper. Jerome presented the young man to his visitors, and Hilary was surprised to discover that the industrious copyist was the Optatus of Marcella's circle, and a very alert-looking young man, indeed.

Jerome turned to his two young visitors. "There is nothing like a fresh mind for a work like this, that goes on year after year. Can you not wait a little while? The winter is not good for travel. Stay until the sea is open once more, and the visitors come. In the next few months we could get a good deal done."

But Maximius shook his head. "There are certain temptations to which a wise man will not knowingly expose himself. This room is, indeed, the forbidden garden for me. I must go on, not back—Sinai and Egypt and Nitria."

Then Jerome turned to Hilary, with a look that sent him back across the years to one of his masters at Bordeaux, asking him when he was going to stop his daydreaming and really get down to his lessons.

Trying to pull what seemed to him a number of strings together at once, Hilary said slowly, "I can do without the rest of the pilgrimage, but I cannot stay long. When things are a little clearer in Rome and Gaul—"

But when, a few days later, he saw Maximius setting off on foot with a couple of Jerome's younger brethren, for the pilgrimage to the desert, Hilary felt a pang of guilt. It was not that he had succumbed to the temptation which Maximius had rejected, for he had not made the sacrifice which Maximius had made, nor did he ever expect to.

Rather it was the same feeling of guilt he had known when he yielded to the Pope's persuasions and started for the Holy Land. It seemed to him that he had taken shelter from a storm which more valiant men were riding out.

Before he left Italy, Hilary had heard of the fall of Stilicho's enemy Olympius. That Olympius should have to flee for his life to Dalmatia seemed a heartening reminder of the justice of God. And the report that Jovius, an old protégé of Stilicho, had taken his place in the Emperor's favor raised hopes among those who still thought that Honorius might be weaned from the fanaticism of the anti-barbarians. But Hilary remembered how contemptuously Serena had spoken of Jovius' opportunism, and he concluded that there was nothing in the news from Ravenna these days that would suggest a world in which he could imagine himself taking a happy part. So for the present he was not sorry to plead the Pope's counsel, and let the studies which he had thought he must relegate to the margins of an active life take the center for a while.

But in the weeks that soon piled up into months Jerome gave Hilary very little time to think of himself. For Jerome, as soon as he discovered that his new assistant combined almost complete ignorance of theological literature with inexhaustible curiosity and a capacity to stay with any intellectual undertaking that engaged his interest, proceeded to pile upon him an amount of work that would have staggered a more experienced student. And for the first time in his life Hilary saw the work of the man who deals in words not as an essay in self-expression or persuasion, but as a battle for the truth, a battle not unworthy of a valiant man's best efforts even with Alaric still hovering on the outskirts of Rome.

For the mind of Jerome still kept, in the most abstruse discussion of theological abstractions, that constant grip on the flesh-and-blood reality of human experience that had fascinated Hilary when he first heard his letters read aloud by Pammachius or Marcella. The result was that as those weeks passed in the workshop of Jerome, Hilary found that he was not only receiving an introduction to a new field of study but reliving a very great life as if it were his own, indeed, with an excitement he would never have expected to find in his own affairs.

Sometimes Jerome took Hilary to visit the little school which he had founded for the promising boys of the neighborhood. After he had listened to them reading their Virgil and had corrected their quantities, he would ask Hilary to read the lines so that they might have some foretaste of the delight that would be theirs when they had really mastered the verse.

Once, after one of these visits, he told Hilary how he had first come to start the little school. "They were all over us, these little urchins, when we were first building here, more like wild animals than human beings. So I decided to teach them," he began. To his surprise he had discovered that some of them welcomed a chance to learn to read the Scriptures. Then he decided he would take a few of the quickest boys and teach them a little Virgil.

"At first, I was frightened," he admitted with a smile, "for I enjoyed reading Virgil again so much. It seemed as if my own youth had come back to me."

"But I am sure it did them good," said Hilary. "So why were you frightened?"

But Jerome looked at him in surprise. And then he went on to tell of the dream of his youth in which he went to judgment and when he cried on the name of Christ, the devil jeered at him, and said, "Do you dare to claim the privilege of a Christian when everyone knows that you are a Ciceronian?" Even as he recalled the story, a shadow of an old bewilderment gave a look of startling pathos to the monumental face. "I told that traitor Rufinus; and later when a lot of mindless barbarians were gabbing like geese because even on sacred themes I could not forget the humanities which had become a part of the very fabric of my mind, Rufinus carelessly repeated what I had told him, and they snatched it to make me out a pagan."

But Jerome's indignation at those who suspected his love of pagan literature paled beside his wrath at those who had accused him of Judaizing; so he told Hilary how he had come to take up Hebrew in the first place.

It was when he was studying the New Testament. He was shocked to discover how poor and bare the style seemed beside that of the classic writers. Then he began to suspect that the back of the cloth was perhaps richer than the front, and that the colors of that richness came from the Old Testament. So he took up the study of the Old Testament, but that seemed to him even worse, for its obscurity offended his very intelligence. So he turned to the commentators for help. But they seemed to have little to offer him but the literalness of the Roman and the fantasy of the Greek.

"And yet," he said, fixing his eye on Hilary with a certain ruefulness that made the younger man realize for perhaps the first time through what agonies a strong spirit hews itself out of the common human weakness, "I told myself that it was not in the rational beauty of Virgil and Cicero that God had chosen to reveal himself, but in this incoherent medley of fantasy and grossness and sublimity. It was then that I made up my mind that I would learn the original language which the Holy Spirit had honored above all others."

And then he told how he had appealed to some friends in

Tiberias to help him find a Jewish master, and how they had sent him the young rabbi, Baranina.

"He is a valiant man," said Jerome. "He had a hard time persuading the rabbis in the schools at Tiberias that this was not a matter of selling the wisdom of the chosen people for gentile gold. It was a long time before he could make them see that it would do no harm to the Jews to substitute for the caricature of their tradition that so often passes for Old Testament studies the beginnings of an understanding of what those writings meant to the people to whom they were first delivered." And then a rarer smile, of amusement at himself, broke on the face of Jerome. "And he was an even more valiant man when he began to teach me. For Hebrew seemed the most barbarous tongue that had ever attempted literature. Even the Gothic that I learned as a boy to shock my family seemed hardly more primitive. But his love for the language overcame even my obstinacy."

So the old man and the young worked together hours on end. But sometimes Eustochium would come over to the workshop with a couple of her maidens, and then Jerome would read the most recent piece of translation, or the latest section of the commentary. And the anxiety would fade from her eyes, and a look of such pure happiness would light her face that Hilary could hardly bear to look at her. For now it was not of Gaia that he thought but of Rhodope reading Pindar with the careless and complacent schoolboy of Bordeaux. For Eustochium played much more than the role of auditor in the workshop. Her praise, given soberly with her customary reserve of manner and word, obviously gave Jerome greater satisfaction than anything anybody else could say however enthusiastically.

And always before she took her departure with an apology for the call of her household duties, she asked some question that left Jerome thoughtful and preoccupied, often for hours after she had gone. Hilary had often wondered whether Jerome realized how much he depended upon the judgment of the young nun until one day he said thoughtfully, "Never have I found any man that gave me so quick and so constant an understanding as this woman and her mother. Wherever in the years to come men enjoy the fruits of these labors, it seems to me only just that they should be remembered who did so much under God to make them possible, the women, Paula and Eustochium."

But the days were not spent entirely in Paradise. Sometimes Jerome took Hilary to visit some point of interest in the neighborhood of Bethlehem, and sometimes, particularly when the site went back to Old Testament times, Baranina joined the party.

On one of these expeditions into the hills to the east they had been looking at a pile of masonry that, Baranina said, was a stronghold that had been old in the land before ever Moses led the children of Israel out of Egypt. Now only the foundations remained, with a couple of trees growing out of them, fresh and green against the blue of the early spring sky.

Hilary asked the rabbi if he did not sometimes weary of their meticulous interest in every detail of the surroundings of Bethlehem. But the bearded face lighted with a grave smile as he said, "You forget that this is David's country, too."

But Baranina, when he caught the sudden compassion in Hilary's face, shrugged his strong shoulders. "It is only for a time. We shall return." And then as Hilary looked at him curiously, he smiled. "The empires come and go."

But Jerome broke in sharply, "You forget that this is Rome."

The Jewish rabbi said nothing but looked over the silvergreen of the olive trees and the pink of the flowering almonds to the bluish gray line of the Dead Sea. Then he turned to his friend, and very thoughtfully he repeated the word, "Rome," and Hilary wondered if he were aware that his warmly pleasant voice had risen ever so slightly as he spoke. Presently they started back for Bethlehem. And as they went along through patches of narcissus and scarlet anemones, Jerome said happily, "Now I can really get at Ezechiel," and they all laughed to think that the return of the spring should give a man appetite for the most catastrophic of all the prophets. But Baranina only shrugged his shoulders and smiled as one might at a loved child who cannot possibly know what his elders are talking about. And then he said gayly, "To Ezechiel by all means. He is older than Rome, and—" but he did not finish the sentence.

The coming of the spring brought visitors, too. Among the first were some merchants coming overland from Constantinople to Alexandria, who reported that Alaric had lost all patience with Honorius and offered the Romans deliverance if they would accept a new emperor. So they had agreed on Attalus and invested him with the purple.

"Attalus!" exclaimed Hilary.

But Jerome shook his head. "A Greek from Antioch! Of course, he would jump at the chance."

And when a little later some monks on their way to the desert reported Attalus' baptism by an Arian bishop, and rumors that he was expected to reopen the pagan temples and turn over some of the Roman churches to the Arians, Jerome snorted, "What else could you expect of a Greek huckster?" And Hilary, remembering the patron of Attis and Claudian, stared openmouthed.

But when later in the summer other pilgrims brought the news that Attalus and Alaric had fallen out, Jerome was delighted, and his satisfaction was in no way qualified when they added that Alaric was said to be leaving Rome for Ravenna. So the fog of rumor continued to drift into the bright sunshine of Bethlehem all through the summer. Some of their visitors talked about the breaking-out of civil war as perhaps more to be feared than even the barbarians, but Jerome refused to listen to them. Heretics and adventurers and renegades were bad enough, but the barbarians were the real foe. And yet it could not be said that Jerome really worried about Alaric. "One of these days Rome will rouse herself," he predicted with confidence.

It was the end of September now, and the visitors were falling off. Even the short distance from the highway along the coast to Bethlehem was to be considered carefully by travellers mindful of the autumn rains. So Jerome was more pleased than usual to hear that an old friend had come to the hostel.

He was Arsacius, a Syrian merchant, who, Jerome went on

to explain, had often, in the old days before their monasteries had become so nearly self-sustaining, brought them goods that they badly needed. Now Jerome imagined Eustochium might have some weaving which the trader would be glad to have in exchange for the medicines which she gave to all their neighbors. "And," said Jerome happily, "he will bring us news of those rascals in Italy."

But the long, sallow face of the merchant, whom they found eating his supper in the guest house with a circle of younger monks standing around him, looked even longer when Jerome asked him for news of Rome. "Nothing much, nothing sure," he muttered uncomfortably, and Jerome made no attempt to stay the younger brethren when the bell began to ring for the evening service. Only when everybody had gone but Hilary did Jerome begin to press his uneasy guest.

Arsacius pushed the empty bowl away and began to crumble the fragment of bread still remaining on the bare board table. Then he answered Jerome's urging in a low, hurried voice as if he dreaded to be overheard. "All I can say is what I heard just before I left Illyricum. Alaric has lost all patience and has entered Rome."

For a moment Hilary was astonished that the familiar little guest refectory with its whitewashed walls and its bare oaken roof beams, and its long board table and benches still stood as always. Only something reeled inside the pit of his stomach, and then he steadied himself to look at the startled face of the Syrian merchant, and from him to the face of Jerome, white as if he had suddenly seen a ghost and could not believe his eyes and could not deny the witness of his shivering spine.

But Jerome steadied, too, and Hilary saw the knuckles of his strong hands whiten as they clutched at the edge of the table, "And you did not stay to check the rumor?"

But this time it was the Syrian merchant who could not believe the evidence of his senses. "Stay to have my little boat sunk under the rush of the fugitives?" And the unmistakably sincere astonishment of the question carried a conviction that could not be denied.

Later that evening when, as was his wont, Hilary went into the monastery chapel for a last supplication before the dim altar, he saw a dark, solid mass huddled in the light of the single lamp. The current of air set in motion by his entrance made the pale light shiver for a moment, and he saw the white head of Jerome fixed and unmoving. And Hilary stole silently from the chapel to his sleepless bed.

III

IT SEEMED UNBELIEVABLE THAT THE BELL OF THE monasteries rang out in the gray dawn of the next morning, seemingly as unaware as the birds chattering in the trees around the great fortress, that the world had ended. But it picked Hilary up from the night's prostration and with the slow swing of its failing sound it moved him like a puppet into the mechanism of the day's routine.

In the chapel Jerome was in his usual place near the altar, his rugged face seemingly frozen in the concentration of prayer. And as the morning office proceeded, it seemed to Hilary that he clung to the performance of the familiar act of worship as a shipwrecked man might cling to a spar in a rough sea. Some whisper of Arsacius' story must have found its way into the monastery, for a shock of excited expectation went through the chapel when Jerome rose in his place at the conclusion of the service and raised his arm for attention. But all he did was to announce that a guest had brought a rumor of the entrance of Alaric into Rome, and he asked them all to kneel and pray with him for the safety, physical and spiritual, of their brethren in Rome. Then he bade them all go to the day's work which God had given them to do, without wasting time on futile speculation.

Jerome set the example himself by going at once to his workshop cave, and taking the Hebrew version of the book of Ezechiel into his hands. But although he held the roll firmly, Hilary noticed that even at the end of several minutes he had made no effort to unroll it. Only when Eustochium came to the door, did he seem to be aware of what was going on about him, and he looked startled when she asked him if it would be all right if she did not buy any parchment from Arsacius this time but took the whole value of their weaving in medicines. As he nodded his approval, he still looked incredulous, but Hilary noticed that when she had gone, he unrolled another page.

Almost a week went by before they had any more news. And then a couple of monks who had been down to the seaport of Caesarea to pick up some books which Jerome wanted from the bishop's library there returned and asked to see Jerome at once. They had talked with the sailors on a boat which had just arrived from Ostia, and they said that when they sailed, Alaric was in Rome, and his troops were putting the city to the sack.

Unable to bear the look on Jerome's face, Hilary tried to remind him of what Maximius had said of Alaric. Surely he who had professed such a veneration for Rome would have made some effort to restrain his troops. Moreover, Alaric and many of his commanders were themselves Christians, even if Arians.

But these assurances Jerome rejected almost contemptuously. "The hatred of the heretic for the orthodox is one of the world's most savage hatreds. And no man who has loosed an army on a city can hope to control it." Jerome looked at Hilary with an indignation in his face that implied that he had dared to defend the indefensible, but Hilary noted with relief that Jerome's anger had at least warmed the terribly frozen look on his face, and he made no effort to defend himself.

Presently, Jerome received reinforcement for his despair from an unexpected quarter. Baranina who had gone home for a couple of Hebrew commentaries on Ezechiel had come in as they were talking. And now having laid the linen-wrapped scrolls on Jerome's working table, he stood listening.

"He is quite right, you know," he said quietly to Hilary.

"There are always a couple of days and nights when an army runs mad. There is nothing that any man can do."

And Hilary thought to himself, "He is thinking of Jerusalem again!"

Jerome must have had something the same thought, for he looked at Baranina and flushed a little. And then he said, "Let us get at Ezechiel." But Baranina shook his head, "Not just now, my friend. It will have to wait."

The stubborn look that Hilary had come to know these last weeks as the sure sign that Jerome was battling with himself came into his face again. Baranina met it calmly as if he, too, understood it. "I have told my wife to have the whole household ready to go to Tiberias tonight. When the storm breaks, it is better to be with one's brethren."

"When the storm breaks!" echoed Jerome, as if he wondered what Baranina thought he was waiting for. But Baranina met his glance firmly, and then his face softened. "You have heard only the report of it, my friend." And then as he took his leave, he said to Jerome in a low voice, "God will not forget his own."

Jerome was still standing by the table on which Baranina had left his rolls, looking at the door out of which he had gone, when Eustochium appeared. As always, her low voice seemed to recall him to his surroundings. But her request startled him.

"Will you ask Paulinian to send some of his men out to bring more grain in from the farms? I have set my maidens to baking all the grain we have." And then as he looked at her in puzzlement, she said, still quietly, "We shall need it all."

The next day Hilary remembered what Baranina had said, for the first trickle of refugees came up the highway to the guest house. Eustochium fed them, and then Jerome came in to talk with them. But it was clear that they gave him no comfort. They were various types of agents and dealers, who had shrewdly taken their measure of the situation in Rome, and had known how in the final panic to get shipping. Hilary noticed that Jerome made no effort to detain them, and most of them moved on quickly enough.

But a few stayed to make inquiries about the possibilities of

trade in the neighborhood. One or two offered to buy up the sur-
plus wheat, and when Paulinian, the procurator, replied that
they would need it themselves for their guests, they raised the
price which they had offered. And when this, too, was declined,
one was overheard to say that he had no idea that even the
Christians in this part of the world were so backward as not to
know a business opportunity when it was presented to them.

Jerome looked relieved when they moved on, and Hilary
thought that this vanguard of what one might call the camp
followers of Rome had accomplished one good thing at least.
They had roused Jerome from his mood of tragic despair to
something like his old indignation at the contemplation of
human rascality.

But the quarters which they occupied had barely been
cleaned out before another crowd of refugees arrived, still in
fair condition but loud in their complaints about the sufferings
they had undergone. These, Jerome soon found, were mainly
rich Romans who had left for their country estates to the south
or their villas on the coast at the first rumor of Alaric's approach,
and had maintained their accustomed way of life through all
the days of Rome's agony. But when Rome fell, and Alaric was
reported to be moving south, they had rushed to the ports
and bought up all the available shipping.

The shipowners, unlike the monks of Bethlehem, had recognized a business opportunity when they saw it. They had sold
the same facilities not once but several times, and some of the
most delicately nourished of the upper circles of Rome had
found themselves herded into dank and filthy vessels that a
careful slave dealer would have protested out of regard for the
protection of his investment.

There had been the terror of the sea, too, and the added fear
of pirates who had carried off several vessels under their very
eyes. And always there had been the threat of the ship captains
that they would sell the whole complaining lot to the slave
dealers, hovering like vultures along their course.

Many of these forlorn wretches bore names that Jerome recalled from his youth, and with the habit of their class they

recalled to him their fathers or their grandfathers, who had always, they swore, expressed the greatest admiration for the man whom they had helped to hound out of Rome. And the monks and nuns of the monastery looked through their ranks to discover all sorts of cousins and uncles and aunts, who embraced with noisy relief the young fanatics whom they had so shamefacedly disowned anywhere from one to a dozen years ago. With the habitual respect of their class for prestige of any sort they stood in awe of Jerome, but they talked readily enough with Hilary. And afterward Hilary and Jerome put together their garnerings of fact and conjecture.

They did not amount to much. None of these people had been in Rome at the time of Alaric's entrance. They had talked with fugitives, and they had been horrified by the fantastic stories they had heard of looting and destruction, of murder of senators and of rape of some of Rome's noblest matrons and maidens. Some of them believed that Alaric had levelled Rome in the three days of his stay there. Others reported that all the slaves of Rome had seized their masters' wealth and run away to join Alaric's army.

"But not even Alaric could level Rome in three days," said Hilary, and, worried as he was, Jerome agreed. But clearly there was something to the slave story, for apparently all the slaves in these parties had been promised liberation, and, to judge from their demeanor, had taken the promise for the fact.

But as they sat talking, the old monk who was responsible for the novices came in to ask if he might speak to Jerome. He was troubled about a number of his charges. They had parents and younger brothers and sisters in Rome, and they had been frightened by the reports of the refugees. Eustochium's young women had been frightened, too, he had learned when he talked with her after Vespers, but she had kept them so busy all day caring for their guests that most of them were too worn-out to lie awake agonizing over their relatives.

Jerome shook his head. "They will have to get used to it," and he looked at Hilary.

"I think," said the latter gently, "that you will find that the worrying now will blunt a little the shock if bad news comes, and it will make them more"—he hesitated—"thankful if it does not." And he looked up to find Jerome's deep-set eyes regarding him inscrutably.

Then Jerome turned to the novice master, "Surely with all this mess you can find enough for them to do to keep them from thinking about themselves."

But what was troubling the older monk was the maintenance of the regular schedule of training and of observance in the monastery. Jerome was clearly irritated by the man's fussiness in the presence of so much greater worries. "I will think about it tomorrow," he said at last.

But it proved quite unnecessary, for the morrow brought such a flood of refugees that, after staggering under the first impact of the deluge, every able-bodied man and woman in both institutions was so busy that there was no time even to think of anything else. For the ships dumping their helpless human cargo on the bare sand of the shore brought men and women who had been in Rome when Alaric came, and who had seen and heard and felt in their own minds and bodies the horror of the fall of the city.

Curiously enough, they were much quieter than those who had heard only the rumor of its horror. They had made no protest when the sailors dumped them pell-mell out of their boats. They seemed to think it only natural that the ship captains should hurry back for those not so fortunate, and they made no complaint of extortion or abuse. Some of them by the time they reached Bethlehem were too exhausted with hunger and sickness to move from where they had dropped by the side of the highway at the foot of the first hill. Others simply sat by their aged or ill, trying to recruit their vanished strength to help them. There were children, too, whimpering in their mothers' or nurses' arms, or standing uncertainly on shaky legs with large eyes solemnly surveying the world out of white, unchildlike faces. For Hilary the mask of the generic passivity of this human flotsam and jetsam was ripped off only when he caught sight of a young girl sitting huddled by the roadside with her face in her hands, shivering so that her whole body shook convulsively.

Starting out in the morning chill, Hilary had thrown a short cloak over his tunic. This he now took from his shoulders and gently wrapped around her, but when she felt the pressure of his hand on her back, the young girl leaped to her feet with a scream. Embarrassed by what he thought his clumsiness, Hilary stepped back and looked around for help. But nobody seemed alarmed. Only an old woman who had been sitting by her rose and wrapped the cloak around her. Then she turned to Hilary, almost apologetically, "I have told her it's happened to thousands of others, but it's no use."

And then as Hilary tried to murmur something comforting, the old woman sighed with unexpected relief, "At least, thank God, she did not jump into the sea as some of the others did."

Eustochium shuddered when Hilary told her about the girl, and then with her usual calm directness went off to find her in the little crowd that the monks had finally brought up on their mules to the guest house. And Hilary went to the grotto of the Church of the Nativity for a brief prayer for those others of whose fate they had as yet not heard.

So they worked that day and many days after. The guest house soon gave out, although the merely exhausted as soon as they had recovered their strength a little with food and rest gave up their beds and staggered down to the beaches to help with the later arrivals.

In spite of the fact that Eustochium brought in some of the women of the neighborhood to help, the linens for the injured gave out, and only rags could be found for the newborn. And medicine gave out, too, and wine for the sick, and oil, and presently there was not enough wheat for the morrow's bread, and some of the older monks went out to beg from their neighbors. And then a day came when there was no bread, nothing but fresh water and kind words to carry down to the new arrivals at the foot of the hill.

That day some merchants came with the promise of a cargo of wheat, which they were ready to sell at a preposterous price.

217

Hilary tried to remember which of their guests had jewels and gold hidden in their rags, which they might be willing to give to the common need, but Jerome exploded when he told him what he was doing. And he went out to where they stood outside the procurator's office waiting complacently in the pleasant sunshine. And he asked them whether they were Christians or pagans. And when they answered eagerly, as if it would make him readier to close the bargain, that they were good Christians, he hurled at them such a flood of invective for greed and inhumanity that they cowered before him. "Rome may have fallen," he thundered, "but God has not fallen. His justice will follow you to the ends of the earth and choke you with the gold you have coined of the pangs of the starving."

So deep was the shock of the men at his indignation that they offered him the cargo on credit for what it had cost them. And the monks stoked the fires in the bakehouse half the night. But Jerome as he turned away with Hilary said, "I think we may do something with Ezechiel yet." And for the first time something like hope seemed to have come into his stricken face.

IV

AS THOSE TROUBLED DAYS PASSED INTO WEEKS, the very air in the monasteries of Jerome and Eustochium seemed alive with rumor and conjecture. But it was astonishing how little that was either precise or comprehensive emerged from the unending talk over what had or had not happened to Rome. It seemed rather as if in the general inundation of misfortune each man had been walled off in his own particular little whirlpool of private terror. If the apartment house in which he lived had been fired, then he thought most of Rome had gone up in the flames. If his own house, more solidly built of stone, had survived, then he was inclined to think that the shell of Rome still stood but that everything of value had been swept out of it.

Almost all had seen some violence, but unless it had been a member of their immediate family who was involved, they had felt powerless to intervene, and Hilary, at least, felt sure that they were right, although there were some romantics among the younger monks who thought they would have done something about it.

It was only in the later stages of the flood, when those who had been through the sack of Rome and had fled from the chaos of the abandoned city came, that anything like a larger view began to emerge. It was clear that there had been a number of fires in various parts of the city, and at the height of the confusion a high wind had risen to blow the flames into what some frightened observers described as a rain of fire and brimstone from heaven. Several refugees arriving at different times reported that the gardens of Sallust had been completely destroyed. And there were two different reports that much of the Caelian was gone, including, it seemed clear, the house where Fortunatus and Hilary had lived.

But some comfort also emerged from this mosaic of personal fragments of experience. There was the fact, attested by a number of refugees, that Alaric had given orders that the shrines of the Apostles must be respected, so that the great basilicas of Saint Peter and Saint Paul became refuges for the women and children who could reach them. And there was the story told by Anatolus, a young Christian poet whom Hilary had once met at the house of Laeta, of the great procession of the sacred treasure.

"It was," said the young man, now at his ease in the workshop of Jerome, "the most extraordinary procession that you ever saw even in Rome." He was not entirely sure about how it had begun. But he had heard that a Gothic soldier had broken into a house in a poor section of the city and found only an old woman there. When he asked her if she had any treasure, she showed him several chests of gold and silver objects, which he, being a Christian, recognized as altar vessels and ornaments.

"She told him," said the young poet, "that since she did not have the strength to keep them from him, she would not make the effort. But she reminded him that the treasure belonged to the Apostles, and God would avenge any sacrilege. That must have frightened him, for he went to Alaric, and he gave orders that the treasure was to be carried to the tomb of Peter, and that all who helped to carry it there should be given safe-conduct."

Then the young man smiled. "Everything was at its worst then, but that got round soon enough. You should have seen the procession, one man or woman to each platter or chalice, holding them high above their heads so that what they carried might be seen. They went in a single file with all the barbarians watching them hungrily but not daring to touch them for fear of Alaric. And frightened as I was, I laughed in my garret to see pagans I knew clinging to a cross or cup they would have scoffed at a week ago. That was funny," said Anatolus, beginning to laugh at the memory, and then subsiding uneasily when no one joined him.

But there were other things that he did not want to laugh at and that filled some of his audience with fresh horror. Only here he lacked any precise information about individuals. Everybody said some of Rome's noblest women had been taken captive, including the Emperor's own sister, Galla Placidia. There was a story that some had been sold to the slave dealers, but he was not sure but that they were holding them for ransom. It was then that he remembered a curious story which seemed to have appealed to his obvious sense of the ironic.

"You know, they say it was Proba Faltonia who let Alaric into Rome, and then she had to give everything she had to save her own granddaughter from rape."

But Hilary protested that he could not believe that; he knew Proba Faltonia, and she would not betray her city. So indignant was Hilary that Anatolus lost something of his look of glib knowingness. But he insisted that a good many people believed the story, recalling that Proba Faltonia had said that the suffering of the people of Rome had gone far enough when there was nobody to bring them any hope of relief. Jerome who doubtless remembered Proba in her elegant youth did not seem much interested. Instead he asked if the poet had heard anything about the Pope, and Pammachius, and Marcella. But Anatolus knew nothing about any of these people, except for the Pope. Innocent had been on an embassy to Ravenna to see if he could not persuade the Emperor to change his mind and send some relief to the city. He certainly was not in Rome at the time of Alaric's entrance.

When Hilary asked him if he had heard anything about Gaia or Thermantia, he smiled again and said, "I never flew that high." But presently Hilary heard from the maid of one of their guests that Thermantia had won much love in the district where she lived, because she had used the respect of the barbarian soldiers for her father to protect her poor neighbors. And when Hilary asked the woman how she knew, she said it was from some Gallic weavers from whom she had ordered some heavy cloth for her mistress. But she could tell Hilary nothing more of the weavers than that when she had gone to collect it before she left, they had said they would stay where they were. They had fled far enough.

It was another ancient handmaiden still faithful to her impoverished and helpless mistress who first mentioned the name of Gaia. She had been telling of her struggle to save her mistress from the barbarian slave dealers who had come into Rome with Alaric's soldiers. Hilary asked her if she knew any of the women who had been carried off, and she named two or three, including the young widow, Gaia Cornelia. Curiously steady now that the blow had fallen, Hilary asked her if she was sure, and she answered she was because she knew Gaia and her house, having accompanied her mistress to receptions there.

In the next few days more women came up to the guest house who had heard of the seizure of the senatorial ladies. It had evidently been etched deeply into the minds of all of them, for as one bookseller's wife said, "If it could happen to them, what chance was there for us?" But none of them had anything more to contribute to the personal question. And again in the night watches Hilary tortured himself—if he had gone back to Rome, if he had remained in Gaul; and again, something deep within his consciousness asked, who was he to think that of all men— and he fell into uneasy sleep.

The flood had now passed its peak. Most of the earlier arrivals, discovering how limited were the monasteries' resources, were drifting off, some to the south toward Egypt, some to the north toward Constantinople.

Then came two visitors who were able to satisfy the curiosity of the monasteries and to give them something like an adequate notion of the extent of the disaster which had befallen Rome. The first was a monk, a messenger from Pammachius. Jerome embraced him with delight, and sent Hilary to bring Eustochium to hear his news. But Hilary and Eustochium, when they returned to the workshop, found Jerome with his head in his hands, and the messenger standing beside him weeping, with a surprised look on his face as if he had not known that he had any tears left.

"Pammachius is dead," said Jerome to Eustochium, but there was a touch of remoteness to his voice as if he could not expect her to understand. And in the distress with which Eustochium looked at him, Hilary was surprised to see how young her face, which he had watched growing so thin and tired-looking in these last weeks, could look. And then he understood how baffled she must feel at this crumpling of Jerome before memories of his youth, so impossibly long past to her imagination.

Suddenly Jerome seemed to get a grip on himself, driven thereto, Hilary suspected, by Eustochium's helplessness. "How did he die?" And then with a sudden horror, "They did not kill him, did they?"

"Not directly," said the man, who seemed to realize for the first time what he had done, and he hastened to add, "Almost the last thing he said to us was that no one was to be blamed for his dying. It was God's will, and that was all he had asked for for a long time. He caught the fever from the sick whom he had nursed in his hospital at Ostia, and he could not resist it, for he was so tired."

And then the monk went on to tell of the death of Marcella, which of all the deaths of the time had most distressed Pammachius. "She was alone with Principia in her palace when the barbarians broke in, and they could not believe that it was so bare because she had given her wealth away. They were angry. And then they saw the young Principia." The messenger paused, and at the horror in Jerome's face he added hastily, "She saved Principia, but she herself was beaten nearly to death. And when they let her take refuge in the basilica of Saint Paul, she lived only a couple of days." But Jerome looked so desolate, so beyond all comfort, that Hilary took the monk away, leaving Eustochium kneeling at her master's feet.

And while Pammachius' messenger ate the slender meal that was all the guest-house refectory could furnish these days, Hilary tried again to find out about the people he knew. But the monk had obviously been too preoccupied with the troubles of Pammachius and his friends to pay much attention to the flood of rumors about strangers. One story he had remembered, however. Fabius had been nearly killed trying to protect his father's letters from some barbarian looters. His recovery obviously seemed to the monk hard to square with the death of good Christians like Pammachius.

The next day brought the second messenger, an old woman who had come to the guest house with some African traders, and asked to see Hilary. She had a letter for him. Hilary, when he went into the guest house, was struck by the dignity of the veiled figure sitting there with the face hidden by the angle of the veil. It seemed to him that all the grief of the last days had frozen in the still folds of the dark gray robe and veil. And then the figure turned to him and sprang to life.

It was Attis, but an Attis so suddenly aged, so astonishingly surrendered to that age, that Hilary stared at her. And something of the old light came back to her face as she smiled a little wryly at him. No, she reassured him, she had not herself suffered.

"You forget, that I had seen the signs of the doomed city

before. So I went down to Ostia just before Alaric closed in. And there I found these people whom I used to know in Egypt."

"But where are you going now?"

"Back to Africa. Rome is all over, Hilary," she said gently. And then she gave him a letter. "It is from Medoc at Ostia. You will be going back to Gaul, too."

He shook his head. "That can wait. From what you yourself said, Attis, Africa is not Rome."

She shrugged her shoulders with something of the old cynical lightness. "I have grown wiser. Civilization is not a fixed thing. It does not stay forever in one place."

"You sound a bit like the Pope, Attis, but," and here he became aware of a certain tension in her usual sureness, "you didn't come to see me just to talk philosophy?"

A look of tenderness lighted the ravaged face. "You had better stick to philosophy, Hilary. She is the only mistress you are likely to have now."

A chill ran through Hilary's mind as he thought of the rumor that had been nagging at every hour of waking consciousness these last days. "Gaia?"

"Yes."

"Then they did take her away?" And remembering the company in which she had come, he cried suspiciously, "Do you know where she is?"

She looked at him pityingly. "My companions are honest traders, Hilary!" And then as he made a gesture of apology, she went on more gently, "But they thought that other boat that kept so carefully away from us might be slavers. It was just before we reached Caesarea. It was a beautiful day, not a bad day for one's last glimpse of this world, Hilary."

"But what happened?" His mouth was dry, and his whisper sounded hoarse even to himself.

"We saw somebody on that ship, two people in fact. The sudden motion startled us, for usually you could see only the helmsman and a couple of sailors. And then one of the figures sprang to the prow of the ship, and for just a second stood there. It was a woman, standing like a figurehead with her robe blowing back from her body in the breeze. The other figure seemed just to touch her when she sprang up into the blue sky like some great white bird, and then suddenly she fell—into the sea."

"But could you see her clearly enough to be sure?"

"No, but that night when we landed, some of our people heard a couple of men talking in one of the waterfront taverns. One was blaming the other for not having agreed to ransom the Cornelia woman. She had said she would kill herself if they did not let her go. And the next day the story was all over the port. At the time I had thought of Gaia, and wondered why I did, for I had not heard of her capture then."

The room darkened, and the face of Attis gleamed and was gone. Hilary clutched the edge of the table between them.

"Hilary," came the voice of Attis from far away, "I didn't know you cared so much."

"She was Rome," he said simply, and then he buried his head in his hands.

When he lifted his head again, he was alone, and Medoc's letter was lying on the table. With trembling hands he broke the seal, but the lines blurred. Finally, with a great effort he managed to hold them still enough to make out their sense. Medoc was going to Campania in the spring, and he asked Hilary to meet him at Nola. The letter ended with its one reference to the troubles of the times, "As for Rome, I think you had better study to forget her."

That night after Vespers Hilary took Medoc's letter to Jerome in his cave. Jerome read it without comment. Only at the end he looked at Hilary and murmured, "If I forget thee, Jerusalem!" He seemed to be talking to himself. Then he sighed. "Sometimes I wonder if men will go on speaking Latin even." But Hilary hastened to remind him of Latin-speaking Gaul.

"I suppose so," said Jerome doubtfully. "One used to think if Rome were only converted. And now—" Then he looked at Hilary. "I suppose you feel you should look after your estates?"

Hilary shrugged his shoulders.

"I had hoped you would stay and help me with Ezechiel. You are sure you ought not to?"

To his surprise Hilary answered quite firmly, "Yes." Jerome looked at him speculatively, "Has it ever occurred to you that God might have preserved you for some special purpose of His?" So put, the question did not seem presumptuous.

Quite humbly, Hilary answered it, "I am beginning to wonder."

V

ONE THING ONLY JEROME HAD ASKED OF HILARY, and that was that he should extend the African break of his journey to include Hippo and deliver a letter to his old friend Augustine. This Hilary was glad to do, for he had still on his conscience the letter which he had promised the Pope in what now seemed a long-distant past to carry to the great bishop. There was, too, a sentence which Jerome had once quoted to him, of which only the gist now remained in his memory, "A man will run all over the creation to look for God, and all the time He is there at home waiting for him in his own spirit." That summed up very well, Hilary thought, what was now slowly emerging from the depths of his own consciousness. He would like to see the man who had found words for it.

As the ship tossed on its way from Palestine to Africa, Hilary lay on deck, pretending to sleep in the shadow of the sail, and trying to bring some order into the chaos of impressions that these last years had brought. In the beginning he had tried to apply some of the things he had learned from Jerome, to organize his experience as the biblical commentators had organized theirs. But something eluded him. He was no philosopher; he was too enmeshed in all the imaginative and emotional implications of what happened to him. He could not even contemplate the experience of other people without this intense personal involvement.

In a way this surprised him. For it seemed to him that it was precisely in the personal world that the slate had been wiped cleanest.

In the clearing sight of these last months he did not have many illusions left. Time had dug a pit between him and his first love Rhodope deeper even than the grave that held his sister. And he had known before he left Rome that Gaia would never marry anyone he could dream of being. But diving into the sea, she had carried with her a whole complex of possibilities that now seemed as closed to Hilary as if she had been indeed his betrothed. It was that realization that left Hilary so empty.

And it was that emptiness that made him so indifferent to the day-long arguments and debates that raged over his closed eyes. For the ship was full of fugitives of all sorts—Romans, and foreigners who had been accustomed to get their living in one fashion or another from Rome. They had all one thing in common. They had fled from Rome in fear of her present and in despair of her future. And like Hilary they were far enough away now from the first impact of the crash of their world to begin to think it over. And although they were for the most part quite unreflective men of action, they were asking themselves how it came to happen.

A few of the Romans still held to the theory that Rome had been betrayed from within by the barbarians. But none of the foreigners would agree to that. They claimed that the betrayal of Rome from within was of a quite different sort, that Rome had betrayed herself. And from the petulance that now and then came into the voices Hilary thought that he could detect a personal resentment that Rome to whom they had transferred whatever loyalty they were capable of should have proved so little worthy of their trust.

Idly listening, to gain a little respite from his own thoughts, Hilary thought of the contempt which Jerome would have felt for them, rats scurrying down the frayed ropes of a doomed ship. But at least they challenged the Romans to look at the disaster again. And now the argument sharpened. For always, however it began, it presently took two directions. There were the pagans who were sure that it was the Romans' failure to continue the ancient worship of their gods that had finally lost them the victory that worship had given them in the first place. And from that it was but a step to laying the blame on the Christians who had destroyed the state's ancient cult.

But the Christians no less passionately rebutted that line of reasoning. It was the paganism of Rome that had destroyed her. The Apostles themselves had brought the Gospel to Rome, and the martyrs with their blood had made Rome a holy place. But the pagans had refused to see the light, and the result was the judgment of God on their blindness.

However, it seemed to Hilary that the Christians were still worried over that pagan argument from success or failure, and he began to wonder if success or failure was a very good argument for Christians to use any way. Irrelevantly his thoughts went back to his youthful puzzlement over providence. It was a difficult business then; now, taken more largely with the fate of the world at stake, he began to wonder if Augustine might have any ideas on that old problem.

But the first sight of the town of Hippo was so extraordinarily different from anything Hilary had expected that it very effectively drove out of his mind the preoccupations of the voyage. A mean little agglomeration of low-lying whitewashed buildings stretched along a flat sandy shore. There was no charm of landscape in sight to give distinction to the setting, no suggestion of architectural grace to break the dull skyline. It was hard to believe that this commonplace scene was one of the great centers of the Christian world, as both the Pope and Jerome had called it.

Equally modest was the low, white-washed pile of the bishop's palace, where a smiling negro youth welcomed him and led him into a small room with a deeply recessed window to wait. Hilary went over to the window and through an opening between high white walls saw the blue sea sparkling in the afternoon sun against an even bluer sky. To the weary traveller it seemed such a miraculous refuge of peace and security that he was startled to hear a light footstep behind him.

There was a sense of great strength leashed and yet something of grace in the keen face with the shadowed cheekbones and the large nose and the full lips so firmly held. It was easy to believe that the man Hilary faced had lived the almost legendary life of the two worlds of sense and spirit, which brought a light to men's faces whenever they spoke of Augustine. And then Hilary forgot the legend in the warmth of the voice, so unexpectedly soft and rich.

"The porter thought you said Jerome," he began as he took the letters from Hilary. Then he smiled at his guest. "Pammachius and the Pope and Jerome are impressive witnesses for any young man to carry with him. Now tell me about Jerome."

He listened with complete absorption while his guest told of the last months at Jerusalem. Hilary scrupulously refrained from any suggestion of personal comment or interpretation, but Augustine guessed quickly enough at what he had not said, for when Hilary finished, he observed thoughtfully, "Jerome has fought so many battles that it is easy to forget how greatly he has loved, too."

Then he asked Hilary when he had left Rome, and how the Pope had been. And presently with deft, impersonal questions he was drawing out the story of those last Roman days. To his surprise Hilary found himself speaking of them as briefly and objectively as if it had all happened a long time ago to somebody else. And Augustine listened with the same warm interest. Only when Hilary came to Stilicho's name, did the bishop look startled, and then he said gently as if to remind himself of something he ought not to forget, "A young man who does not at some time or other defend a bad cause will probably never do much for a good."

But when Hilary began to plead for the dead general, Augustine stopped him with the direct question, "Did the Pope know about this relation with Stilicho?"

"Yes," said Hilary stoutly, "and everybody else"—and then he added with sudden embarrassment—"who knew me." Augustine smiled, and his face grew more thoughtful, as if he were weighing evidence in a very finely adjusted balance. "The Pope has always been interested in the barbarians, as of course he should be. But it has been more than that. I think he has been more hopeful of them than any man I know."

"Hopeful," Hilary repeated in surprise. And Augustine nodded, "And God grant that he may be right."

And then clenching his long hands, he went on, "They can hardly be worse than some of the Romans we have seen here, even in high place, who saw in this catastrophe only a chance to pick up a little wreckage for themselves." The sensitive face with the moving light on the firmly molded features hardened. "They robbed the refugees and held them for ransom. They even sold them to the slavers. Romans sold Romans to Romans for slavery among the barbarians and the enemies whom Rome once held in awe!" The warm voice shook with horror.

But he stopped at the sickness in Hilary's face, and he went on more quietly, "It is like an earthquake; when one thinks the ground firm again under one's feet, then the after-shocks begin, and the buildings one had thought shock-proof crumble before one's eyes. And then one knows how happy was the wretchedest of the days that are past."

But, as he spoke, the sea breeze came in the open window and fluttered the papers on the table before it. Augustine sat down, motioning to his guest to take a low chair on the opposite side.

"Now and then, I do a little with this," he said wistfully, pointing to the manuscript.

"What is it about?" asked Hilary.

"I am not sure." And then, becoming aware of his guest's surprise, he leaned forward as if he would try again to get straight something which still baffled him. "With all you have seen of the refugees, you must have heard them arguing yourself."

Hilary smiled, "I tried to sleep, but I am sure I missed very little of it, for they went round and round the same point like a chariot race. The pagans said it was because they had abandoned the old gods that Rome fell. And the Christians said it was because Rome had been obstinate and rejected the one true God, that Rome fell."

"And what do you think?" The voice of the bishop was gently insistent.

But Hilary hesitated. "I am not a philosopher, you know. But it doesn't seem to me quite so simple as either made out."

"That doesn't sound at all unphilosophic to me," said Augustine, "at least for a beginning."

"That is really all I thought of then," said Hilary. "But since we have been talking now, I have remembered what Jerome's Jewish master, Baranina, said. He said, 'The empires come and go.'"

The speculative look on the face of Augustine sharpened. For a moment he watched through the open window a dozen or so small birds in a trailing rope of flight across the sunset. Then he looked at Hilary. "What did Jerome say to that?"

Hilary tried to remember. He could see the face of Jerome clearly enough, but how much of it was words and how much look he could not tell. "I am not sure. I think it was something like, 'But this is Rome.'"

Augustine smiled ruefully. "And I suppose Baranina thought that we are as bad as the heathen!"

"No, I don't think so. But I am afraid that he thinks Titus was at least as bad as Alaric."

"Titus? I suppose it doesn't seem so long ago to him."

Augustine's voice had fallen as if he were thinking aloud Then he seemed to remember his guest.

"I have a young man here, Orosius, who has been gathering all sorts of evidence that even when Rome worshipped the gods, disasters as bad as this befell her because of her wickedness."

"But none of those other times were so"—Hilary groped for the word—"so final as this."

The bishop looked at his guest curiously. "What makes you think it is so final? Alaric is dead, they say, and his hordes after threatening us have gone back to the north."

Augustine had turned to the window and was looking out at the ocean, as if he could see to the northern world that he was thinking about. And then Hilary remembered the north of his childhood, the forests across the Rhine where the mysterious German tribes moved dimly out of range of the long spears of the legions. And then the ultimate dread of these last weeks came into the focus of his vision, and he looked into its face.

"I think that is it," he said slowly, trying to grasp the outlines of the idea that was slowly emerging from those shadows. "Alaric is dead, but it is not like the defeat of Hannibal. When Carthage was ploughed under, one knew that no one could spring from its ashes to take his place. But no one knows who will come now after Alaric. For the sources of his power are intact up there, or if not his, then somebody else's."

Augustine looked at Hilary without speaking for several moments. Then he said gravely, "You have put it very clearly. Is there no hope then for Rome?"

A few minutes ago Hilary would have had no answer to that question, at least no answer that he could have borne to consider. Now to his surprise he saw the answer very clearly. "It is there," he said, "that we must turn to the Pope. For I think that is why he pays so much attention to the barbarians. We must get hold of them before they come down on Rome." He stopped. Was that why his wandering father had gone to Dacia?

But Augustine shook his head. "Alaric was some sort of Christian. Perhaps if he had been the right sort, but I do not think that we can be sure of that." And then as he caught sight of the disappointment on Hilary's face, he smiled. "Not that I do not agree with the Pope on the main point, and if you are thinking of going up to convert the barbarians, I hope you will go. For there is nothing more important than that to be done."

Hilary felt the blood surge in his cheeks as Augustine dragged out of its hole deep in his consciousness the thought which he could hardly acknowledge even to himself. But Augustine was driving ahead. "It isn't what is to be done that I am thinking of now. It is rather the foundation of it all, the thinking that we must get clear if we are to do anything at all. For what are you going to carry to your barbarians? Rome? Even Christian Rome?"

Incongruously, Hilary thought of the chapel of Laeta. And then he began to his surprise to defend Christian Rome. "But the actuality always falls short of the ideal. Even Plato knew that."

"I want something more than Plato," said Augustine. "I am not sure that Baranina is not wiser there. The cities of this world always fall, even Rome, but there is another city that does not fall. It is the city of God."

The light was fading in the small, low-ceilinged room, but the face of Augustine seemed to have its own light from within. He turned now to Hilary. "Not Rome but that city you will take to your barbarians, my son, and that is what I shall write my book about, 'The City of God!'"

VI

SO MUCH OF THE PAIN OF THESE LAST MONTHS had been in the turmoil of his own mind, beyond the reach of words, sometimes it seemed even beyond the reach of imagination, that Hilary was surprised that any reality could be worse than the thought of it. The first sight of Nola disabused him of this illusion. He had been watching for some landmark that he might recognize even from the unfamiliar approach of the road coming up from Baiae. But the fresh green fields stretched to the blue sky without his being able to identify any fold in the level plain, any break in the sharpening skyline. And then he caught the curve of the apse of Paulinus' new basilica against the sky, and the supporting mass of the clustering buildings of the monastery. And the memory of the beauty and peace of the house of Paulinus, which had made an armistice in the agony of the news from Gaul, came back to him with a sweetness that in this very different desolation seemed almost as miraculous in its promise.

Suddenly the mass of the town lifted above the plain, and Hilary thought it must be some trick of the morning shadows that made it look so somber in the Campanian sunshine. And then the light fell more clearly on the curve of the apse, and Hilary saw with horror that it was only a hollow shell. All the finely timbered roof was gone, and the fabric of the church was torn and jagged as if some gigantic hand had tried to tear it apart and had been stopped only by the clutch of the earth.

Hilary riding ahead could hear behind him the exclamations of the little company from the ship who had come with him, but they meant no more to him than the sound of the wind rippling through the olive trees by the road. And suddenly all the bright scene dazzled in the mist of his tears.

After that, he saw other broken walls and the haunting skeleton of a timber roof laid bare by a starved fire, black and sinister against the radiant sky. He reminded himself that he had often enough seen in various places of his pilgrimage the debris of time and man's destruction, but never with such rawness, such ineluctable immediacy. And never had destruction worn so commonplace an air as in that balcony hanging crazily from a torn wall and that column of stairway screwing up meaninglessly into the unfloored sky. But these were the wounds of strangers. The ache in his flesh was that jagged shell on the low height.

And yet to their astonishment they found Nola joyously en fête. There was nobody at the burned-out road station on the edge of the town to run out and take the tired horses, but the air from the town was loud with cheering and singing. And all the angry shouts of his companions could produce from the cavernous shadows of the neighboring ruins was a single aged cripple hobbling slowly forth on a crutch, and blinking in the sunshine.

"What has happened?" yelled the captain, who had come to see relatives in Nola. "Did Alaric take all the town off but the fools and the madmen shouting their heads off up there?"

The old man scratched his head thoughtfully, and then he answered slowly, "Well, he did pretty much at that, but the bishop has brought them all back, and they are going up to thank Saint Felix."

"Thank Saint Felix!" exploded the captain, who had been grumbling that in twenty years of calling at Nola he had never seen anything like this. "What has Saint Felix done? He couldn't even keep the roof on his own house!" And the captain thrust out a jeering arm to the height above the town.

The old man scratched his dirty poll again. "You may be right at that," he conceded grudgingly, "but the bishop says it was Saint Felix, and he ought to know. If it isn't Saint Felix, then it would have to be the bishop. And he's no saint; he's alive." The old man's cracked voice rose triumphantly on this conclusion.

The captain laughed, however, and leaving the horses in the care of his servant, led the way up to the town. Here the newcomers were just in time to catch up with the end of an extraordinary procession in which not only the town but seemingly the whole surrounding countryside had joined. For a number of old farmers and country women with children clutching their robes were straggling along, evidently still hoping to catch up with the procession before the day's festivities ended. Hilary joined one of the last of these stragglers, a stalwart old fellow, taking his time.

"We're late anyway," he said cheerfully, acknowledging Hilary's greeting. "I hadn't meant to come, and then when I saw everybody going by, I thought I might as well come along, too.

But when Hilary asked him what it was all about, he seemed uncertain. "Most folks say it's the bishop did it, but he says it was Saint Felix. I don't think it matters," he added tolerantly. "All the folk those savages took away have come back, or most of them. It's a miracle any way you look at it."

When they reached the low rise of ground where the great basilica had stood, Hilary was startled to find the shell filled to over-flowing with a vast crowd, standing in the grass that had begun to push up through the pavement, sitting on heaps of broken stone and rubble, slipping uncertainly in the thick mud left by the winter rains. They were singing a hymn, and though they seemed to feel that they must fill the blue vault of the sky, now the only roof over their heads, they were clearly beginning to flag a little. And looking at them more closely, Hilary was startled to see how many of those people, who had earlier looked so prosperous, were thin and worn, while their clothes were little more than dirty rags. But they sang with a fervor of thankfulness that made any pity for them seem quite irrelevant.

Hilary found the base of a broken pillar from which he could see over the heads of the congregation into the apse, but the high altar had vanished, and so had the bishop's throne. Only the great Christ still sat there on the inner shell of the apse, a little dimmed by the winter rains so that He seemed to be seen through tears. And where the roof had been broken away, the four rivers of Paradise flowed out into the blue sky.

Hilary thought of the Pope, and wondered if he had come back to Rome yet. And then there was a stir all around him as men and women tried to kneel. And far off Hilary heard the low murmur of Paulinus' voice, faint as if he were speaking from a great distance, intoning the words of blessing.

Since there was clearly no use in attempting to see Paulinus just now, Hilary sat on the base of the pillar and watched the crowd move slowly out of the enclosure of the basilica. Many of them were clearly in a hurry to get back to their homes. But others stood around aimlessly as if it made no difference where they went. And then the report began to spread that there would be free food and drink in the town in honor of the miraculous return. That seemed to give a sudden destination to some of the aimless.

But every so often the slow progress of the departure would be held up as old friends recognized each other and embraced in an eddy of the crowd. From such encounters Hilary began to get some clearer notion of what had happened, for over and over he heard the same question, "How was it?" and usually the same answer, "Oh, not too bad, now that it's all over." But now and then he heard more intimate whispers, once from a woman, clinging to a man, "I am so thankful. I don't think I could have held him off for another day," and the other from a young man to a group of his contemporaries, "I shall never beat a slave again." Hilary tried to see the face that went with that passionately earnest voice, but all he could see clearly was a companion, laughing carelessly, and saying, "That is silly of you, Marracinus. After all you were not really a slave." Still Hilary could not quite see the face of the young man; only he could hear the same conviction in the swift retort, "I tell you that brute of a Goth did not know the difference." And then the crowd closed in.

To judge from the way people were speaking of the bishop, Hilary felt sure that it would be some time before he could reach him. Apparently everybody within reach had been going up to ask for his blessing; he would certainly be tired. So Hilary drifted back with the crowd to the market place where people said the free food was to be had.

There he found a stout, middle-aged woman standing proudly on the steps of a ruined temple with huge baskets of bread on either side of her, and beyond, tables with jars of wine and pottery cups. She was laughing and chatting gaily as a couple of slaves took the small round loaves of bread and passed them out to all comers. On the steps below her a rather weedy youth in an elegant toga, new and white in contrast to the torn and dirty tunics around him, lounged casually, chatting with his contemporaries, and now and then responding rather sulkily to some request for attention from the woman above.

As Hilary came closer, he heard the woman greet some friends excitedly, and as they came up the steps to her side, she cried out so that all could hear, "It is wonderful, and I say that my Paeonius is really responsible for it all. If the barbarians had not taken him, then the bishop would not have been taken captive, and there would have been no miracle."

By the time Hilary reached the basilica again, he felt he had a fair notion of what had happened. It was quite like Paulinus to have given every thought to his flock until the disappointed invaders had lost patience and sacked and burned his heart's pride, and taken his people captive. And then the confident almsgiver in the square had undoubtedly looked very different weeping her widow's helplessness at the bishop's feet. Even the most ignorant of barbarians must have jumped at the chance of Paulinus rather than that limp youth. It was grotesque, and yet out of that grotesqueness—

Hilary found Paulinus quite alone in a corner of the basilica, trying to fit two fragments of carved marble together. He looked old and frail and tired, but his skin was brown as if he had been outdoors a good deal of late. And his face lighted as he caught sight of Hilary.

"I heard you had got out of Rome to Bethlehem, and then I was sure Jerome would never let you go," he said, holding Hilary off and looking at him.

Hilary smiled. "Let us say that I know my limitations rather."

"You were grieving for Gaul, when I saw you last."

It had not occurred to Hilary that it was so long ago that he had come to Nola. He smiled. "Let us say that the great flood has engulfed the little. And let us not talk of little things any more, but of big like—" He was going to say "you," but he could see the incipient embarrassment on the face of Paulinus, and hastily, he added, "this."

The bishop looked around the ruined church and then back at the great Christ. "God has been good to us even in this. The best thing in the whole basilica is still here, and I think it is a lesson to us that this is all that really matters."

For some minutes the two stood there contemplating the great figure. The marks of the conflagration and the rains were on it, as the grief of the time was on everything man looked at these days. But the majesty and the compassion of the great figure shone through them.

"How many of your monks have you?"

For the first time Paulinus looked troubled. "About half of them," he said. And then as Hilary waited curiously, he tried to explain. "Some of them died, a few here, and a few in the south where they took us." A look of amusement came into his face at some recollection. "It was then my master began to suspect his gardener, when they sent for me."

"I have seen the woman and her son whom you saved," said Hilary, trying to keep the amusement out of his voice.

But the bishop stood his ground. "Then you know that she was quite right when she feared that any master would kill him. She thought, poor thing, that he was too spirited."

"What did your barbarian master say when he found out?"

Again a look of grave consideration came into Paulinus' face as if this were something on which he had thought a good deal. "He freed me on the spot, and he asked me what he could do for me. I told him about the three or four hundred of my flock in the neighborhood, and he said he would see what he could manage." And then he seemed to gather up all his resources as if it were very important to get this right. "They really had no heart for staying in the land after Alaric died toward the end of the year, and I think they would have turned most of their captives loose on the way back."

Hilary smiled. "Do you think it becoming a Christian and a bishop to take so much pains to disprove a miracle?"

Paulinus looked alarmed. "It was a miracle all right. I never wanted to deny it. But it was God through Saint Felix. I had prayed to Saint Felix all the way."

And then the two fell silent, looking again at the great figure of the painting. But now it seemed to Hilary that his eyes were always leaving it to follow the rivers. Finally, he said to Paulinus, "It is almost a pity you have to close it in. Those rivers seem to be free now to flow quite out of the picture."

Paulinus seemed surprised, and then he looked at Hilary. "That is curious. When I first saw that, I thought of my barbarian master—he is a good man, and I shall always pray for him." And then as a new idea came to him, he looked closely at Hilary. "Is that why you did not stay with Jerome?"

"Yes," said Hilary. "I must wait for Medoc here and see what I can do for Cerealis, but when that is done, I am taking one of the rivers."

Paulinus nodded as if he had expected it. "God has a way of making things clear to us if we will only give him a chance," he said quietly.

VII

IMPATIENT AS HE NOW WAS TO BE ON HIS WAY, Hilary did not have long to wait. Less than a week later a fisherman from Naples brought word in the morning of a large boat approaching Nola, and that afternoon a tradesman from the town reported that it was said to be from Gaul. Hilary went at once to the shop of the cloth merchant whose address Medoc had given him.

There he found his old friend sitting over a glass of wine in a fire-scorched room behind the shop, as calm and unchanged as if two worlds had not passed away since Hilary first remembered him sitting like that in his grandfather's library. And Medoc greeted him with the same easy affection with which he had first won the boy's confidence long ago.

"Yes," the old trader said in answer to Hilary's first query, "it was a hard trip. It's not only the uncertainty about the ports, but the pirates. There is nothing they are afraid of now." And then a speculative look came into his deep blue eyes, as he added, "If there is anything you Christians can do about it, you had better set about it fast."

Seeing Hilary hesitate, Medoc must have decided that he had spoken too sharply, for he smiled at Hilary and went on more gently, "You, I know, will be doing your part on your estates here. I heard from a friend in Ostia how you had shaken them up, even on your first visit." And then his face shadowed as all men's faces shadowed these days, when they thought of the past. "Of course, it's all very different now. Everything's different," he added almost apologetically.

"I am not staying here; I am going back to Bordeaux," said Hilary quietly.

It was not Medoc's habit to be surprised, but for a moment he simply stared at Hilary. Then he repeated the word, "Bordeaux!" incredulously.

Hilary nodded.

"But there's nothing to go back to. Cerealis has managed to recover the hill top, but there's nothing but ashes there and the foundations of the old Druid fortress. Barbarous they may have been, those ancestors of yours, but they knew how to build better than their descendants."

Hilary smiled at the unconscious echo of the old argument over the comparative advantages of Druid and Roman Gaul that had raged so often about the dinner tables in the brightly decorated dining room of the burned villa, but still speaking in a low voice, he said, "It will be enough."

"For what?" Again Medoc's voice had sharpened. And then it relaxed, as he smiled. "What will that fine Roman wife they have been talking about do there?"

At the stricken look on Hilary's face, Medoc put out his hand, and Hilary said only, "Dead. She is dead, too," and then his voice steadied and very briefly he told the story which he had heard from Attis; only he told it as if he had been there and seen that beautiful figure shining against the blue sky. There was admiration for that vision as well as pity in the eyes of Medoc when he had finished.

"But there are other women in Rome," said Medoc very gently.

Hilary shook his head and repeated what he had already said to Attis, "She was Rome."

Medoc shrugged his shoulders. "And your Campanian estates?"

It was Hilary's turn to smile wryly. "Gaul is not the only place. Things are so confused they can hardly grow worse for waiting."

"Surely, whatever it is you want to do at Bordeaux, you can do in Campania, and have something to work with."

But Hilary shook his head. "I should always be trying to restore the pattern of the mosaic when half the pieces have been lost. It is a fresh start that is needed."

Medoc looked at Hilary with a quick flash of surprise that steadied to respect. Then he returned to the attack. "But what can you do on that ruined hill? The slaves have fled, and the farmers that have stayed are too frightened of the bandits to stir beyond their own barnyards. And everywhere there are the barbarians, who would not know how to work, even if they wanted to. You can't hope to rebuild those old walls alone."

Hilary laughed at the picture. "I shouldn't even dream of trying. The Druid stronghold was levelled for the Roman villa. Why should I go back to that?"

To his astonishment that idea conjured up out of ironic mockery did not seem so preposterous to Medoc. "That is exactly what men who have anything left to protect are trying to do. I had not thought of that before."

"The treasure I am thinking of," said Hilary, "will not be preserved in a hole in the ground." And then he was ashamed at the shadow of hurt in the old trader's eyes.

"Neither the fortress nor the villa," he said more humbly. "Only the little chapel by the old fountain of the Three Women—"

"But that is gone, too. Surely, Cerealis must—"

"I know—that is the one thing I would restore, or perhaps better replace, with something much poorer, I know."

For some seconds Medoc said nothing, and then he seemed to accept what he knew he could not understand, and with his life-long habit of undertaking implausible commissions he began to think about how this incredible business could be set in motion. "Perhaps," he said at length, "you could get your father to come back."

For a moment Hilary wondered if it were a grim jest, and then he remembered that the individual fate must often have slipped through the meshes of the great nets of rumor and report that carried the destinies of cities and empires these last disastrous months. He told his old friend of what he had learned from Nicetas.

And when Medoc murmured something warmer than the conventional condolences, Hilary reminded him rather sharply that he had never known his father. He said this in embarrassed defence of his own matter-of-factness, but for some reason he seemed to have put Medoc on the defensive, and presently he discovered to his astonishment that it was his father whom the trader was defending.

"I don't suppose it makes any difference now that they are all gone," Medoc said slowly, "but whatever you think of Martin of Tours and the old shrines, he was a man you would not be ashamed to follow. And whatever your grandfather said, there is nothing to be ashamed of in your father." He looked thoughtfully at Hilary. "I never cared much for religion, not my business; but it has always seemed to me that if a man is to have a religion, he might as well do something about it." For Medoc it was a very considerable statement, more than Hilary could ever remember his making on an abstract theme.

Medoc must have thought so, too, for he looked a little sheepish as he went on, "They say that when Desiderius drew his sword in front of the oak that day, Martin said, 'It is not for a tree that I have come, but a man, Desiderius.' And even those who cared least for Martin agreed that when out of the whole countryside he picked your father, he chose well."

"Why are you telling me this?" asked Hilary.

Medoc smiled and went to a chest, standing half open behind the table. From it he took a little bundle and unwrapped it. It was a picture on a wooden panel.

"One of my men was up in the Dordogne last year, and he stopped at the monastery on the cliff at Primuliacum. It is a picture of Desiderius, which somebody made there before he went east. The artist took it up to Tours, and then when the barbarians came, somebody brought it back. They thought his family should have it. They did not know what had happened —either way," he added softly.

With a quickened beating of the heart Hilary took the picture. It was a rude enough affair, almost as rude as the picture of Pope Corneilius in the catacombs. This, too, was a man who would carry what he undertook to the death. But there the resemblance ended. For there was nothing old or embattled about this countenance. Rather, it was an astonishingly young and eager face, as if Desiderius, setting out for the adventure that was to cost him his life, still found the hazard good.

"Has nobody ever told you that you have a look of your father?"

Hilary looked up to find Medoc smiling a little. "Nicetas did, his bishop in Dacia," he explained.

How incredibly young his father looked, he thought, feeling suddenly very old. In the crashing of all the worlds he had known, he had gone out to meet his death, still looking like this! But aloud, he said only, "I shall hang it up in the chapel—when I have rebuilt it, and I shall bury the bones of the others in a chest beneath." His voice fell.

But Medoc seemed not to have heard. "You are like your father," he said musingly, "but you are moving in the reverse direction." And then he seemed to rouse himself. "Still there isn't much in the way of sacred oaks or heathen temples left to pull down. They went with the churches and the villas, quite indiscriminately."

"I wonder how many were caught in the falling of the sacred oaks"—Hilary was astonished to find how remote that old shock of Patricius' death now seemed. And then as Medoc looked startled, he went on with a smile, "I am still going to where the barbarians are; only it is not Dacia now, but Bordeaux."

For a moment Hilary wondered if he should tell Medoc about the two cities of Augustine. The trader was not a Christian, and he might find it all rather mystical. But even more than that Hilary suddenly realized that to Medoc as to Attis the fall of Rome, however disastrous in terms of personal relations and personal fortunes, was not the final and unique catastrophe that it was for Jerome and Augustine, and even for the more easy-going Paulinus.

So he began to talk soberly of what he hoped to attempt at

Bordeaux—the restoration of the chapel, a school for the countryside, perhaps even a hospital. But as Medoc raised his eyebrows, he hastily added, "Nothing of course like those great buildings of Pammachius at Ostia. Timber will do for the very small beginnings." He stopped, appalled at the way his imagination was already straining at its leash. Had he learned nothing, was he still the same man—

But the trader could be counted on to pull him back to earth. "There is plenty of broken stone everywhere," he said dryly. "But that can wait. The question now is what can we get here for your return, and perhaps even at Ostia later."

Suddenly, though he had not thought of this before, Hilary was quite clear on the answer. A passage on the earliest ship possible, the most practical travelling clothes such as one of Medoc's young agents might wear, and a little gold for food. The rest could wait. But again he did not think it necessary to begin to explain what Medoc could hardly be expected to follow. And yet as he looked at Medoc's worn face, he realized that he, too, must have seen many plans fail, and somewhere in his trader's electicism he must have found the barer and grimmer equivalent of a trust in Providence.

All Medoc said, however, was, "You are wise. A ship is due any day now, and I'll arrange it."

So Hilary took his leave and went back up the hill to the shrine of Saint Felix. God would find his workman—surely, that must include the provision of the workman's tools. Now that his decision was made, all that seemed of little importance. But it seemed to him that there was still something he should do.

He thought of it as he made his way back to the ruined church. When he reached there, the light was fading, but there was still enough to see the face of Christ.

"I wish, Hilary," said the soft voice of Paulinus from behind him, "that I could give it to you to take to Bordeaux."

Hilary turned, and as he did so, it seemed to him that the last piece in his puzzle fell into place. "There is something even better that you can give me. There is no question of my ever being good enough. And even if I should never be in any danger for Jerome's Cicero, I shall always be remembering Virgil. If knowing all this, you still could bear to think of me at the altar—" And he knelt down at the feet of the bishop.

For a moment Paulinus stood there, and then his face lighted in the shadows, and he threw his arms around Hilary.

"There is no man—" he began, wiping away the tears from his eyes. But Hilary shook his head, as he slowly rose to his feet.

"It isn't that," he said hastily. "It is simply that with Him," and he nodded at the great figure fading in the twilight, "to bring to them, I shall not worry about anything else, Rome, or Bordeaux, or even myself." The great figure was hardly visible, but at the crumbling edge of the apse Hilary could still make out the four rivers, flowing into the roofless sky.